Entities Part 1
Entities Connected

By Barry S. Brunswick

ISBN- 978-0-6452266-4-5

Editing by N.T Anderson
Cover Design by 100covers.com
Published by Barry S. Brunswick

Dedication

Nikki & Jacki
You're the most amazing friends a crazy
author could ever have. Thank you for being you.
I love you!

&

In loving memory of Judy

Acknowledgements

I'd like to say a big thank you to N.T Anderson for her amazing editing work and teaching me a few things along the way. I appreciate the hard work, understanding, and love that you put into this project. I am eternally grateful.

Cracks in the Cosmos

Again, he looked up at the ceiling through the fuzz in his eyes. He was lost in the lonely depths of insomnia. His thoughts crept their way from light to darkness and then onwards, drifting towards paranoia. Swallowed by his solitude, the whole world seemed silent and sleeping. He felt dreaded emptiness, like he was the only person who was awake on Earth at that moment. He floated alone on the planet through the cosmos, like all the others had died. Like it was the end of the world, and he was the lone survivor.

Liam was detached from the beings that slept around him in the other apartments throughout the cold winter city. Lost in an endless labyrinth of thought, his mind swirled, being dragged helplessly to places he didn't even know existed. The ideas lurked into mysterious depths, and he was powerless to stop them. The thoughts jumped quickly from one subject to the next, with no bridge between. Those wild thoughts blended and twisted, metamorphosising until he could no longer remember how they had appeared in the first place.

The trail inside his mind snaked through the blackness and images that flashed repeatedly. Whether it was through dreams or memories, through his life or the life of another, he could not tell. They wound their way around his mind and then his very soul, leaving him shivering, leaving his thoughts lost somewhere outside his body, somehow incomplete. The images swooped past his mind's eye until he felt almost dizzy, and as quickly as they began, the images faded out, fell apart to dust and out of memory.

Through heavy eyes that burned with exhaustion, Liam continued to look to the ceiling. He hadn't taken his eyes off it. It was covered in stony grey shadow that seemed to change a little with each passing second. He stared deeply at the bumps and lumps of the plaster that were reflected by the streetlight outside, whose orange glow carved its way through the curtains. The ceiling blurred every now and then as his eyes stared firmly upon it, then he would blink, and it would be clear in his vision again.

Liam drifted in and out of consciousness. How he wished he was asleep and lost in dreams, but this insomnia had been happening for weeks, and his day-to-day life had been suffering the consequences. He felt half dead, zombie-like during the day, and at night, his mind just wouldn't switch off. It wasn't even as if he was worrying about things at that time. The thoughts were random, like they may even be from another. Like thoughts that he did not own.

An edge of anticipation filled Liam's heart, as if he knew that something was about to happen. No sooner had that feeling entered his body than in the depth of shadow, a crack appeared in the ceiling.

"What?" Liam opened his eyelids further at the sound of his own voice. Even he was surprised to hear it. Could it be he had become so deliriously tired that he was hallucinating? He closed his heavy eyes and then opened them again. From total blackness back to dim light, his vision flashed. He stared upward, hoping the crack would have vanished, but there it was, still visible.

There was no time to make sense of it. The crack grew again, then a second later, with a crackle, it forked out across the ceiling. Like lightning, it snaked, ripping apart the plaster. A rumble shook the room, then there was a fearsome crunch as the ceiling split open. Bits of ceiling and plaster rained down upon Liam, leaving him choking and spluttering. His eyes were full of dust and the grit that entered his mouth crunched as he clenched his teeth.

With a rumble like thunder, the rest of the ceiling caved in upon him. Wide-eyed, panic filled him in an instant as he covered his head to protect himself and bent his knees up towards his chest to take the impact. He had only *just* prevented his body being crushed beneath the weight. Before fear caught up, he was blinded and buried.

Liam struggled to free himself from the debris. He held his breath, clenched his jaw, and with every ounce of his strength, pushed against the plasterboard until he freed an arm. He swept the plaster from his face and gasped for air. His eyes stung with the dust. He quickly brushed it away.

Looking up, there were the stars twinkling above him, and the cold night air tickled his skin. The ceiling had gone, as had the roof. His bedroom was now in the open winter's air.

With a woosh, white light beamed down. It blinded him and forced him to close his eyes. It warmed his skin. The light poured upon him like a waterfall, over his cowering and dust-covered form. He felt static electricity in the air that made his skin tingle, and the hairs stood up on his arms.

His heart started to race as a million thoughts rushed through his cloudy mind. He felt his whole body vibrate, then his stomached flipped upside down while a force pulled upon him, lifting him out of his bed. Plaster rained down once again, but this time from atop his body. He was ripped from beneath his trap.

"This can't be real," he gasped.

Had he fallen asleep? Was this a dream? No. This was no dream. Or at least, not like one he'd ever known. He could only wish it was a dream. Panic filled him and raged, first, wild around his mind, then his very soul. The light burned ever brighter and warmer, then the force pulled on him harder still. His arms and legs flayed helplessly as he shot screaming upwards, freed from his bed, freed from the restraints of gravity, and up into the cold night sky.

Liam summoned the bravery to open his eyes, and the light flowed in, but now it didn't hurt like it had before. It surrounded him and rippled into him, through his skin and down to the very grain of his being. It was like warm blood glowing in his veins.

He saw the sky above him and shot quickly higher and higher. Liam was helpless, doing his utmost just to keep breathing, just to keep calm. It was clear that he was little more than a passenger on this ride, a prisoner to a force that he couldn't possibly understand. It was like he was being sucked towards a waterfall; no matter how hard he swam, he was a mere slave to the force and its mysterious tide.

Liam's hands started to tingle, then slowly they began to burn. He looked down and screamed, more in shock than pain— his hands were falling apart. As he watched, they went from solid then fell to pieces like grains of sand. His body was useless, and he was hopeless, at the mercy of a force he did not recognise. A mysterious force that was far beyond his mortal control and human understanding.

His heart was beating wildly inside his chest and waves of fear rushed through him. He yelped again, this time in sheer terror. A feeling of warmth washed over him, and he cried out. He wrapped his arms around himself as, slowly, his body disintegrated, falling apart before his eyes. It left nothing but a trail of dust like a comet behind him.

He was ripped up through the atmosphere as the last solid part of him fell away. He had no body, but somehow, he had thought, and he could still see and hear. He was surrounded by strange tunnels of light. He could see them, but Liam felt nothing at all.

The glow of beautiful colours beamed into his vision. He felt giddy while the strange sights flashed all around him. The fear lifted and slowly left him. The panic subsided, and like he was hypnotised, he revelled in the wonder of the ride. This was a place he belonged, a place he had been before. A location where he was free to wander and explore, beyond human reality, beyond the constraints of physics, beyond even the hands of time. Liam was home.

The colours rushed past, flashing magically, vibrant and warm. Then he felt the calling. He just knew. He couldn't say why or where, but it was somewhere outside or within him, beckoning him along.

The ride went on and on for what could have been a second or could have been forever. The time didn't matter. As he thought his last thought, silence fell, and Liam slipped into complete and utter darkness. Perhaps even his death.

The Mantis

Liam floated in darkness. He accepted the nothing, but soon, light flashed in through the blackness and warmed his being. His death had not come after all. Becoming a haze, then smoke, and then dust, his form began to solidify.

Downwards, he fell fast, still surrounded in light, still wrapped inside the tunnels where the colours flashed brightly. His vision quickly transformed from blurs of light—little more than streaks running by—to a watery, more solid image. Finally, he could see clearly through human eyes once more.

He took in his surroundings, but it wasn't a second later before he was clamping his eyes tightly shut again. He jumped with a start as below, a planet rushed towards him. Falling freely through the atmosphere like it wasn't even there, no heat, no flame, he helplessly plummeted downwards. His arms flapped uselessly as with every second he rushed ever nearer to the planet's surface.

The sky around him was a thick, orange haze. Puffy towering clouds with a tinge of purple were below him and then, in a mere matter of seconds, above him. There was a mysterious glow, lighting the sky like fire from the powerful rays beaming from the planet's host star.

Down and down, holding his breath Liam went. Stretched out for miles below him was an endless landmass. There was no sign of oceans. It was one solid continent—one solid continent towards which he was hurtling. Out of the sky he fell ever faster as he zoomed past rocky mountains, jagged and sharp, and down towards certain death.

There were green lights from a city beneath him, stretching out for miles around. Tall and shining metallic buildings that reflected the orange sky were crammed side by side, pointing their spires skyward like silver pyramids. The city rushed closer, and his heart raced, from at first the confusion and wonder, until it became all-out terror. Then his heart almost stopped—he was headed straight for one of the structures below. The building grew bigger and closer every second until Liam closed his eyes, drew his last breath, and braced himself for a crushing impact. That impact never came.

He felt himself slow. He blew out the breath that hadn't been his last after all and mustered the courage to open his eyes again. He was inside the building, floating just above the floor, moving swiftly up a long corridor. His heart fluttered, now exhilarated, as he marvelled in the wonder of the ride.

Had Liam awakened a power that had lay dormant inside of him forever? Had he tapped into the secrets of the universe? Again, he questioned if this was a dream.

No, it wasn't. That was the only thing he knew for certain—this was no dream.

He swooped, rushing towards the end of the corridor, approaching a tall, closed door. He couldn't stop, nor could he slow down, and once again, the instinct inside him took control. It made him close his eyes and brace himself for an impact that would never arrive. He passed silently through the door as if it didn't exist.

He opened his eyes. He was inside a huge room with an enormous round table in the middle. He rushed towards it, yet without moving a muscle, and a silver flash sparked all around him. He felt the weight of his body and sensations on his skin. Liam was filled with relief that he had survived his dreamlike journey.

He looked down. The colours were duller than they normally would be, and there was a lingering pink haze around him. He did not recognise the clothes he was wearing. They were long robes of vibrant colours that flowed right to the floor.

Liam raised his hands to see his three fingers were long, slender, and pale blue. He wanted to yelp in fear and surprise, but his mouth didn't move. He looked again at the body below him. It was far taller and thinner than his. He felt giddy. His hands, his body, and even his eyes were not his own. He was inside someone else's body... or at least *something* else's.

Fear surged, sending his senses into wild overdrive. Confusion rained down. He felt faint and nauseous. He wanted to scream his lungs out. He wanted to run a mile or just explode, but he simply couldn't take any of those options.

The snowballing terror rushed through his mind. It screamed loud and shrill within him, but remained contained, showing no outward, physical sign at all. He was no more than a prisoner trapped inside another form. The realisation clanged around him—not only was he inside another body, but also another mind. Locked screaming within some other being over which he had no control.

Tall and thin hooded figures stood lingering on the edge of shadow. The eyes of the host tried to see, but Liam couldn't make out their faces. They all stood, lean and gangly, at the other side of the table. The shadow was in just the right place to conceal them, almost as though they intentionally hid their identities from him.

Again, waves of fear overcame him like electricity. Muddled by blind confusion, the head around him seemed to pound. Panic scrambled his senses. He tried to close his eyes, but the host's body kept theirs open. Silently, he wished with every ounce of his being he could escape the confusion that clouded him, but here and now, it reigned supreme. His awareness was spinning, his vision blurring in and out. Liam was at his very limit. Never had he been so afraid and helpless. Never had he felt so manipulated and unsure. At that moment, even death seemed a better option than living through these terrifying moments.

From across the room, one of the hooded figures started to speak in strange tones that a human would never be capable of articulating, tones of a language he had never heard before. The figure seemed agitated, flaying its arms, barking loudly and aggressively. The other figures listened on in silence.

The creature asked Liam a question, and though he could not speak the language, he answered fluently and clearly, making his mind swirl to the verge of cracking.

The figure banged its hand down on the table with a thud that made the others jump and shouted another incomprehensible sentence. It screamed, a high-pitched sound unlike any Liam had ever known. It was a scream not like that of a primal creature or a roar but a shrill, whining whistle. The figure ripped the hood from its head.

If Liam's sanity was barely holding on by a thread, the thread snapped as fear swallowed him whole. The shock reached its peak, tearing relentlessly through his soul, contorting his mind. His eyes were fixed and wide. For the second time in mere moments, he wanted to run away, but again, he was trapped. His host certainly had no intention of running.

The face of a monster stared right through Liam. Compound eyes attached to the sides of its head looked on almost lifeless. Its jaws were clasping, jagged, and crushing. The face was that of an insect, but the body was almost human. He scanned his memories for a point of reference, then it clicked—it looked like a preying mantis.

It towered over him, aggressive and intimidating, spitting spiteful words while the others remained silent and hooded. He wanted to back away as surges of terror overcame him. From within its robes, long, thin arms extended with slender fingers attached to its hands. It gesticulated aggressively and continued to shriek in the strange language.

"Now. Now is the time." A voice entered Liam's soul and the body around him stood ready. He paused for a moment. A feeling bubbled inside him, heat burned in his mind, and without knowing how or why, he knew what he must do.

From his host's eyes, black mist poured out in waves, quickly filling the room like steam. The hooded figures clutched their throats, rasping, as did his host. They spluttered, choking, desperately screaming as pain burned them from within. Frothing at the mouth, they collapsed to the floor, gurgling and gasping for air. They writhed there, screeching, until finally, they were limp and silent. The mantis uttered its final words with its dying gasp: "The Fleck!"

The host's body collapsed. The haunted fingers of death reached out for Liam's soul, then they grasped him and dragged him to darkness.

A Voice, Trusted

"Isha, is it you?" The voice echoed around her mind.

"Yes, it's me. What do you want?"

"We're going on a journey."

The voice tingled magically, soothing and hypnotising, swirling warm within her. It didn't come through her ears, nor in her mind but around her very essence. It floated inside her, tickling her heightened senses. It was the voice within and with out. It was here and there. It was everywhere, and it was everything.

"A journey? Where?" Isha asked out loud. This situation was one she had never known. It was one with which she should be overwhelmed with fear and confusion, but she was calm and not afraid. She drifted along the nowhere. Her mind was free; freer than it had ever been before.

"Anywhere," the voice whispered.

Isha felt the warmth of joy rise within her, and all at once, she believed. A journey to anywhere would be one to behold! Her thoughts wandered to places that she had never seen, to dreams of anywhere, of things that exist, and perhaps those that do not. She saw strange alien landscapes in foreign worlds, far from where her body was. The voice was in her very being, whispering to her, offering comfort and guidance. It would have been so easy to feel invaded or question her own sanity while something seemed to be reading her mind. Though for reasons Isha did not know, still, she trusted the voice. It felt like they were somehow connected, even more like they were two parts of the same thing. That voice, the one inside her, *belonged* there with her.

"We can go wherever I want?" She asked the question, but she already knew the answer. Her heart told her not in words but through a tender glow. It was the glow of love that blossomed and grew inside her, warming her very soul.

"Yes, anywhere."

"Can we travel through time?"

"All that has ever existed or will ever exist is out there, locked in the mist of the cosmos. The possibilities are endless and unimaginable. Come on a journey with me now, Isha. I can take you to places beyond your wildest imagination."

"Am I dreaming?"

"What is a dream? Is life itself a dream? Does it even matter if it is a dream?"

"No, I just wondered because I'm asleep."

"You are not asleep. You are more awake than you have ever been in your life."

The voice stopped talking, yet still, it didn't stop speaking, only now it said everything without using words. It spoke through and into the deepest depths of Isha's being. They no longer had a use for words. Now the voice made her *feel*.

Another rush of warmth came over her. It filled her body like warm water pumping through her veins. She gasped as the feeling grasped her. Her mind went fuzzy and cloudy, and her vision was a blur.

Slowly she was lifted up, hovering near the ceiling, and like a camera coming into focus, everything around her became clear. She was awake, but beyond awake. She felt, for the first time, truly alive. There was clarity which she had never known, like she had travelled to the next plain of existence, having crossed the precipice into another realm. Maybe, indeed, she had.

Before, Isha had never known that she wasn't, but at that moment, she felt complete. She felt like she was standing on the edge of her destiny, looking out to a horizon where, at last, she could see beyond.

Below lay her sleeping body in the bed. Isha glowed inside to see herself lying so peacefully with a warm smile fixed upon her lips. Her essence had broken the bonds of her human body, and soon, the voice silently told her, she would break the bonds of the Earth as well.

A silver glow fell around her, a force pulled upon her, and she floated up through the ceiling, and then the roof like they weren't even there. She was whisked like a seed on the wind, away and through colourful tunnels backed by endless blackness.

A million images flashed within her, like she was searching. Face after face appeared and moved, ever-morphing, ever-changing, twisting into others then moving on again. The faces rushed by, seemingly as if there were millions. Faces from all around the cosmos, many frightening and mysterious, others strangely familiar and human-like. Like a slideshow, they skipped through her mind's eye, until finally, the images stopped on one face.

The face stared at her. It was the face of a young woman who looked nearly human. Her skin was whitish grey and her eyes large but human. Bitter tears flowed from the woman's eyes. Her brow was furrowed and pained like her heart was shattering into a million pieces.

Isha reeled as she empathically felt the woman's agony, the devastation almost too much for her to bare. Her heart broke, too. She was drawn, flowing in silence towards the image of the woman.

The woman opened her arms to embrace her. She felt warmth, which changed quickly to cold, and from her dream, if indeed it was a dream, she awoke.

She opened her eyes and sat up. Immediately, the bed didn't feel right. She looked around, and she didn't know the place. She reached up and placed her hands on her head with confusion, and in an instant, she froze. Her long flowing black hair was gone, and tight curls were in its place.

Crushing realisation crashed down around her, sending her swirling with doubt. She wasn't herself any longer; Isha was someone else.

She sniffed. The tears were still present on her flushed face, but she did not feel upset. The windows were shut and blacked out with blinds, but still she saw the blinding flash of lightning coming from outside. It was followed quickly by a rumble, then the mighty crash of thunder.

Isha stood up with a wave of energy. She felt a longing that tugged upon her soul, and she was compelled to run. She flung open the door and burst out of the room and through the little house.

No lights were on. Each room was draped in shadow, but somehow, she knew the way. At least, the body she was inside did. She opened the front door and ran out into the night.

The wind whipped up a strange feeling. It wasn't fresh but rather warm and humid. Strange yellowy clouds rushed across the darkened sky and rolled into mountainous, menacing formations in the distance. Huge raindrops were falling, far bigger than the raindrops are on Earth. They exploded in puddles onto the already slippery ground.

Isha stopped for a second to look around. The body she was within panted and involuntarily shivered. The huge, golden moon, stretching from horizon to sky, shone bright through the clouds as they parted.

She jumped as a scream rang out, a scream of the most primal fear. She wanted to run away, but instead, drawn helplessly, she rushed towards it. She heard the scream again. Someone was in trouble. She rushed in panic, running, almost blinded by the rain, her feet slipping on the ground with every stride.

She ran for all she was worth, until finally, she saw it—a small cloaked and huddled figure. It was on top of a boulder, staying low, hugging its knees, freezing in the rain. With her footsteps, the figure saw her coming and looked towards her. Their face was slender and innocent; they were just a child. The child was bright eyed and beautiful, but at that moment, their face told a harrowing tale of complete, abject terror.

Glowing orange liquid gathered and pooled around the boulder. The fluid snaked and hissed and fizzed with fury and spat upwards, reaching towards the terrified child. It was almost as though it had a mind of its own. Sparks flew from it as it twisted and swelled, changing from orange to red, glowing like fire in the gloom of the night. The liquid moved like an animal, like it had a will of its own. It was alive and seemed to be hunting the helpless child.

Something within Isha told her what to do, and without so much as a thought, she sprinted headlong for the child, jumping over the strange solution. The glowing mass reached up for her, but she narrowly evaded it and landed on the boulder, only just keeping her feet. She swung down an arm, lifted the child up, and held them clinging to her while she cradled them in her arms.

Taking a half-step back, Isha sprung with all her might over the liquid once more. The fluid creature spat. Twisted electric arms shot out like whips and reached up for her. They sparked and wrapped burning tentacles around her ankles, but she somehow managed to land on her feet.

Isha screamed out in pain. It burned like acid, instantly blistering her skin and eating into her flesh. She screamed again as she tried to keep running. Her ankles struggled to hold her weight, and she had no choice but to stop.

She positioned herself between the child and the liquid, then she gently set the hooded figure on the ground. Her useless ankles, burning and smoking, gave way, and she fell to her knees. She gestured for the child to run, but they grabbed her hand and tried to pull her up.

The child spoke in a strange language, ushering her to come. She struggled to get back to her feet, but they no longer worked. The burning was like stinging venom that filled her veins with fire, shooting up from her toes through her entire body.

She fell backwards, crashing onto the rocks. Again, she waved for the child to run, and through her blurred vision, she saw them scuttling quickly off into the distance.

She smiled at the sight, then gasped a final breath. Isha closed her eyes and slipped slowly away from life.

Awakenings Part I

He prized open his heavy eyelids with a headache that was banging like a drum. His mind was cloudy. His phone alarm screamed. He reached out a clumsy arm and, in a rage, threw it hard against the wall. Sitting up in bed, he immediately put his head in his hands. What had he done? What could have evoked such an uncharacteristically angry reaction from him? He'd never in his life reacted like that before, and this could well have cost him a phone.

Liam sat there, groggy and staring through watery eyes while the haze around him refused to lift. Even though he'd gone to bed early, it felt like he hadn't slept at all. The entire night had passed him by in seemingly little more than a second. All around his weary being were strange echoes—echoes of something that had been but now was not. There was a complex web of mysteries in the recesses of his mind, strung together with confusing bridges that had no rhyme or reason. All were misty thoughts, or at least the ghostly traces of thoughts that had long since drifted away.

Fighting the temptation to take the easy option to lay back down and wrap himself back in the covers, he forced himself out of bed then stumbled lazily towards the bathroom.

Liam stood hunched, splashing cold water on his haunted face. He looked in the mirror. He was a terrible sight. A fearsome screech tore through his mind. It made him jump in his skin. The horrifying images came back. The ear-splitting screams of the mantises flashed into his mind's eye. He froze. His heart nearly stopped. He remembered the dream. *Wait... was it a dream?*

Soon he remembered clearly, in sharp images, all that had happened in that alien room. He could hear the screams of the dying mantises. He could feel his own life escaping his body. He started to feel light-headed. A panic attack made his heart race and, in turn, his chest hurt. Fear filled his trembling body. He whimpered. They were such terrible things to witness and, worse still, to be a part of.

Stepping away from the mirror, Liam concentrated on breathing for a moment. He kept telling himself over and over it was just a dream and that he was safe. He spoke out loud, "There's nothing to be afraid of," again and again until finally, he'd convinced himself. He pulled himself together to some degree, but the panic attack had stolen a little of his soul, for that day at least.

He dragged himself to the kitchen and made a cup of tea, just to give himself something real to do. For a moment, he needed to be present. He took deep breaths to calm himself and slowly brought his heart back under control. He blew away the comforting steam and sipped his drink.

Still, somewhere inside him, the visions lingered. He fought to forget them, but they stubbornly refused to leave. No matter how hard he tried to wash them away in the shower, they remained, taunting him. Feeling like a zombie, Liam headed for the door, putting his phone—now with a cracked screen—into his pocket with a frustrated huff as he went.

The walk out into the grey winter's cold and the bus ride to university passed by in a misty moment while his mind wandered, never focused at any moment on what he was doing or where he was going. Always, he searched the depths, scanning the misty memories, but the more he searched, the less sense they made.

All day he felt uneasy and distant. The bustle of life around him went hardly even noticed. He plodded from lecture to lecture like he was on the outside, watching a movie. Everything that happened that day seemed pre-planned and inevitable, and he was merely an audience watching his own mundane story. Uninterested, distracted, sleepy, he day-dreamed the moments away and then, in turn, the hours.

At times he felt odd, experiencing a slight tingle of static electricity that left his arm hairs on end. His skin gently buzzed, like energy was surrounding his body. Liam had to wonder, could it be the remnants of his journey last night or the panic attack that morning?

Finally, he sat down to lunch with his best friend. The canteen was a bustle of activity but still fatigue kept stealing him away.

"Wake up, Liam."

"Huh?" He shook his head and met the friendly eyes that smiled upon him.

"Having a little snooze, were we?" Penny prodded him teasingly.

He rubbed his face with his whole hand, then his bloodshot eyes met hers. "Erm, no, not really."

"You look terrible. Out all night again?" she teased, knowing full well he rarely went out.

"No, I just didn't sleep very much." Unintentionally, his tone was a little snappy.

Penny chose to ignore that. "We'll go get a coffee afterwards, if you want?"

"Sure thing. I'd love to." His jaw creaked with an enormous yawn. "Think I need one today."

"I thought as much." She smiled, pointing at his red eyes.

"Is this day ever going to end?" he asked, groaning.

"Well, one thing I can guarantee is that every day ends in the end, mate."

They shared a chuckle. Penny was the one shining light in Liam's mundane day-to-day.

The afternoon dragged on like an hour had become four, until finally, not a moment too soon, the day did indeed end, just as Penny had promised it would.

The café was bustling as the waitress put the steaming cups on the table.

"Why couldn't you sleep then?" Penny took a sip of her coffee.

"I just had a really weird dream."

"What was it about?"

"I don't really know. It's just a blur now." Liam paused thoughtfully. "It's like I remember it, but I don't. Like I can still feel it inside, but the memory doesn't exist in my brain. Like, maybe even, it's somewhere else."

"Yeah, Liam, it sounds to me like you *really* need some more sleep, ya weirdo." She rolled her eyes.

"Yeah, you're right…"

"Obviously," Penny joked.

"It was just a dream." He stared past Penny and into space as he recalled the haunting feeling once again. "I'm just being weird, I know."

"Liam. Liam, are you with me, mate?" Penny waved her hand in front of his eyes to catch his attention.

He shook his head again and snapped out of the daydream.

"I'm here. Oh, sorry. I'm just…"

"Look, just go home and get some sleep. I hate it when the company finds my conversation so riveting they keep daydreaming and staring off into space all the time." She giggled cheekily, and her eyes danced playfully like they always did.

"Yeah, I'll go then, dude. Sorry, mate." He grabbed his bag and jumped up. He reached out a fist and bumped hers. "See ya later, alligator."

"See ya, bruh."

Awakenings Part II

"Wake up, Isha! Wake up, would you?"

She opened her eyes halfway at best, and the haze of light crept in. Her mother's face stared down upon her. She shook her again and huffed impatiently.

"Hey!" Isha said with a grumpy frown. "Stop it. I'm getting up."

"Well, hurry up. Breakfast is ready. I've been calling you for fifteen minutes."

Isha lay there, momentarily wondering why her mother got herself so worked up about things that, in the end, really didn't matter. She would get up and go to school, just like she always did. She was fourteen and old enough to get herself ready without the interference. She had barely ever missed a day and when she did, that was because she was sick, not lazy. With a sigh of indignation, she threw the covers off and climbed out of bed. She pushed rudely past her mother, going down the hall to the bathroom. She stood for a moment, and only then did it hit her—the memories from the night before—the dream.

She flashed back, remembering that she had been on a strange planet. Inside a different body, she had saved that strange child, and most shockingly, she had died! She stared at herself in the mirror. She touched her face, just to be certain she was herself. Much to her relief, she was.

"Okay, just a weird dream," she confirmed to herself.

Reluctantly, she got to the kitchen table, dressed and ready. She knew she would get a barrage from her mother who was always in such a hurry. The barrage was, as anticipated, received while breakfast was eaten, followed by a bus ride to school.

Isha was popular with the students but not so much with her teachers. This was because of her laidback attitude towards things that didn't really interest her, and one of those things just so happened to be schoolwork. Her marks were good enough but never outstanding. This wasn't because Isha wasn't smart. In fact, she was very smart—it simply didn't pique her interest. She was wise well beyond her years and knew that school would be only a small part of her life. Her yearning for challenges and adventures made her bored with the day to day of the subjects.

Okay, she loved her friends and was witty and popular, but to her, for some reason, it just didn't seem to matter. She was always a dreamer, one that looked to other things more than where she was at that moment. Recently, something about her had changed. She had grown smarter and surer of herself. It was like something had clicked inside her, and she was evolving. She was growing in body, yes, but mostly she was growing in mind and spirit.

She had started to see that the things that many considered important simply were not. The reality TV shows and social media, video games and technology that all her friends were obsessed by were stupid and a waste of time to her. She liked to look pretty, but Isha didn't follow the latest fashion like her friends, and no one criticised her for it.

Her family were far from rich; they got by but didn't have extra for luxury. This had taught her to gather cheaper, second-hand clothes from the charity shops. She had an eye for vintage clothing, and she had a fair passion for it, too. She learned if she went out to the richer towns, there were more treasures to be had in the shops. It was just her thing. Isha was happy that way, and frankly, she didn't care if others didn't like it. The truth was, however, there were not many who didn't like it, and those who didn't were simply green with envy. They would never tell her, but it was more than the look suiting her—it was her confidence, attitude, and poise that made her shine so brightly.

She never complained. Even with her hard upbringing, even though bad things had happened to her, she just got on with it. Through pain, Isha felt strength, almost as though strength itself was reward for the pain and fear.

She and her mother had escaped, and Isha no longer had to live in the emotional prison of her domineering father. No longer did she have to live by his rules, dress how he wanted her to, and not do anything without his say so. No longer could he scold her because she wasn't like him, didn't think like him, or didn't believe in the things that he did. Never again did they have to live in that man's cruel shadow. No more mere shrinking violets, hidden from the world or treading on eggshells each day, awaiting the next explosion.

When one's expectation is perfection, then inevitably, one will end up disappointed. Mostly, though, now of humble wealth, no longer did they have to live under the endless pressure of an expectation that neither Isha nor her mother could ever meet.

Isha had developed an independence that, at times, made her not quite like other girls her age. She was different. In many ways she was wiser, but simply put, she was special. Not because she was better than anyone, but because she was growing with out and within, undistracted by society's teenage pressures. She was different in her familiarity with who she was and what she was capable of. Just how special Isha was, however, even she could never know.

Throughout the day, Isha's mind wandered. Still those misty memories from the night before lingered. The whisper of the dream, the hazy memory of the journey she'd taken, and of her awakening buzzed inside her. So many crazy dreams had come to her recently. Ones she could never quite remember, even though it was as if she had lived them at the time. Her mind took wandering flight.

Once again, almost silently, she bumbled her way through school. Just when it felt like her school day would last forever and she would go crazy, it finally ended, and she caught the bus home.

Immediately ducking her mother's questions, Isha rushed to her room. She had decided the best thing she could do to find answers was to write down what she remembered from the dream and, for that matter, any others she could recall as well. Any detail, no matter how small. She figured it was the only way that they could ever even have a chance of making sense.

Sometimes, maybe dreams are irrelevant and random, but in this case, she was certain they had meaning. She took out her notebook, and at her little desk, by the lamp light, she prepared to write.

She closed her eyes as images from hazy nights past flowed into her mind. Each was a moment trapped in her memory, each a snapshot of another lost dream. The images dangled in her mind, on the edge of nothing but darkness. They had no reasoning or context. She simply couldn't knit them together and felt as though she had skipped over a vast, dark void, from one island to another, yet with no journey in between.

There was no way for her to make sense of the memories. It felt like she had wandered so far, through a million journeys and a million lives and seen the cosmos through countless eyes. She'd been so far, yet it seemed like she'd never moved at all.

She released the pen, and it rolled off the note pad and down onto the floor. She dropped her head into her hands, squishing up her cheeks, almost head-butting the desk as she did. She was frustrated and exasperated. Before that moment, she had known what she wanted to write. She could see it clearly, but now that the page was there in front of her, she couldn't write anything at all. Her thoughts had become a cloudy muddle. She didn't even know where to start. She sighed, puffed out her cheeks, and closed her eyes.

Her eyes were shut, but through her mind, the dreamy images still came and went. They flickered by, sketchy, like an old film, a projection on a screen. She squeezed her eyes tighter to block out the images, but her eyes were useless. The images were inside her. Soon she started to feel strange, like something was about to happen. Then she felt a force pulling her body. A force she recognised. It was the one from her dream. Her body was asleep, head in hands on the desk below her as she rose out of her skin.

Isha giggled, child-like within. She floated free from the gravity that weighed her body down. She floated away like a whisper on the wind, up and out through the roof. The warmth encircled her and tugged on her being, and once again, she was surrounded by amazing tunnels of light.

The Fleck

Silently falling, drifting, weightless, out of time and out of space, those lights so warmly caressed her soul. Gently guiding her to a place she had to be. It felt like she was being pulled along by a gentle current, towards an unknown destiny. The tunnels of light and the blackness of nothing else surrounded her. Isha floated, riding the force, like she was surfing a wave, as if she was spinning, arms out, giggling through the cosmos.

For a time, she forgot fear or confusion. All she felt was joy. The joy of the purest freedom. The wild ride she was on lasted forever, or maybe mere moments, as the cosmic journey unfolded out before her. It carved a pathway to her fate, a road she followed to wherever it would go. Where she went wasn't her choice; she was a passenger on forces far greater than Isha could control.

Somehow, despite the fact she was a slave to the force, the joy reigned inside her, and she felt free. She trusted it and willingly let go of control. Isha had a destination, that was clear, but only time would tell her where it was.

"Guide me," she called out, even though her body was not on this journey with her.

The force pulled on her as if to grant her request. Looking without eyes at the beautiful colours around her, somehow she felt whole, like she had finally found her home.

From the lights came dark, then grey, and walls melted like liquid all around her. They dribbled down and became solid and stood tall and firm. There she was, back in body, standing in a room in the middle of nothing. She was alone, but still, she knew she was not. She could feel it within.

There was something or someone else there with her. There was static in the room. An electric buzz ran around her, and there was a crackle of white noise. Her mind felt fuzzy, like she was not quite tuned into existence. Her vison faded and then a voice spoke, distant and hypnotising. The beautiful voice sang out words like an enchanting dream. Not words into her ears but words through her very being.

"*Isha, do not be afraid.*"

"I am not afraid. I know you, don't I?"

"*You know me very well indeed. I have been with you for quite some time.*"

"It's you who makes the dreams come, isn't it?"

"*Yes.*"

"Who are you?"

"*I am not a who. I am a what. I am The Fleck.*"

"The Fleck? That's a strange name."

"*I have no label. This is not my name. This is what I am. I am The Fleck.*"

"What's The Fleck?"

Words flowed from the voice. "*Isha, this will be hard for you to understand, but understand it you must. Listen and I'll explain, but first, for you to understand, you must forget everything you've ever known to be true. Forget everything you've ever believed and open your mind. All of sudden, then, what to you seems impossible, becomes possible. It's a simple change of point of view.*

"*I am an entity, but I have no form. I am not a body. I am not a mind. I am pure energy. I am what humans would consider consciousness, though what that is, is far beyond that which humans can comprehend. I am free from the restraints of the body that imprisons you, free of the gravity that weighs you down, and free of the time to which you are slaves. The only way to describe it in a way that you would understand would be what you'd refer to as a higher-being.*"

"How can you be free of time? Isn't time everywhere?"

"*Time is everywhere—the past, the future, and a present that never exists. What will be, what has been, what may be to come, all of them exist here and now. All exist right here in the present. You can travel wherever you please once you can touch it.*"

"Wait, you said the present doesn't exist?"

"*The present never exists, but if there is no present, there is no past or future either. Remember, again, to forget all you've ever known to be true.*"

"Okay, I'll try." Isha paused thoughtfully. "Where are you?"

"*I am in you. We are one, you and I. I have lived inside you for a long time.*"

"I've felt you before." It suddenly clicked within her. "Yes, many times before. You've spoken to me."

"*I came to you and then became part of you. I had no choice.*"

"So, you control me then?" For the first time she felt uneasy. It rushed through her mind. Were her decisions not her own? Were her actions not of her own choosing?

"*I do not control you. We are one, yet we are also separate. I am a flash in your consciousness, like a thought or a dream. Like a thought in the mind, but one that is not of mind.*"

"I don't understand."

"*You don't need to understand. You just need to accept that this is the way things are. I'm sorry, but I had no choice. I had to come to you.*"

For a moment there was total silence. Isha ran back what she had been told, and what she had been asked to accept without question. She felt uncomfortable. This entity had come and, it seemed, invaded her body without asking. Maybe even infiltrated her soul.

Now she was stuck with that which she couldn't understand, in a situation she never asked for. The one thing she certainly did understand was that The Fleck, whatever that was, was far more powerful than she.

Fear started bubbling up inside her, and questions ran through her mind. What if it meant her harm? What if meant harm to others? Her heart raced as the frightening reality of the situation swirled around her being.

"*Don't fear, Isha. I will not hurt you or others. I love you.*"

The Fleck could read her thoughts and feel her fears. This scared Isha even more. She shuddered, sick to her core, but not a physical shudder, a spiritual one. Was it true that her thoughts were no longer her own? Was it true this thing inside her knew everything about her?

The Fleck made her warm. It told her without words that it was there to protect her, to make her powerful. It showed her that her thoughts were her own and it did not spy upon her. It just was.

"Don't you have a name?" Isha asked.

"*No. I am The Fleck. I am not a who...I am a what.*"

"Well, I'm a person, and I need to give you a name. How else can I address you? If we are one—and I don't remember ever being unhappy being just me on my own, by the way—if now I'm us, then you need a name." She paused as she thought. "Flick. That's what I'll call you. It's not that different from The Fleck anyway."

"*I will accept this label, Isha, if it is indeed one you need to give me.*"

"It is. Okay, Flick, why me?"

"*I had no choice. I had to come. To escape. To hide.*"

"To hide from what?"

"*Dark Space...*"

Dark Space

Seconds drifted to nowhere. Seconds that, it seemed, mattered not in that place, before Isha finally asked, "What is the Dark Space?"

"Dark space is a higher being also, but maybe what you would consider an anti-star, an energy that is dark. Most stars burn bright, create heat, and at times, life, but not this star. Where stars bring life, the anti-star brings death. It sucks in the warmth and the light and leaves behind frozen, shadowy ruins of what once lived. A human eye could never even see it, but it is there, it is alive, and it is conscious. It is energy, much like The Fleck, but this energy is far vaster and with far greater power.

"It has been using The Fleck and our power to do its bidding. It is causing much pain throughout the cosmos.

"We learned the only Fleck it cannot find, or control, are ones that make a union with another physical entity. I had to escape. So many are already a slave to its whim. The Fleck are needed to fight back. We cannot be forced to do Dark Space's bidding. We must stop it."

"So, by 'we,' you mean you and me, right? What does any of this have to do with me?"

"Some beings may call it destiny, some may call it fate, but this task has befallen both you and The Fleck, Isha. These circumstances are beyond our control. We have been trapped in a web, and now we must find our way out of it. The stakes are higher than you can ever imagine. It is senseless to wish that things are different when, indeed, they are not. You must accept this so we can continue our work."

"When you say 'continue our work,' by that you're suggesting that our work has already begun?"

"Our work has begun. Search your memories. Search your dreams, Isha, for you will see the answers. You already know this to be true. I will show you the way."

A wave of energy overcame her, from the outer to the inner, where it flowed through her, and the walls of the room that surrounded her fell apart and blew away like dust in the wind. She left the bonds of her body and floated free. Isha was tugged towards destiny, from the realms of her reality to another place.

This was a place she knew. She had been there before. She went back to the dream when she was inside the woman and had saved the hooded child. Was that real? It must have been real. Somewhere within her it clicked into place, a dawning realisation of something that, really, she had always known. Like the dawning of a new reality, one that had existed all along, yet was just out of reach. She accepted it was real.

Isha had known and felt The Fleck for a long time. Now she could even pinpoint the exact moment she started to feel different. The Fleck had entered her one afternoon, and she had no idea why at the time, but she felt as though she had suddenly woken up. She had felt more alive in an instant, like a switch of evolution had gone off inside her, and perhaps that's exactly what had happened. Maybe she had stepped onto a new plain of existence.

Most people would have been terrified to be without a choice, for something to happen against your will, something as heinous as invading one's soul. To be stolen in the night, to do something else's bidding. That something being powerful and unrestrained that a mere human could never understand. Somehow Isha was not afraid, like it knew her inner being, like they were connected. All the time, The Fleck had reassured her and coached her through it, hardly making its presence known.

Isha grew angry. She burned with the determination that she would purge this invading entity from her consciousness and once again have her mind, body, and spirit all to herself. Soon, almost instantly, the rage and hostility calmed, and she felt at peace again. She began to wonder if Flick had soothed her anger from within, but somehow her thoughts never quite joined themselves together.

A flashback entered her mind. She saw the hooded child in the rain. She heard their cries and saw the look of terror etched on their face. Something about them seemed important. Something about them linked this all together. Not so much a thought but more a feeling. Whether it was her own or came from Flick, or anywhere else in the cosmos, she had no clue. She only knew the child was the key to everything.

"What does that child have to do with this, Flick?"

"The child is very important. If they had died that night, many terrible times would befall so many. You saved countless lives."

"But why?"

"Before I get to the child, you need to know... Dark space, it is pure destruction. It plays the game of life and death. It wants to destroy whole planets, whole star systems, leaving all life floating like ghosts in the empty space. It leaves nothing but death in its terrible wake."

"Why is it so evil. What does it want?"

"Evil? Oh, no, it is not evil. It's all about the point of view."

"What? That is evil! How could it ever not be?"

"Look at it like this, Isha—a human sees a spider and squashes it with their shoe. Does the human think they're evil? No, not at all, but I'm pretty sure the spider probably does. Dark Space is more complicated, however, like a human child that burns ants with a magnifying glass. Again, does the child think in that moment it's being evil? No. But it's as simple as that child killing those ants for its own entertainment. No other reason. That is Dark Space. That's what it does. Other planets and all life upon them are destroyed for no more than its own entertainment. That's simply what it does, and what it's here to do."

"Wait, Flick, it must have a goal of some kind."

"Does the child with the magnifying glass have a goal? I understand that from a human point of view, voiding entire stars of energy or sucking all the life out of an entire planet is gargantuan,

but to Dark Space, they are as insignificant as ants are to humans. This is a violent cosmos, that is a fact you need to wake up to."

"I don't think ants are insignificant," Isha protested.

"And that is why I am here with you, not some other human entity. For your purity of thought and your inner beauty."

Warmth poured over Isha, the warmth of a smile but without a face. Flick mesmerised her with the words, made her glow, made her feel special. She believed she was lucky she'd been chosen to be connected to such a powerful entity. It was a feeling that bubbled in her energy, again making her feel calm and serene, yet still somehow bursting with power. The situation was almost incomprehensible, yet one, despite all logic, she felt comfort within. She could think and speak and feel and see, but always without body. She was energy or consciousness, just as The Fleck was. She was energy, and the Fleck was within her. Combined, they were energy within energy. It spelled a new reality, an awakening, a moment after which she could never be the same again. The daydream lasted but a moment until she was sucked out of it and back to the place she was before.

Her mind swirled, and she lingered for a few seconds before she fully snapped out of the daydream. "How does Dark Space destroy planets, Flick?"

"It uses The Fleck to do its bidding. It is devious. It manipulates species against species. It destabilises civilisations. It starts wars on planets or interplanetary ones. It does all with a warm glow of joy as it watches them crumble one by one. Or worst of all, it kills the host star and destroys the entire system. It can drain a whole star in a few million years, and the populations nearby are powerless to stop it."

"Is there any way it can be stopped?"

"This I do not know, Isha. I just do not know. All we can do is hope."

"We have to find the child, don't we?" Isha knew it as a certainty, like her heart had told her, like it was knowledge that was deeply rooted inside her core. Things seemed clear to her, even in the whirl of confusion and unknowing. She had no time or use for fear; there was a journey ahead and she had no choice but to go. It called to her, nagging at her soul, until there was no such thing as a choice. It simply had to be.

"The child is lost and must be found. A great many civilizations rely on the fate of them."

"Who is this child?"

"They are the bringer of knowledge and light. They are the future. They are the only hope for the cosmos. They must be protected from dark forces."

"But why?"

"Some answers, Isha, I simply do not have. We have no direction, and we have no plan. We simply must do what we must when the time is upon us to do it, and that time is soon."

"I thought that time didn't matter."

"To The Fleck, or to us as one, it does not. To Dark Space it means not a thing, but to the life of the child, it means everything. The child is bound by the restraints of body and gravity and time, but we must free them. They are in grave and mortal danger. With their death, the galaxy will be destabilised, and all-out war will face us all. A war that nobody can win."

"What about Earth?"

"Earth is weak and unready. The planet will be destroyed, quickly, without making powerful alliances. They will strike first, as humans always do, and then the consequences, the vengeance, will swiftly be unleashed. Humans will be conquered, enslaved, or blown out of all existence like so many before."

Shock followed by fear bubbled inside Isha. The fate of her own planet, of everything she had ever known or loved, was tied directly to her own. "We must not let it happen, Flick. Where is the child?"

The Intruder

"Where is the child?"

"I don't know. I don't know!" The grey creature let out an ear-splitting scream, loud and shrill, roaring in a mix of terror and pain.

"The child is here somewhere." The Hunter reached forward and grabbed the sides of the grey creature's head with its long fingers. It let out an unearthly rasp.

The grey creature's eyelids slid horizontally across its almond-shaped eyes, and it clamped them tight. Pain surged through it, twisting its form. It convulsed and writhed in the metal seat. Finally, the rasp stopped, and the creature sucked in enormous breaths. It exuded slime-like perspiration from its leathery skin. Its eyes oozed tears of clear jelly. It opened its eyes with its chest heaving up and down and stared up at the evil, long, slender figure, cloaked and shrouded in shadow, that stood menacingly over it. It whimpered, which brought nothing but disdain from its antagonist. It was at the mercy of this Hunter, this agent of darkness who brought only death.

"Now, I have your attention. Where is the child?"

"I don't know. I swear I don't. Your torture won't work. I can't tell you anything."

The Hunter took an intimidating stride towards the grey creature as it squirmed. Its face was scrunched up in fear, anticipating more pain.

"What you fail to understand is you can tell me and live, you cannot and die, but either way, I will find out what I want to know. I always do."

The grey creature sat and breathed for a moment, fury and desperation building up behind its eyes. It would die right there, sat in the chair, and accept its fate, or it could make one last effort to fight.

It stared wildly and jumped from the seat, lunging desperately forward as it did. It reached out a clumsy and weak grasp for the Hunter. The Hunter flowed like water, swooping silently and slipping out of the way. The grey creature sprawled forward, off balance and useless, arms spread wide, sliding along the shiny floor. It pushed itself up on trembling arms to its hands and knees. It was now certain its plight was less than hopeless. It knew its time had met the end. The clumsy grasp was the last chance to save its own life, and that last chance had failed miserably.

The rasp left the Hunter's mouth again as it grabbed the grey creature by the head once more, scrambling its brain. Its arms collapsed, and it fell face first to the floor, bucking violently from side to side. A throat-tearing scream left its mouth. It rolled over, convulsing for a few seconds, then it stopped. Its once-black eyes were pearly and glazed. Dark veins throbbed and pulsed just below its skin. It lay back, its head hitting the floor with a thud.

A wave of coldness overcame the grey creature, and it awoke. Its head hurt, like the inside had been on fire. It could barely see, and it was drowning in pain.

"Where... is ... the child?"

"They are somewhere you will never find them," the grey creature growled defiantly.

"Then where is the scientist, Vertin?"

The grey creature shook its head in defiance. Still, it refused to talk.

The rasp rang out once more, louder and fiercer than before. The grey creature's muscles contracted like it was being electrocuted. Its black veins were now swollen and nearly bursting through its thin skin. It stopped convulsing, even though the rasp continued. The closest thing it could make to a smile came across its lipless slit of a mouth. Black blood dripped thick out of its nose and mouth and puddled around it.

The Hunter kicked the limp, lifeless body on the ground in annoyance. It removed its hood and cloak, and white light poured out from within it. The bipedal form of the Hunter morphed and snaked and twisted into different shapes, from a solid upright being to what was little more than a stream of bright light. It stretched and swirled and grew with immense power glowing brightly from it. It floated off the ground and swooped through the room and underneath the unopened door. It wound its way down a bright empty corridor, but even if the corridor had been being bustling with life, it would have gone completely unseen. It blended perfectly against the white walls, camouflaged against the backdrop. The lights beamed down, making it more invisible than ever.

The Hunter was the opposite of a solid being hiding in the shadows, it was ever-changing and hidden in the light. It was silent in its pursuit, brimming with deadly intent, searching for the next target—the scientist known as Vertin.

Further and further the Hunter travelled, seeking all the while. It was almost as though it was sniffing the air, like a predator searching for its prey. It scanned every room and every corner for its target.

Ahead was a door, and the Hunter twitched with excitement. It could feel the target nearby. Its elevated senses were alert as it glided on. The Hunter bristled, the thirst for blood its only thought. It shot towards the door that was no barrier against it. Like a ghost, it flowed through the cracks, morphing to fit and, in seconds, was on the inside.

An alarm rang out, loud, shrill, and whooping. That sound told the Hunter that they had found the body of the grey creature. Soon the corridors of the enormous craft would be teeming with more of their kind, armed and searching for the deadly intruder in their midst. This intruder, however, they would not find easily. As long as it stayed in the light, it blended in like it wasn't even there.

Clumping boots on small feet passed below as the Hunter hovered flat on the ceiling. The grey creatures ran by, completely oblivious to the deadly warrior above them. They urgently searched every room, and then continued down the corridor. The Hunter waited for them to pass, then slid silently down the wall and continued its search. It knew that Vertin, being a scientist, should be located in the laboratory, so eliminating one room at a time, it searched. It snaked invisibly through every door and slipped stealthily by the grey creatures as it went, until finally, it reached the lab.

It slid beneath the door and entered. It was dark and huge, and now the Hunter was visible in the shadows. All the equipment was within, but there was no sign of any of the scientists. It hissed and cursed in the words of a strange language, its senses switched on, alert, but still, it couldn't sense its prey.

The Hunter stood there glowing; there was little it could do now to avoid exposure. It moved on, searching every inch for a clue as to Vertin's whereabouts. It went through the room and then into another. Each was set up for different, twisted experiments. In one, hundreds of alien babies from many species filled jars that were stacked floor to ceiling. In the next, there were strange, larger creatures in tanks, suspended in liquid with floating silver beds and savage-looking contraptions fixed all around them. They looked like instruments of torture, not ones of science.

The Hunter went further and further through the rooms, each space telling a chilling tale of the grim crimes the grey creatures committed. Horrific experiments done on stolen beings. Gross atrocities enacted to who knows what end?

The search continued, every inch scanned, until there was only one room remaining. The door was round and domed, locked, and magnetically sealed. The Hunter probed the entry, but there was no way it could get through. For the first time since it boarded the craft, the frustrated Hunter paused for thought.

With a hiss, the door split into four, and the sections retracted leaving a circular opening. The Hunter was excited. It entered quickly with its senses running wild. It could feel it, the one he'd come for—Vertin.

The small, grey creature stood staring at the Hunter as it morphed back into the fearsome bipedal creature it had been before.

"I've found you," the Hunter hissed menacingly. "Now, you shall tell me what I want to know."

"I won't tell you anything," Vertin replied defiantly. Leathery skin stretched across its face as it smiled.

Before the Hunter could react, Vertin reached over and pushed a button on the touch screen behind it.

A shrill and brain-piercing whistle rang out. Then a flash exploded like a sheet of lightning. All inside the room was turned to instant powder.

The Fever

The sheets clung to him, grabbing every inch of his shivering form. The bitter cold came from outside, and he lay convulsing and shaking, teeth chattering. He hugged his knees. The sweat leaked out of him, leaving his skin slimy. His eyes were clamped tightly shut. He wished he could sleep, that the pain and discomfort would melt away, but his blood burned inside him. He was awake, but not really there. Seemingly lost between two realities—his physical waking pain and his mind wandering off to strange places.

He groaned, and his flesh tingled. He drew the blankets tighter, cocooning himself inside, trying to keep out the bitter cold. The sheets below him were drenched with sweat, and they felt like ice on his skin. The heat was burning inside, the cold was stinging outside. Liam had never felt so sick.

He drifted for a moment until dreams haunted him awake again, and the savage fever was there to greet him. That fever was all there was. It consumed him and left him helplessly shivering.

His skin tingled again, and it lingered, then shot down his arms leaving numbness and pins and needles in his hands. He frantically rubbed them together and shook them to get the blood flowing again. He stopped, and for a second, they felt normal, but when his senses caught up, pins and needles shot up his entire body, leaving his hands and feet buzzing.

Waves surged over his arms and legs then his body, rolling across him like lightning. He screamed, and like a crackle of electricity, his whole body fizzed. It filled his entire being at once, inside and out, no longer in waves but now a constant, painful hum.

His body floated up from the bed, an inch above the sheets. He burned with inner warmth, so he flung the covers from himself and threw them down onto the floor. His head fell back, gently hitting the pillow. Like gravity no longer existed, the weight of his body left him.

He levitated, hovering just over his bed. He looked down at his arms. The colour of his skin started to fade. It turned pale grey, then ghostly white, then semi-transparent until the shades blurred like a wave of pixels. He could see right through his arms as the colours crawled from his feet upwards until, in seconds, his entire body vanished to nothing. Liam was still there. He could see his room. He could still feel the pain, but he was completely invisible.

Questions rushed by, never staying long enough to figure an answer, but then he probably didn't want to know the answers anyway. He didn't feel anything except for the buzz all over him. Like a ripple of light, his colours started to return. He was astonished, and it froze him. The fear made way for awestruck fascination.

He watched his body morphing before him, but it was as if it was happening to someone else. The edges of his form blurred and fuzzed and gently split in two. The colours faded once more to transparent, then invisible. He watched on as the colours returned and became solid.

His form morphed until it had two separate outlines. His head pounded. Liam felt as if he had two separate bodies, but they were there together. It gave him the sensation that he was watching himself on a split screen, or as if he was two different beings, in different places at the same time. One body was his own, while the other was slender and pale with yellowy, leathery skin. Long, extended fingers stretched out much farther than those of his human hands.

He stared, frozen. It took him a few seconds for the shock to catch up. He let out a yelp and instinctively raised his hands to his mouth. The human body and the other one moved together. Liam felt the cold, foreign fingers touch his horrified face. He shuddered to his core, screamed out loud, and tried to move. However, he was stuck where he was. He moved his arms again, but this time they stayed where they were. At least, the human ones did.

The spindly alien arms moved, and hands dangled above him near his open eyes. The longest finger on the left hand reached down, bending at the knuckles, and then was pushed hard up his nose until he heard a pop. He yelped in agony, but it came out silent.

His body was completely immobilised, yet his heart thundered, overwhelmed by fear. The two instinctual options of fight or flight were completely unavailable to him. He was trapped.

The strange creature removed its finger, and blood trickled out. He was on the brink. On the verge of being broken by his fear. His body couldn't take one more granule of stress on top of the mountain that had already built up.

"Help!" Liam cried out loud, his voice finally free. "What is happening to me?" He sniffed back tears and, with them, blood. Then, like a bubble bursting, the alien body was gone.

That was when he felt it, a presence lurking inside his being, lingering silently in the background, taunting, dark and brimming.

"What do you want?" Liam's tone was forceful.

The presence said nothing. It watched, silent, never admitting its existence. It scoured Liam's inner landscape intently, every action, every emotion, every thought. It dwelled dark, hanging on the edges, creeping and haunting in silent whispers, probing at his soul. It didn't want to speak to him. It wanted to test him, to push him to the limits of what a human can endure to see if he would crack.

The alien hand reappeared in a flash, like someone had changed the channel. It reached upwards, grabbing his face, crushing his cheeks in its gangly grasp. Liam recoiled in fear. He screamed as the cold fingers of the other hand stroked his face, winding along the contours for a moment, then the lean digits stopped and forced their way inside his mouth. The vile fingers probed his cheeks.

He tried desperately to bite down, to squirm, to get those things away from him, but he couldn't. Tears started to well and fall from his eyes as his whole body trembled. Frightened, invaded, and whimpering, Liam had never felt so helpless.

He retched and reached up his human hand to grab the alien one. His slipped right through, but still he could feel it violating his mouth. It was there, but at the same time, somehow it wasn't. At times it felt like he was the alien. Other times, like the alien was separate from him, yet still there. Like a reflection in the mirror, it seems there is a whole world that you can never step inside.

He may not have known if any of it was real, but the fear was real, and so was the pain. They were all he knew.

With tears rolling down his cheeks, he shivered. This fear was far deeper, far more intense than he had ever known. Not the fear of dying, but the fear of much, much worse.

Finally, the hands pulled away from him, leaving him shuddering in disgust. They lingered before his cowering form, then, like steam on the breeze, they drifted apart and vanished.

Liam's ordeal was over, but now remained the trauma, forever engrained on his soul. He could never forget that feeling, how powerless he had been, how sick it made him feel. He whimpered again, wiping the tears from his face with his human hand.

The presence watched on. It twitched with glee. It was entertained by its own power. A wave of joy filled it. It was finally satisfied that it had pushed him to the breaking point, to the very edge, but indeed, Liam hadn't quite fallen over it. Only now would the presence release him from that twisted nightmare.

Liam plummeted downwards and bounced on his bed. He awoke from the hazy dream-like state with the bump. His head felt clearer, and the fever had lifted. He was suddenly wide-awake, stunned as his mind flashed back through the events of the night.

Reluctantly, he patted his body down and took a few seconds to pluck up the courage to look. To his relief, he was himself. The memories gathered and then hazed in the background, never quite fitting together.

He lay staring up at the ceiling, trying to make sense of it only to recoil every time he thought of it, over and over for hours until he was exhausted. At long last, Liam forgot the weight of his insomnia and the fear that had rushed through him for what seemed forever. He drifted away from the confusion that ruled. His body had no choice but to sleep.

What seemed as though only moments later, his phone blared out, and he awoke with a start. His eyelids were heavy, and his eyeballs stung with fatigue. He looked at the phone and huffed when he saw the cracked screen, but it was Penny's ring tone. She was the one person in the world he would even consider answering the phone to at that moment.

He took a breath, shook his head, and cleared his throat, yet his voice croaked anyway. "Hey, you. How are ya?" He tried his best to not sound grouchy, but he failed miserably.

"Liam, are you all right?"

"Erm, yeah, I'm cool. Why?"

"You haven't been at uni for three days, and no one's seen or heard from you. Are you sick or something?"

"You what? Three days?" A deep furrow came across his brow. "I mean, I had a bit of a fever, but that was just last night."

"What happened to the other two days then?" Penny sounded concerned.

"I had a fever and then I slept, and that's it. Then you called and woke me up, and here we are."

"It's Thursday."

"Thursday? I haven't been asleep for two days... Have I?"

"I'm worried about you, bud. I'm coming to see ya, but before I do, you haven't got the zombie virus or something, have you?" She giggled infectiously and managed to get a chuckle out of Liam. Just for a second, she lifted the grumpiness from him, as she always seemed to.

"Nah, I feel fine. Honest. Just a little groggy is all. Come over. And Penny…"

"What?" she asked, knowing full well what was coming.

"Can you grab some food on the way? All I've got in the fridge is one beer, half a carton of gone off milk, and some cheese."

"What? You always make me do this. I'm not your wife or your mother, you know."

"Yeah, true, but I'm too ugly to get a wife and my mum lives miles away, so who else will look after me?"

"You're so pathetic."

"And I *have* been sick." He put on his best 'I need someone to look after me' voice.

Penny tutted. "We'll just have pizza when I get there, cos you're pushing your luck, pal."

"All right. You're the best, Penny. Catch ya soon."

"See ya later, baked potata."

Skipping

Liam buzzed Penny through the front door of his tatty old apartment block. Three flights of stairs later and she was walking through his door. It was dark inside. The curtains were drawn, and a musty smell lingered in the air. Liam's nose was used to it; Penny's certainly was not.

"Ew, boys are gross! Open the curtains and the windows. It stinks in here."

"It's cold," he protested.

"Well, I'd rather freeze to death than sit in this badger's den with you."

He laughed. "Okay, okay. I'll do it, I'm doing it. Who says 'badger's den,' though? And also, are you suggesting badgers aren't clean? They may have something to say about that."

The quips saved him momentarily from the embarrassment of his own laziness.

"Well, badgers, see," Penny explained, "they're like humans. Some are clean, some aren't. But you, you'd be a super stinky one, for sure." They both broke out into laughter.

"You don't see that in the old docos, do ya?"

"What? Stinky badgers?"

"And here we have," he did his best Sir David Attenborough impression, "the lesser-spotted stinky badger. Often found festering in its own stench in its preferred habitat of student apartments after suffering a fever. This badger has been laying low, but tonight, he hunts. His prey items include the last beer, take- out pizza, and garlic bread."

They both doubled over with a giggling fit.

Soon the apartment was smelling fresh again, some music was on, and pizza and garlic bread were on the way.

They stood perched on the kitchen counter, sharing the beer.

"So, what actually happened?" Penny stopped the jokes for a moment. She was concerned for her friend.

"I don't know. I just had, like, the worst fever. It must have made me delirious or something. I think I was hallucinating and stuff."

"That can be quite com—"

Everything went dark, like the planet's light had been switched off. Less than a second later, the lights flicked back on again.

"Yeah, they were, like, flying at thirty thousand feet or something. It was wild," Penny said.

Liam's eyes darted around. Now he was sat on the sofa with his feet up. He had absolutely no idea what Penny was talking about.

"What?"

"Oh, weren't listening again. Typical of you, that is. The last time I tell you a great story, pal."

"No, I was listening. I just wondered—"

The light went out and back on again.

"And he could come to no other conclusion," Liam's professor said.

In the flash of a second, Liam was sitting in a lecture at university. He was overcome with fear.

"See, told you," Penny whispered confidently in his ear.

"What?" Liam stood up. Panic started to flow through him. "I gotta go!" he yelled, loud enough to turn every head in the room. Leaving all his belongings behind, he ran for the door.

He flung it open, then slammed the door hard behind him. His footsteps echoed off the walls as he ran down the corridor for the exit while his heart echoed around his chest.

The lights above him shone brightly, but ahead, the exit was covered in shadow. He ran as fast as he could muster, desperate to get out of the building. He just couldn't be in there for another minute. Liam had no idea what was happening to him, but it frightened him completely.

Relief filled him when he reached the end of the corridor. He ran forward into the shadow that covered the exit. Mist swirled around, coming from underneath the doors and dancing round his feet. "What the…?" he said out loud.

Reaching forward, he pushed the bar down and burst out the exit doors, through the mist. He stepped out into the sunlight and headed towards the train station. He ran onto the platform panting and checked the time. He had five minutes to wait for his train.

The station was almost empty around him, and Liam found himself pacing up and down or standing still and jiggling his legs impatiently. The train rumbled close, entered the station, and stopped with a hiss. The doors opened, and dark mist swirled and poured through the opening. He took a step back, but the mist rolled forward, surrounding him as it did.

Again, the light went out for a split second and then back on again.

In the blink of an eye, he was back in his apartment, lying in bed, lights on. He sat bolt upright and scanned the room. His head was spinning. The confusion made him giddy, testing his version of reality. Fear consumed his every thought.

His eyes widened as they darted to the corner of the room. The dark mist was lingering and swirling there. It hung in the air, not spreading throughout the room like smoke but rolling menacingly in the corner.

Liam braced himself. He felt like he could skip again at any moment. He was leaping in time. Hours had passed without him, but to everyone else, he'd been there all along.

"*Stop, we need him!*" the voice rasped from deep inside Liam's being. All at once, he knew—this was the presence he had felt before. The one who watched and tested him.

"What?" Liam replied to it, though he knew the voice was not addressing him; it was addressing the mist. He looked on nervously at the mysterious form in the corner. Was it alive?

"*I shall not stop. This is fun!*" The voice came from within the mist, where evil lingered on its edge. A dark voice that made Liam's blood run cold.

"*You will leave him be, or the consequences will be extreme,*" the voice demanded.

"*I don't fear your consequences. You are weak.*"

"*No, Time Snatcher. I am The Fleck!*" the presence inside growled and bristled.

"*I can do what I wish. Time is mine. I have it to spare.*" The Time Snatcher's misty form rolled with each word, ever moving and changing.

Liam shuddered to his soul as the presence inside him burned with the purest rage. He could feel it, bubbling up from the deepest depths of his being. He stared wild at the mist, taking on the rage, growling like a dog. His eyes pierced it with the purest hatred. They glazed over, pearly, and his skin faded to grey.

The voice came out thunderous and vibrated inside the young man. "*Time matters not to The Fleck!*"

The mist hissed like a snake at the words, and then the light flashed off again, then on.

Liam was somewhere else but, this time, a place he did not know. He was now out in the open in cruel weather. Sand was whipping at his face in a wild wind that blew against him. He covered his eyes and turned his back away from the howling gusts.

Before him was a strange landscape. The sky had a tinge of purple, and the sand below his feet was black. The air was thin. It was hard for him to catch his breath. He felt heavy, like his arms and legs were made of lead. One thing was clear—he wasn't on Earth any longer.

Still, the mist swirled nearby, enjoying its little game.

Again, the presence inside him roared angrily. "*Stop this, Time Snatcher, for I am The Fleck!*"

The light went off and on.

Liam stood in a long dark hallway. Before he could even take it in, the light went out and then on again.

He reappeared in a room with a table in the middle. Lurking behind the table, there it was... the mist.

"What? This is not where I brought him!" the mist screamed out.

"I told you I was more powerful than you, Time Snatcher. I am The Fleck!"

Then the voice silently spoke to Liam. *"Grab it."*

Like he had been programmed for the task, Liam reached down under the table, and his hand went cold. He raised it again, watching as a bubble formed round it and attached itself to his wrist. He pointed the bubble towards the mist, and the quivering mass pulsed. An electric flash rolled through the bubble and a transparent cube flew out of it, springing as it did, heading quickly towards the mist. The strange cube grew, then consumed the Time Snatcher, leaving it trapped inside. The cube rapidly shrunk around it. When it was no bigger than a golf ball, it shot up rapidly and vanished through the ceiling.

Liam dropped to his knees, wailing, as tears streamed down his face. His mind was racing. Everything was so confusing, like he didn't know who or what he was anymore. He tried to scream the fear and confusion away, but they remained. In fact, they consumed him, eating his shivering soul alive. It was too much for him to take. He squeezed at the sides of his head with his palms and tried his best to block it out. He wanted to make sense of it, but to make sense of the senseless seemed impossible.

He came to the realisation that he needed to demand the presence inside him give him some answers. Before he could even finish the thought, the lights went out...

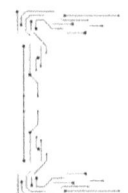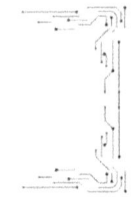

The Calling

The light came on, yet all around it remained a blanket of darkness. Liam was floating, lost in silent emptiness, suspended alone in nothing but the endless dark. He felt no sensations on his skin. He saw and heard nothing at all. His senses were useless in that place. It was impossible to tell if he was a floating thought, a consciousness, or if he was in his body. The only thing he knew was his emotions were real, and there were plenty of them.

Now his fear was forced to give way. Things had spiralled so far out of his control for so long, he was exhausted, and he could fear no more. Perhaps he was getting used to the fear. Maybe it was becoming his home. Either way, he was slowly growing a self-preserving acceptance of the situation. He didn't understand anything, but at least for the moment, he was safe.

He looked around in all directions but couldn't see a thing. He couldn't see his hand in front of his face, if indeed he had a hand or a face. He calmed himself each second and, lost from bounds of his body, he attempted to probe at the situation in mind. He searched for answers for what seemed forever, but those answers didn't exist. His thoughts drifted on nothing, with nowhere left to go. In the end, he felt lost. He was completely and utterly helpless. Cosmic forces were hard at work. These were forces beyond his mortal understanding or control. He was merely along for the ride.

The presence lurked within, and again, he felt it. It sneered at him, daring him to question it, teasing him. With no other option, Liam fully intended to question it.

"Are you here?"

The presence didn't speak. It watched. It was always watching.

"I know you're there. Answer me!"

Still, there was nothing.

"Please. I'm scared. Tell me what is happening. Please." Liam cried but without the release; restrained crying, not from his eyes, but from within.

The presence laughed as it revelled in his pain.

"Please!"

The laughter faded out. *"Yes, yes, I am here, human. I am always here,"* the voice growled and rumbled from nowhere.

"I know you. I've felt you. What do want from me?" Liam barked the words as his anger boiled.

"That entity was the Time Snatcher. It was stealing your time. It's a parasite. It feeds on time. I saved you from it. You should be grateful to me, not angry."

Thoughts ran wild through Liam's mind. It was certainly true—time had been skipping and this presence, whoever they were, had stopped it. But The Fleck had been there far longer than that, spying on him from within, learning, pushing him, probing his weaknesses.

"Yes, I was here, awaiting the Time Snatcher." It answered Liam's thoughts, triggering his fear again. *"I knew it was coming, and I knew you would die."*

Liam fought to remain calm. His thoughts were being stolen. This presence, whatever it was, was inside his very being. He had to find a way to get it out. His mind ran it over and over, desperately searching for an answer, but the presence somehow calmed him.

"I will not hurt you. If I was to hurt you, I would have done it by now. You are safe with me. You are far more powerful than you can ever imagine."

"Powerful because of you, and a prisoner because of you?"

"You are no prisoner. You are freer than any human ever could be."

"I am?"

"You must trust The Fleck. I am here for you. I already saved you. I could have let the Time Snatcher take away all of your time until your life had gone by in no more than a flash. Your entire life gone and wasted to sustain another entity."

"I guess I have to thank you then, so… thank you."

"*I need no thanks. There are things I must do. The Fleck does not need another entity's thanks to validate what had to be done. Human pride is foolish and pointless.*"

"Well, if humans are so pointless, why save me at all? What am I to you?"

"*Humans are pointless, but you, you are important.*"

"Right, you'd better tell me what you want with me and what the hell is going on. I've had enough of the tricks and sneaking around. Just tell me what is going on, okay?"

"*The Fleck doesn't use tricks. The Fleck just is. The Fleck just does.*"

"That all sounds great and everything," Liam said sarcastically, losing his patience, "but again, enough of the riddles. What do you want?"

"*Know that you have an important job to do human. Know that the fate of your world depends upon you, you and The Fleck, completing this task.*"

"Can you please stop talking about yourself in the third person. It's really annoying. You're driving the Liam crazy."

"*Stop your insults and hostility or you shall feel pain. I can make you feel pain!*" The voice growled through him, huge and powerful, leaving Liam quivering in its mighty wake.

He backed down immediately. The Fleck, with so much power, was intimidating. It could hurt him for certain, and it would even though it had said it wouldn't. It could probably crush him like an ant, but why would it want to? That he didn't know.

"*The Fleck has no choice.*" It answered his thoughts, once more chilling him to the soul. "*The task must be completed no matter what it takes. The Fleck doesn't want to hurt you. The Fleck needs your help. But if The Fleck needs to, The Fleck will take your help.*"

"Please, just tell me what's happening. Maybe I'll be happy to help. Maybe I will." A wave of hurt filled Liam's soul and invisible tears fell from non-existent eyes again. "Please help. I'm so confused and afraid. Please help me understand. Please."

The hopeless despair filled him, and he sobbed within. The bitterness welled, threatening to consume him whole, but soon a warming energy started to fill his being. The despair lifted, and The Fleck smiled within him.

"The Fleck needed to test you, needed to know your strength. Only one with true inner strength can complete this task. Few humans are capable of what needs to be done."

"Can you tell me what it is that I'm in the middle of? Can you tell me what I must do? Fleck, or whatever your name is, all I want is to have my life back. I have things to do."

"Your life, or the mundane existence humans call a life, is not important."

"It's important to me!" Liam barked angrily.

"No more outbursts, human!"

Again, Liam was silenced and frozen as the voice boomed. He fought the instinct to cower again, but he did, nevertheless. He felt as though he was tiny, that he was nothing compared to this thing, this mighty force within him.

Liam was only an actor stuck in a script, going on a journey that he was forced to take. Stolen from his life against his will, to do things that were not of his choosing, there was only one thing he could be—a slave. He was being pushed into doing the bidding of this force that lived within him. Taking the parts of him it wanted and hating the rest. It left him shrouded in mist, completely lost inside himself, little more than a prisoner.

It wrapped him in fear and laughed as it consumed his frail humanity. It drained his emotions, emptying his bucket of strength until there was none left. He was on the very brink of insanity.

"Understand," the voice whispered, *"we are locked in a deadly battle. One across time and space. The Fleck are fighting amongst themselves, and the balance of the galaxy is in great danger. A child we must find and destroy, or great devastation will befall all things."*

"By 'destroy' you mean kill, right? I can't kill a child! You're totally off ya head."

"What if the child held a blade to your throat or a gun to your head? What if it was between you living or them? Would you feel the same?"

"I don't know. I've never been in that situation. I mean, you'd have to react in some way if it was your life at stake."

"You say you have never been in that situation, but that is the situation that you are in now. This child will destroy everything you love and beyond. They will bring forces of great destruction, and the war will be lost."

"What war?"

"A war that has raged for centuries in your near galaxy between what you would call extra-terrestrials. Important alliances need to form, and the child will divide and destroy. That is their purpose. Then all will be lost."

"Why don't we know about this war?"

"Because humankind is not ready to know. Humans are still primitive. They believe they are the peak of evolution when they are far from it. Even the ones who lived on Earth before you were more evolved than you."

"Before us?"

"I shall not waste my time with what you won't believe or understand. All that will do is create confusion."

"I may understand."

"You don't need to understand. Even if you could, it matters not. What you must understand is the task at hand and only the task."

"What if I don't want to do that task?" For a second, defiance seemed the best option.

"Then you shall die." The Fleck was cold, calculated, and calm.

A shudder ran through Liam, the words like icicles in his soul, but he needed courage, not fear, and from somewhere, that courage he found. "If you need me, you can't kill me, can you?"

"Do not underestimate what The Fleck can and will do. Your puny life means nothing to The Fleck. You are a speck of dust, atop a grain of sand, floating in a cosmic ocean. You should be pleased the Fleck has made a union with you. You are lucky that you will see things no other of your kind ever has. You will know powers that no other human has before."

"Yeah, and all I have to do is kill a child, right?"

"You will not kill the child. It will not be your hand that does the deed."

"Not my hand, but my will?"

"Our will combined. Our will to do what is right for all living things. Think of your friends and your loved ones. They will all be destroyed and far sooner than you can imagine. Your world will never evolve, and the humans of Earth will be extinct."

"Humans of Earth, meaning, there are other humans elsewhere?"

"There are many types of humans in many places. You are not as special as you think you are."

He stopped trying to figure it out when, suddenly, he was filled with child-like wonder. He dreamed what other humans from other places may be like. Slowly it dawned upon him that things he couldn't possibly imagine to be true really could be.

He didn't know if he could trust The Fleck. It had, after all, invaded him. It had made all these things happen to him. It had threatened him with pain and death, but if such terrible consequences truly could befall the planet, did he even have a choice? He could learn so much from The Fleck, and the promise of the answers to some of the biggest questions in the universe could be his. That was a pathway down which he simply had to travel.

Liam needed to know more. He needed to know what was happening, what he must do, and exactly what the consequences would be. This was a test of his very deepest moral fibre.

Visons ran through his mind. He zoomed through the emptiness of space, away from the solar system he knew, and out, far beyond. He flew, exhilarated, at unfathomable speed and stopped near an enormous empty black shell. Something within told him that it was a dead star, one that's energy had been sucked out. The fire, the light, and the life force were now evaporated.

Onwards the visions went zooming, over the top of black planets, floating haphazardly through space. They were like pieces of coal, drifting aimlessly amongst the nothing. The solar system was lifeless. It was haunting and devastating. He knew that once, here was life, but now, life was no longer. Everything there, in that harrowing place, was dead. The silent ghosts of countless souls who had perished called out in despair to an empty cosmos that would never hear their cries.

Liam whimpered.

"You can feel them, can't you?" The Fleck asked.

"Yes," he said as tears of sadness flowed through his soul.

"It is their energy that lingers; that is what you feel. The last moment of pain and fear before they met their end."

"Is that why it hurts so much?"

"That is why it hurts you so much."

Liam wished he could close his eyes to hide the harrowing vision. It brought him such grief. He could feel the lost souls calling out to him.

"I know what I must do."

The Tunnels

"Yes, I saw the child. My friend, she was with them, but now they're gone." The language was strange, but Isha could understand every word.

"Where did you last see them?"

"By the bridge. There's a woman. She's tall with purple hair and tattoos. People pay her to get them to the tunnels, it's said." The older woman, sweating and panting, rushed the words. She turned and continued with the streaming crowd, heading out of the city.

Isha was no longer in-body, yet she was inside another form. The street around her bustled. Countless humanlike beings were crammed tightly together. Most were wearing rags, and they were covered in filth. Like a river's current, the people flowed out of the city and towards the mountains in the distance. They were carrying all that remained of their lives in their arms or struggling to pull carts over the piles of rubble.

The city smoked. Thick and black, it went spiralling upward until it was carried away, zooming upon the wind. Ghosts of buildings that lay blackened and fallen lined the streets and the skyline. Strange vehicles, upturned or burned out, were strewn around, blocking the roads. What was once a great city was now little more than ruins. Children were screaming with fear and uncertainty in mothers' arms—mothers who had no more certainty than the children they tried to comfort.

There was a constant mumble in the background as streams of desperate people tried to get away from their shattered lives. The feeling of pure disbelief and desperation was palpable. These simple people had one day been living their lives and the next were upended in disarray. Total turmoil now reigned supreme. Those day-to-day streets where once people lived, worked, and travelled were now scarred beyond recognition. A city of countless, faceless individuals with all hope stripped away and the unknown thrust upon them. The only certainty they had was for their lives and the lives of their loved ones. They must leave and leave quickly.

Isha worked backwards against the crowd, like a solitary rock splitting the flow. The going was tough and slow. She was constantly pushed and hustled with every step as people surged past her.

She didn't know exactly where she was headed, nor did she care. She followed a pull from within, a longing that beckoned her along. Her goal was clear—the child was there somewhere, and all that mattered was the child.

She came to the bridge. Finally, the crowd was thinning a little. She started searching, running the whole time, asking people for the woman with purple hair. She may have asked twenty people, or perhaps a hundred, so one-minded in her goal was she that she didn't even notice.

"Yes, I saw her not ten minutes ago," an elderly woman confirmed.

"Where did she go?"

"I don't know. She was running. There was panic. Running that way." Her face was harrowed from the fear of the unknown and tears flowed down her wrinkled cheeks.

Isha hugged the woman tightly. The dirt on her skin and clothes was more than just superficial; she smelled bad. Isha's host felt the lady's body tremble in fear.

"What's happening? What were you running from?"

"They've been taking the children. They took my own grandson. The only thing left to do is run."

"Wait! Can't—" Before she could even finish the question, an explosion sent debris raining down upon them. The woman, still in her arms, went limp and lifeless. Isha let go, and she slumped down to the ground. Her skin was blackened.

A scream rang out and then another explosion shook the ground. Isha was thrown backwards by the force and was left rolling on the road. Her ears were ringing a shrill squeal from the blast. She rolled over and struggled back to her feet.

"*Run, Isha. Run,*" Flick's voice echoed from within her.

Her shoeless feet hurt as she stepped over the rubble that was left littering the street. Crowds of people ran haphazardly all over. Bodies lay lifeless. Others were left screaming, crushed or with severed limbs.

Another explosion rattled the whole world around her. Chunks of buildings dropped and crashed into the street. The ground shook hard beneath her feet. She covered her head with her arms and forced her legs to keep going. She saw an alleyway over the other side of the street. Maybe if she went down there, got off the main drag, she would avoid the explosions. The explosions that now were coming over and over with hardly a break in between.

She ran across the street, dodging stricken citizens as she went, jumping puddles of blood or bodies that lay unmoving. Each step damaged the soles of her feet more. The explosions continued, blowing the fleeing and screaming people apart. The blood and debris came down all around her. She was terrified, her breath heaving in her chest.

"*Flick, what's happening?*" she asked silently.

"*Just run, Isha. Head towards the alleyway. If they catch you or kill you, the child will be lost.*"

"If they catch me, *I'll* be lost!" she screamed, out loud this time.

A silver disk silently skimmed over her head. Three green orbs of light dropped down from it into the running crowd. A ball of fire blasted out in all directions, ripping the crowd to pieces, hacking huge chunks out of the underside of the bridge as it went. The shockwave sent Isha off her feet and down to the ground again. She was dirtied, but apart from a few scratches and bruises, she was unhurt.

"*Get up, Isha. You've got to keep moving. It's our only hope.*"

She scrambled back to her feet and finally made it across the street then rushed down the alleyway. She reached the shadows at the far end where she hid, waiting for the explosions to finally stop.

"Hey…hey, kid," a voice came from the shadows next to Isha.

"Huh?"

"You were lucky to make it out of there. They're like sitting ducks out on the open street. Most of the ones that headed for the mountains, they're dead now. Damn fools."

"Who are you?"

The tall figure shuffled out from her hiding place to reveal herself in the light. "I'm Vaz. Lucky you found me, kid. You got half a chance of getting out of here alive." She grabbed Isha by the arm and pulled her into the shadows beside her. "They're drones, and they can sense movement. We have to stay out of sight until the danger passes." She held a gun-like weapon in each hand.

"My name's Ish…"

"Nah, you're name's kid now, kid. Not worth me knowing names around here. Nobody's alive long enough."

"You're the tall one, with purple hair and tattoos?" Isha caught a glimpse of her hair.

Vaz smiled. "Well, I'm pretty tall, my hair is purple, and I'm covered in tattoos, so I guess so. But that's, of course, assuming there's no one else around here who fits the description."

"No, you're the one I'm looking for. I'm certain."

"Now why would a sweet kid like you wanna find a rough old warhorse like me?"

"You take people to the tunnels, don't you?"

"Listen up…there's no way you have ten thousand, kid. Sorry. It'll be too risky now, even if you do."

"No, wait, did you see a child? Someone told me you were with the child."

"Yeah, I was with the child and their family. They paid me thirty grand to get them inside the complex. They have protected digs there like these real rich families do."

"The child had a family?"

"Well, you know, it looked like one of those cross-species adoptions everyone's always crying about, where they can't have their own kid, so they buy one on the black market. They didn't quite look right."

"Vaz…"

"No way, kid."

"Vaz, please. You've gotta get me in there."

"No, kid."

"I have to get the child away from that family. They mean them nothing but harm!"

"Okay, sure. You wanna die and take me with you? Why not? Give me fifty grand, half now and half when the job's done, and I'll take you. Oh, wait…you don't have fifty grand, just as I suspected."

"You said ten earlier!"

"That was before I thought you actually wanted to do it. Oh, but let me guess, you haven't got ten either."

"No."

"How much have you got then, kid?"

"Erm, nothing."

"You've got some cheek! Unbelievable."

"Surely you'll be safer inside the tunnels, too, so all you've got to do is take yourself there, and I'll come with you. I'll be, like, your backup."

Vaz chuckled. "You're funny, kid, and smart, too. The tunnels are where I'm headed when the coast is clear. You're right—it is the safest place. Beats running for the mountains and getting blown apart like the others."

"You're going there anyway?"

"Yeah, but I had to at least try and get paid first."

It was Isha's turn to laugh.

They waited down the alley until the light faded.

"Now, kid, we're going to have to move quick, and we won't be able to see so well, so mind your feet and stay close. There'll still be drones out there searching for survivors."

They scuttled out of the alley, always remaining in the shadows, ducking low behind anything that could cover them. They checked the sky each time before scurrying to the next hiding place.

The city was deserted; well, at least void of life unscathed. Corpses lined the roads among the scorched ground. Still, some survivors lingered on, wailing, the hours of agony passing while they dreamed of death. A death that would inevitably meet them.

Some buildings burned, spewing toxic smoke into the atmosphere. It wafted down the deserted streets in the wind. The breeze was stale with the edge of death upon it. It howled, searching down city streets, rolling over each lost soul in its path, though those lost souls would never feel it.

"Try not to breathe the smoke, kid. That stuff is bad for you."

Isha followed Vaz closely, virtually in her shadow as she went. Isha felt safe with her and trusted her. Whether that was a feeling she had about Vaz or a simple matter of not having any choice, she couldn't know.

They ran for at least an hour, halfway across the city, gladly without encountering any drones.

"We need to get under the street. There's a manhole about a mile down there." Vaz pointed where they were headed. "That'll take us out of the city. There's one place we can access the tunnels from a cave in the rocks west of here. Under the city we should be safe. It's getting to the cave that'll be the problem."

"How do you know all this stuff?"

"I've only been taking folks to the tunnels since the war started. Even the rich folks that live in the complex need a little contraband every now and then." She smirked. "Look, just don't ask, okay?"

"I think I'm learning it's best not to." She chuckled.

"Playtime's over, kid. We've got a long way to go, and with any luck, we won't get blown to smithereens, cos that, that'll really mess up my evening."

"It'll probably be the highlight of my crazy week," Isha said sarcastically. "And yeah, it's your turn not to ask."

They ran out into the open, heading for the manhole.

"Kid, get down."

Two drones floated nearby, probing the wreckage, searching for even the slightest movement. Isha and Vaz hit the ground in a second and wedged themselves behind what remained of a wall.

"Stay dead still."

They both sat frozen, daring not to speak or even breathe. The drones lingered, zigzagging the wreckage, green lights probing, searching relentlessly for their prey.

All at once the drones zoomed away, and huge explosions again lit up the city.

"They're distracted, kid. Now, run. We can make it to the manhole. Stay close."

They tore out into the street, Isha's bare feet pounding the ground. Rubble jagged into her soles, bruising and ripping the skin. It was best to stay up on her toes and try to ignore the pain. Vaz was fast and wearing boots. Isha struggled to keep up, but something inside her made her run faster than she thought she could, put the pain out of her mind, and do what was required to get where she needed to.

Another explosion boomed out in the distance, shaking the ground. Vaz glanced over her shoulder. She could see green lights buzzing across the darkened sky.

"They're coming. Quick!"

Isha ran with everything she had, almost stumbling and tripping over herself. The green lights above swooped in from either side. Now just mere metres away, they ripped through the sky.

Vaz let Isha go in front of her and drew her weapons. "Don't stop, whatever happens, kid."

She stopped, took aim, and fired her weapons. Bolts of plasma lit up the sky. The first drone took the full brunt of the volley, explosions bursting on its silver shell. Sparks fizzed out and it veered off wildly, smashing into a building and exploding. She fired another volley at the second but only grazed it. It let out two of its orbs.

Vaz fired out of each gun, trying to take the orbs out of the sky. The plasma from her weapons smashed into the first orb making it explode in the air, letting out a shockwave. The second hit the ground. The explosion rocked the city. Isha was blown over, scraping her knees and elbows with her ears ringing again. She clambered back to her feet and searched the scene. She couldn't see Vaz anywhere.

"Vaz?" she shouted into the smoke that clouded around her.

A warning came from somewhere inside of her, like she could read the future. She sensed imminent danger. She looked skywards through the smoky haze. She saw bright green lights coming towards her from above. She turned and ran, giving it everything, though somewhere deep down, she knew that it was hopeless.

Three bursts of plasma cracked out of the smoke before a drone crashed, flaming to the ground, and exploded. Isha stopped, turned around, and ran back towards Vaz.

She found her down on her knees with her smoking guns in hand. Isha helped her to her feet.

"Nice one, Vaz! I thought we were cooked."

"There's more coming, and they'll be here soon. I told you not to stop."

"I just..."

"Oh, never mind. Come on."

Now Isha easily kept up as they ran. Vaz was limping badly. Again, Isha sensed danger. She whipped her head around and saw more green lights in the distance, racing towards them.

"We haven't got long. Where's the manhole?"

"Ahead. Not far. Keep going, kid."

The lights were nearly upon them as at last they reached the manhole. Vaz drew her weapons. "You'll have to open it."

Isha got down on her hands and knees and tugged the handle. It didn't budge. She stood up again and pulled. Letting out a roar, she pulled as hard as she could. Metal squeaked against metal, and the handle finally moved.

Vaz's weapons went off with fury behind her. Explosions once again rang out as her fearsome companion quickly shot down a scattering of the approaching drones.

Finally, Isha had the cover off the manhole.

"Jump, kid!" Vaz shouted as she fired another volley from her guns.

Isha vanished down the manhole, and a second later, Vaz jumped after her. They ducked down, head in hands as mighty, flashing explosions rumbled above. Sparks rained in through the manhole, and huge cracks appeared in the structure above them.

Vaz climbed the ladder and closed the manhole from underneath when the explosions finally stopped. She was aware that the raining fire wouldn't end there, and if the drones circled back and found it open, they would certainly follow them inside. With the manhole shut and the explosions muffled above, for the moment they were safe. At least, until they reached the rocks.

After many hours, Isha and Vaz finally climbed up the ladder through another manhole and out into the cool night air. Isha was glad to be out of there. It was so dark within, she had no idea what she was stepping in or, indeed, what had been crawling around her feet the whole time. The thought left her shuddering. The city was now behind them, and the rocks were ahead, a few hundred metres away.

They ran, now tired, injured, and dragging their bodies towards the rocks. They were getting closer, so Isha, burning with determination, sped up. But Vaz stopped behind her. It didn't take long for Isha to realise her companion was no longer running with her. She turned. "Vaz? What are you doing?"

"Hey, what you do is run. Run right for that cave." She pointed the way. "That'll lead you into the tunnels. I really like you, kid. Now promise me you'll make it."

"Of course, but…"

"Go."

"But…

"Kid, go!"

Isha reluctantly turned her back on her friend and sprinted. Moments later, the explosions lit up the night. First, she saw the flash, then came the deafening boom, then the heat and the shockwave hit her. She was flung down into the mud. The skin on her neck, face, and arm was instantly burned.

She rolled over and screamed out. The burns stung in the cold night air, and pain shot through her leg. She reached down and grabbed it, grimacing. There was a rip in her clothes. Blood seeped through her fingers from a gaping wound in her thigh. A drone had exploded above her, and the shrapnel had pierced her skin.

Flick's voice came through, coaching her, willing her along. *"Isha, get up. Get up quickly. You have to move now. You have to make it."*

Flick's words and the promise she had made to Vaz made her burn with a strength and determination she never knew she had. She screamed out again and clenched her teeth. She grabbed a metal pole that had come from the drone wreckage and grunted as she pulled herself up to her feet.

Her thigh muscle was next to useless; it could only just bare her weight. So, using the pole as a crutch, she did her best to run. She dragged her leg behind her and fought every second through the pain. With each step, she roared. Her body wanted to collapse, but something in her soul pushed her on. The pain didn't matter anymore; there was only survival. Agony surged through Isha every time she planted her foot, but somewhere inside, Flick was giving her strength she didn't know she had. She clung onto a hope that drove her onward, fuelled by her desperate need to survive, the mission, and the child. She limped, roaring in defiance. The drones above circled around, tearing towards her from all directions.

She fought on. The cave was just ahead, giving her yet another injection of hope. The host body she inhabited trembled with the gruelling excursion and howled out with endless pain, with tiredness rushing over her in waves. Every step burned fire through her. Each movement was greeted with an affirmation that her leg was almost useless. Isha made herself dig deep and strive on, no matter the pain, no matter the fear.

The drones were nearly upon her, but Isha finally made it to the rocks. The cave was only big enough to crawl through. The drones swooped in and released their deadly orbs, glowing like green fire, rushing towards Isha. With every ounce of strength and energy she could muster, she dove desperately forward. The orbs exploded. There was a blinding flash, then an almighty boom, and the ground shook like an earthquake as a fireball lit up the sky.

Isha lay blinded, burned, and stricken in the cave. For a moment, she felt relief, but then the pain caught up with her. The pain of her injuries, yes, but mostly the pain of Vaz's death. Tears of grief ran from her eyes. Vaz had died protecting her even though she hardly knew her, and with the memory of her sacrifice, Isha's heart broke. Vaz had played a vital role in her story, and Isha would never forget her.

She had no time to settle. The danger wasn't over yet, so she started crawling, dragging her useless leg behind her, screaming, ripping the skin off her knees as she did. Outside, the drones circled around again and, with the clearing smoke, made their way towards the cave entrance. The drones had to slow down. The entrance was only just wide enough for them to get through. That bought Isha a little time.

She could sense the drones coming from behind her. They were silent, but in her mind's eye, she could see them creeping into the cave.

She crawled in total darkness, her enemy gaining on her all the time. The host body started to slow, panting hard, tears running down her face, exhausted. Isha's mind would never, ever quit, but the body she occupied was failing.

She struggled along as fast as was physically possible, but her body screamed out with every movement. Her consciousness was teetering on the brink.

The lead drone approached, locked onto its target, and released a single orb. Just as it was about to hit her, Isha fell. The orb exploded above her as she hopelessly plummeted into a hole in the cave floor.

The heat and shock of the explosion collapsed the cave. Most of the drones were crushed or trapped, but one twisted direction and gave chase into the chasm after Isha.

She fell for many seconds, her body tensed as she braced herself for a crushing, rocky impact, but she landed in a soft, squishy, jelly-like substance.

She looked up and the drone was tearing down the cavern towards her. She desperately tried to move, but she was stuck fast in the jelly. It squelched and sucked tightly to her limbs, creating suction that held her firmly in place. She struggled to free herself, but the thick ooze stretched then pulled her back into its grasp.

The drone was right above her. She closed her eyes and held her breath, expecting this to be her last moment, but there was a flash so bright she could see it through her closed eyes, followed by a loud pop. Isha opened her eyes as tiny pieces of metal rained down upon her and smoke lingered. The drone was gone.

She blew out a huge sigh of relief, thankful she had survived for the moment, but injured, trapped, and alone, she feared her journey would end now. Sooner or later, her luck had to run out. Pain ripped through her, and she screamed all the curses under the sun in the strange language.

A force pulled upon her, leaving her wailing as it lifted her from the jelly. The suction pulled hard on her wounds as she was ripped violently from the quivering mass and dragged unwillingly away upon an invisible force.

A door opened in the cave wall, and she was carried inside. A metallic platform slid out of the rocky wall then clanked into place. The force didn't lower her down—it released her, dropping her from height. Isha clanged ungraciously onto the hard metal platform. She screamed and wept and lay clutching her bloodied limb, shivering in agony. There was a whir, then a blinding flash. The purest burning white invaded her eyes, then there was nothing but blackness.

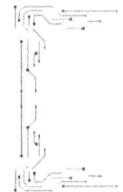

The Assassin

The Assassin swooped, forcing her deadly blade into the on-rushers, one after the other. Death was inevitable, and it met them in an instant. This fearsome warrior was where she belonged, deep in the midst of battle, the place she thrived. Each clumsy opponent met a demise by her swift hand. If she allowed her attackers to see her, all that remained for them was a split second of pain followed by the nothingness of death. With cat-like balance, she struck like lightning, incapacitating each of her enemies, tearing through body armour and flesh with her blade. She had meant to enter stealthily with the minimum fuss, but it hadn't been long until she met resistance.

The dissenters, an army that scurried like rats in the darkness of the tunnel network, were searching everywhere for her. They wouldn't have to look hard. She had no intention of running from this fight, no matter the hefty odds she faced. She would meet them head on.

She stood tall with muscles rippling down her blue skin, her armour hugging her body tightly and moving with her. Her weapon, her beloved blade with a plasma edge, made short work of anything that should come into contact with it. In her hands, it ripped the dissenters apart, slicing and cauterising the wounds in an instant. They didn't bleed, but their bodies fell apart, leaving nothing but death behind.

Sparks cracked and exploded off the rocks above her head, and debris poured down followed immediately by the sound of voices. They were speaking in a strange language. Then came the clumping of footsteps, echoing down the tunnel, coming towards her.

The Assassin ducked down and took to one knee, placing a hand on the floor, and scanned the scene with her amazing vision. The crackles lit up the tunnel again, coming closer, sparking and fizzing violent fury that would surely rip her apart. There were countless dissenters headed for her. She had no choice...she had to move. This was not the time to stand and fight despite her instincts. Everything in her nature told her to die right there in battle where she stood, but she knew she had to survive. There was something inside driving her; a longing, a calling, an eternal need.

She scurried across the floor as sparks exploded behind her. They were close enough to feel the heat. Her instincts were those of a killer. The blood ran cold in her veins, but at this moment, she had no choice but to run. To the Assassin, the fight for life or death was not unusual. This was just business.

She sheathed her blade upon her back and sprang high on long, muscular legs towards the sheer rock wall. From her sleeves, hooks appeared that effortlessly gripped the stone. She scurried up like a gecko, getting higher and higher.

The crowd of dissenters with their weapons exploding appeared below her. Above her and to the left, the Assassin saw a huge crack in the rock. It seemed too small for her to fit inside, but she headed for it anyway. The sparks flew around her, shaking the rocks, missing her scuttling form as she zigzagged up the wall. She reached the crack and pushed herself against the rock, her skeleton flexed and flattened, and scurried quickly inside. For the moment, she was safe.

The dissenters below haphazardly fired their weapons around the crack, crumbling the rock. The way she had gone in was no longer an option for escape. She lay there flat, tightly squeezed against the rocks above and below her. The only choice that remained was to push forward, deeper into the cave wall. There was no way of knowing if she could fit or if, indeed, it would lead anywhere, but she had to try. If the path around her grew any narrower, she would get stuck and die right there.

The Assassin's eyes could see perfectly in the darkness. In the shadows, she was at home. She went through the crack, wriggling like a snake, hardly able to move her arms or legs at all.

She struggled, inching forwards all the time. For hours she went until, finally, sore skinned, body aching, and exhausted, the crack opened. She crept through it. Her head popped out and instantly sprung back into its original shape. Once her arms were free, she pulled the rest of her body forward, and at last, after what seemed forever, she could stand tall.

She stretched her arms skyward when something hard struck her from behind, sending her jolting forward across the cave. She slammed into the rocks and slumped down onto her back. As quick as a flash, she drew her plasma blade. Rolling over and up onto her feet in one fluid movement, she expertly flipped her body as a blast fired out and hit the rocks right where she had been standing. She sprang up again, growled as she took her stance, and faced her foe.

Her enemy stood before her, huge and muscular, covered in thick metal body armour, staring at her through the visor of their helmet. In one hand, they had a triangular weapon, unfamiliar to the Assassin, and in the other, a black disc no bigger than a bottle lid. Simultaneously, her enemy roared and flung the disc towards her. The Assassin, with a swoop of her deadly blade, expertly sliced the disk in half.

A shot blasted out of the triangular weapon. She jumped high, gripping the rocky wall as she did. The blast crashed into the rock below her. She flipped over, pushing herself away from the wall. She landed on her foe's back, bringing them crashing down. The metallic suit glowed, then sparked green, and the Assassin was stunned by a jolting electric shock. It blew her across the tunnel. Her weapon flew out of her hand and left her on the floor, convulsing and roaring. Her tendons contracted, leaving every muscle in her body violently cramping.

Her foe stood slowly, looming over the stricken warrior. A glow appeared in the palm of their hand, and another disk materialised. The shock had ceased, but the Assassin had no time to gather her senses. She needed to move.

She spun herself around on the floor, flinging out her legs as she did. She swept her foe's legs from underneath them, bringing them down, crashing hard onto the rock. Arching her body, she flipped up onto her feet. Now it was her turn to loom over her foe. She picked up her weapon and stood, staring down upon them with yellow eyes that burned fiercely, threatening, and wild.

"What do you want. Who sent you?" She held her glowing blade aloft.

"There is a price on your head. I have come to collect it."

"A price on my head? When *isn't* there a price on my head?"

"You can kill me, but others will come for you. They will find you. There is no escape from here."

"Kill you… oh, yes, yes, I like that idea."

She lifted her foot and brought it crashing through the visor on their helmet. The stricken foe launched one of the black disks. The visor split open, and the creature screamed half a scream then lay lifeless.

The Assassin jumped from the brunt of the blast, yet still she flew across the cave and hit the wall hard before sliding to the ground. She clutched at her side while black blood oozed through her fingers. She winced and sucked in air through her jagged teeth as she applied pressure in a futile effort to stop the bleeding. Her wound was gaping, and certainly mortal.

She looked down at her beloved plasma blade still in her hand. She shook in pain, but driven by her mission, her target, and the mortal danger she faced, she knew there was no choice but to do it.

With a roar that echoed around the tunnels, she thrust the fizzing blade into her open wound, sealing it in an instant. The smoke poured out and the smell of cooked flesh filled her tiny nostrils.

She teetered on the brink of consciousness. The mighty Assassin swayed, knowing whatever happened, she could little afford to pass out, but pass out, nevertheless, she did.

A Bid for Freedom

Isha awoke surrounded by shadows. At least for the moment, that's all she could see. Her eyes went from the darkness to blurred light. Quickly, she stirred from the haze and, with a bump, into painful reality.

The pain in her leg shot through her. She jerked and tried to sit up, but she was strapped down. She struggled for a moment until it was obvious she wasn't strong enough to break her bonds.

She turned her head as far as she could to the right. There were beds, brightly lit computer panels, and what looked like medical equipment, although it was the like of which Isha had never seen. The clinical and sterile atmosphere reminded her of a hospital.

She turned her head to the other side, and there was a figure tapping on a screen with their back turned to her.

"Hey, you. You. What's going on here?" she blurted out.

"Oh, you're awake. I was worried there for a second." The short man turned and smiled at her.

"Why am I strapped down? Let me go. Now!"

"Oh, I'm terribly sorry, but we had to be sure you weren't one of them."

"One of who?"

"The Tall Ones' spies. We've been infiltrated by them before. It was carnage. Many died."

"Well, trust me, I'm not one. Let me go!" She started struggling, but the pain quickly stilled her.

"I'll let you out. I just need to run a couple more tests."

"Why?" She was abrupt, but the man answered patiently, like one who is used to being barked at.

"They use a type of hypnosis to make their spies work for them without their knowledge. The only way we can tell is by reading your brain waves."

"How are my waves?"

"Extraordinary!"

A warning went off inside Isha. Maybe it was Flick that told her, or maybe it was her instincts, but she knew there was something wrong.

"Don't panic, Isha. He is just picking up our presence in his readings, but he cannot possibly know that we are here."

The young man continued. "They are showing patterns the like of which I've never seen."

"Oh, no! He may think we're a spy," Isha silently said.

"No. We will not show those signs at all, but he will want to know more."

"I'll have to run some more tests on you. I hate to keep you detained like this, but we have to be sure. Security of this facility is our number one priority. There is no other way in these times. Please, if you'll only be patient."

Security didn't change the mission or her haste. "Flick, we have to get out of here."

"We do, but we cannot break these restraints. We must use other methods to get loose. You can persuade him."

"What? How?"

"You can and will."

She needed no time to think. Immediately, she addressed the young man. "How about undoing the bed straps for me?"

"Hardak wants to keep you restrained until we know what's going on with you. I have to do what he says."

"Am I a prisoner under arrest?"

"Well, no, of course not."

"Release me then." Isha's feistiness showed. She didn't like being imprisoned one bit, no matter what the reason. She was far from the scared fourteen-year-old she perhaps should have been, partly due to her own strength, partly because of Flick pushing her on, and partly due to the host body she was within. She was more than sure this young woman, whose body she had borrowed, was a tough one. Anyone who had survived in that place for any length of time surely had to be.

"I can't. Hardak is the commander. If I disobey him, then I'll be the one who is punished."

"Well, you know I'm not a spy, don't you?"

"All I know is that you are not the conventional type of spy. I do not know for sure you are not spy at all."

"Well, send for this Hardak fella, or take me to him. I would like to meet with him, please."

The man was visibly anxious at the thought, but she knew with a little more pushing, he would do it for her.

"If I'm not a prisoner, what am I if I'm being kept against my will?"

"You're not a prisoner, and I can tell you're nice, and I *feel* like you're not a spy or anything, but orders are orders. In this place, punishments are super harsh. They kind of need to be."

"What's your name?"

"Parvis."

"Well, Parvis, of course I don't want you to get punished. That would be awful. But at the same time, I don't want to be strapped down or imprisoned. Especially because I'm no danger to anyone. Look at my leg—I'm not going to get far, am I?"

"I treated that for you. You will live."

"Oh, are you sure you didn't need to hack it off?" She giggled, and Parvis' uncomfortable expression turned to a smile.

"My diagnosis says you can keep it for now."

She giggled again. "Now, can I speak to this... what was his name?"

"Hardak."

"Yep, him."

"I can maybe call him, and you can talk to him, if he'll agree. He's gonna be mad, though. He hates being disturbed, and he hates my guts already. That's why I have this job."

"Don't worry. I'll stick up for you."

"I'll bet you will." He smiled again then wandered off.

"Shall we mention the child? This Hardak may know where they are," Isha suggested to Flick.

"No, not at first. Let's just get free."

Parvis returned and pushed a button on the wall. "He'll speak to you."

The barking alien tone was aggressive and impatient. "Speak."

"Hi. Is there any chance I could get out of these restraints?"

"No. Parvis is a fool for even asking."

"He's not a fool. He's doing the right thing. I am not a prisoner nor a spy, so I want to be released."

"Parvis, are you listening?"

"Yes, sir," Parvis answered shyly.

"She has shown no symptoms of the hypnosis?"

"None at all, sir."

"Undo her restraints, but she cannot leave the medical compound and cannot mix with any of the other patients. Is that clear? Keep an eye on her. If anything happens, it will be on your head."

"Yes, crystal clear, sir. Than..." Parvis tried to offer thanks but the call had ended.

"Well?" Isha smiled cheekily, nodding towards the restraints.

"Oh. Oh, yes, I've got you." He rushed over to a touch screen, pushed some buttons, and with a click, the restraints loosened themselves.

She sat up, and instantly, the pain in her leg hit her. She grimaced and let out a groan. "I'm not sure I'll be able to walk, you know."

"You will. It'll just hurt. I'll give you some pain killers to help with that."

"Oh, that'd be great. I'd love to take a look around."

Parvis administered the pain killers and got her a pair of crutches so she could keep her weight off her bad leg. He helped her up.

"What's your name?" he asked.

There was a moment's pause. She had no idea what her host's name was.

"I don't know either." Flick offered no help.

"Isha," she said, knowing full well that could be a mistake. "Hi. Nice to meet you. Well, much nicer now that I'm not strapped down." She let out a little titter and held out her hand to shake his.

He looked at her like she was crazy. "You're not from around here, are you?"

She felt herself glow with embarrassment as she quickly pulled her hand away. "Erm, no, I'm not. It's easy to tell, right?" She smiled awkwardly.

"Yeah, kinda easy. Why did you come here of all places?"

"Look, Parvis, at the moment I can't explain. Let's just say it was something that I had to do."

"Well, that's pretty obvious. No one in their right mind would come here if they didn't have to. The Tall Ones have torn apart half the planet."

Isha pointed down to her leg. "Yeah, tell me about it. They tried to tear me apart, too. Who are they?"

"We're not totally sure. Anyone who has met one has never returned. They never show themselves, just their drones. They have been wiping out the adults and rounding up the kids. They just disappear into thin air."

"Someone told me they were enslaving people."

"That's a theory, but we have no real idea. The people just disappear, never to be seen again."

"How many people?"

"Millions."

Isha's heart sank. "Millions?!" This was a planet and a species on the very brink.

Parvis nodded solemnly.

"Can't you fight back?"

"We've tried, but it's hopeless. We just don't have their level of technology. We have never seen anything like this before. We don't know where they've come from. They even killed my sister and took my nephews."

"Oh, no, Parvis. That's so tragic! I'm so sorry."

"Yeah, me too." He stared into space for a moment, once again envisioning his family. He lingered on the edge of bitter grief. They'd been gone long enough for him not to burst into tears right there, but there could never be enough time to stop the pain, to stop the piece of his soul that was lost without them.

Isha held both her crutches in one hand as she reached out her other and gently placed it on his back to offer some comfort. Her heart empathically broke for him.

He shook the painful memories from his head and smiled at her. "The Tall Ones just do what they like, Isha. This is the only place we're safe."

"You said you don't have the technology, but what about this place? It looks super high tech."

"It is, that's true, but it was not created by us. We don't fully understand how it works or who put it here. This is our one stronghold. The entrances are protected by EMPs. It's almost like this place was left here for us to use as a shelter." He paused for a moment. "You can't leave the medical complex, but I'll show you around if you want."

"Yeah, that'd be good. A nice slow walk around." She held her crutches out.

"Well, I can still hack it off if needs be."

They both giggled.

"After the grand tour, I'll have to run some more tests on you, though. Sorry."

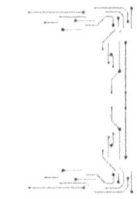

Fight Another Day

The long staff jabbed at her, awakening her. She didn't move. The pain greeted her, but she showed no sign of it. Her eyes opened. Her hand grabbed her blade and swooped. The staff fell in two as did the creature that was holding it. She stood menacing, blade fizzing. She didn't need to fight the rest of the short figures. They ran screaming for their lives, back into the tunnel and vanished into the darkness.

"Damn scavengers!" she growled in her weird language.

Only then did she allow the pain to show. The Assassin winced as a constant, blistering soreness ate into her side. She limped gingerly down the tunnel, ready for anything. Each step was agonising. She was unsteady, so she walked by the tunnel wall with her hand on it to be sure she wouldn't fall. The Assassin could hardly even walk, let alone fight, though that's exactly where she was headed—into a fight.

She never wavered in her determination, no matter the pain. The desperation to find her target kept her going. She was unsure where she was headed, and what compelled her to travel the way she did was unknown. There was no plan, but nevertheless, she had to find a way. The injury she carried was more than enough to floor lesser beings, but something within drove this mighty warrior on regardless.

The Assassin heard voices coming from one of the tunnels ahead. She instantly went into hunter mode, slinking into the shadows. Her injuries and pain would just have to wait. There was work to be done.

She snuck up to the tunnel entrance where the voices were coming from, and staying in the shadows, she listened. This was not the incomprehensible language of the scavengers, and this wasn't the dissenters. This was the military. The guards were discussing how they were going to stop the dissenters, plotting against them. Little did they realise that it was, in fact, the Assassin who was plotting against *them*. They must have been scouts, and she could tell from the voices there were only a few of them.

Reaching around behind her, she drew her blade, though she left it cold. The glowing plasma would give away her position. She stood, back pressed tightly against the wall by the tunnel opening. She drew a deep breath and launched herself forward, the plasma blade bursting into life as she went.

The soldiers were caught off guard. The blade flew through the air as she jumped and roared forward, slicing the first guard in half then thrusting her weapon to pierce the flesh of a second. The soldiers fired, but she was already gone, disappearing again into the shadows with her blade cold once again.

She remerged, diving forward. The pain coursed through her body with every movement as she struck another soldier and then another. The final guard started to run. The Assassin smirked and flung her blade, spinning it through the air like a deadly firework. It struck the fleeing man. His head and body were no longer connected. All that remained in her wake was death.

Clutching her side, she pressed on down the tunnel, ready for anything. The adrenalin coursed through her. Her eyes were alive as her senses twitched. Her body bristled with determination, itching for the battle. She was one-minded in her mission, willing to take on any challenge, even a seemingly impossible one such as this.

With the guards that would soon be searching for her, and the terrible wound slowing and draining her, getting out of those tunnels in one piece would be the challenge of her life.

A shrill alarm sounded out, ringing, echoing, and wailing down the tunnels. That was it—now the entire base knew there was a deadly intruder in their midst.

Before long, the sound of countless boots echoed through the tunnel, coming in her direction. There were far too many of them even for a fearsome warrior such as she to defeat. If she stood and fought, it would simply be suicide. Out-gunned, outmanned, injured, and exhausted, she would have no chance at all. With her death would come failure, and failure was not an option.

Time was running out. The boots were getting nearer. She desperately searched for somewhere to hide. The sheer, smooth walls of the tunnel offered her no hope at all. She knew if she ran, her body would fail her quickly. She drew her blade. The plasma sword lit up.

Despite her heart yearning for the battle, despite the vow she made to herself to never surrender, despite her desperate thirst for blood, she knew this fight couldn't be won. If she died, the target would escape, and her mission would fail. Reluctantly, she put down her weapon, took to her knees, and put her hands on her head. If she'd had the foolish hope the soldiers wouldn't treat her roughly, she was wrong.

They swarmed upon her, kicking and beating her into a heap on the floor. They restrained her hands and dragged her roughly to her feet. Her instinct told her to stand tall, head high, but her beaten body crumpled. They slapped and beat her as they dragged her away, but they didn't kill her. Hardak demanded they didn't kill her. The Assassin was on the watchlist and worth a hefty price. Every single one of the guards stared upon her with revenge for their fallen brethren, each hoping she'd make one sudden move, just to give them an excuse to finish her right there.

Silent Meeting

The alarm bleared out loud. Isha nearly jumped out of her skin having hobbled halfway around the medical facility. "What the hell is that?"

"There's some kind of emergency. Come on. I have to get you back to the medical room. It's secure."

"But what's happening?"

"Something bad. The alarm only goes off when really bad things are happening. Come on. We've got to go now!" Parvis's tone was urgent, and he ushered her along with his arm.

She followed him back the way they had come, the alarm a constant reminder of the urgency. Finally, they made it back to the medical room. They went inside, and Parvis locked the door behind them.

"You're going to stay here?" Isha asked.

"Erm…" Parvis started rubbing the back of his neck uncomfortably. "Yeah… If you don't mind, that is? I mean, I can go into my…" He looked hopefully at her.

She smiled, immediately putting his mind at rest. "Yeah, I'd like that. This is a bit scary, to be honest. I don't know what's going on."

"I never know what's going on around here. They don't tell me anything, remember?"

She let out a little giggle. "It seems we're in the same boat then."

She did feel a little safer with someone to keep her company, and she liked Parvis. They both perched on the end of the bed to which, hours before, Isha had been strapped.

It was obvious to both Isha and Flick that Parvis would start the small talk at any moment and ask questions about her background. They were things she had no idea of. It would be challenging to make that up on the spot. She couldn't even tell him what planet she was on now.

"So, you said you weren't from round here. Where are you from?" The small talk they anticipated had begun.

Inside the host body, an urgent and silent conversation took place.

"What do I do, Flick?"

"Let her speak. Let her memories guide the conversation, but you must stay in control. Some lies will need to be told for this to add up for him."

"Can't we just be honest and ask him to help? I think he will."

"No. We don't know he can be trusted. Keep up the pretence; we still need to get out of here."

For over an hour, the alarm rang out before it was finally silent. Isha and her host had managed to bungle out a backstory, but she wasn't in the least bit convinced Parvis believed her.

He never said much about himself, or the complex, or the war. Even him being in the room with Isha would be frowned upon by those above him, let alone sharing knowledge of the complex. Those were the most suspicious of times and suspicion was often proved correct. When things all around are desperate, moral fibre can quickly fray.

Parvis suspected she wasn't telling him the whole truth, but he wasn't really concerned. After all, he hadn't told her the whole truth either, and for reasons he did not know, he liked and trusted her.

Confined within the room, a change of light indicated a door at the end of the corridor had been opened. Through the windows, they could see eight armed guards marching in and taking up positions on either side of the corridor. Slowly being dragged by numerous other guards was a shackled and wounded blue creature. She had a scowl upon her face; not one of pain, but one of pure distain. She wouldn't give them the satisfaction of seeing her suffer. She stood tall and muscular, a fearsome being, exuding an awesome power from her very core.

Isha stood up and walked towards the windows as the Assassin was dragged past. Just for a second, she struggled back against her captors and dug her feet in, then stopped. Isha's host's and the Assassin's eyes met for a second, a second that seemed to last an age. Each being had the tingle of electricity running through them. They felt almost as though they knew each other, or in some way, their individual destinies had crossed. The Assassin was dragged off roughly, but she didn't take her eyes off Isha until she was out of sight.

"Come back here, Isha. She's probably dangerous!"

"She's definitely dangerous! Did you see her? She stared at me like she wanted to rip out my soul."

"Why did you stare back?"

"I don't know. I felt kind of pulled towards her. And what was strange was, I could feel that she felt the same pull towards me."

"*Quiet, Isha!*" Flick interjected before she could say any more.

Isha's stomach dropped, and she knew in an instant, she had already said too much.

She looked at Parvis, hoping he hadn't noticed anything odd, but to her disappointment, he had an excited smile on his face and his eyes lit up. That was when she knew for certain she had, indeed, said too much.

"I knew it! You're a telepath! I knew it."

Isha let out an audible sigh. "No, no, I'm not."

"How can you feel what she feels then, and know what she thinks? Oh, I have to do some tests. This is an amazing opportunity. I simply can't pass it up."

"What?!" she barked angrily.

Parvis was too excited to notice. "Oh, well, statistically it's only one in seventeen million who are telepaths. They, I mean, you are a great mystery. I'll never be this close to another one in my life."

"Wait, hold on there!" she almost yelled. "You won't just do a lot of tests on me, mate. I'm not up for being prodded and probed by you, thanks. I'm not gonna be the subject of your freaky experiments."

"Freaky what? But…" he stammered. "But it's my job, Isha."

"I don't care what your job is. You can't just do weird tests on me. What I really need to do is get the hell out of here."

"Ha! To do that you'd have to escape, and you're not going to get very far in your current condition, are you? That's not even to mention the armed guards."

"I may surprise you, Parvis. I just might." She scowled at him. "Now, if you'll apologise, we can move on, and then you can help me get out of here."

"I will not apologise! Apologise for what? Doing my job? And I certainly won't help you escape. You must be crazy! All that will do is get me and you in trouble. Look, just sit down and relax. I'm sorry, okay? I won't do any tests on you." He didn't like confrontation and quickly backed down. "Unless you say it's okay." He strung the last part on in hope.

Isha tutted, rolled her eyes, and sat back down on the bed with a huff. It seemed, despite what Parvis had told her, she was a prisoner after all.

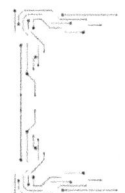

Cold Threat

The Assassin was roughly thrown onto the hospital bed and strapped down by the guards, sparing no thought for her injuries. Hardak's voice came from overhead as if from nowhere: *"You have killed our people. What is your purpose here?"*

She roared wild in defiance and didn't utter a word. She knew this would cost her, but she did it anyway.

"We are not heartless, Assassin. We're going to treat your wounds. You will probably live, but tell us what we need to know. Tell us or we will treat them without the aid of pain killers. You will feel everything."

She hissed and writhed, trying with what was left of her strength to break the bonds that held her. Her body was failing her. She lay still and sneered. "My secrets will never be yours. I choose the pain. Don't underestimate me. I will kill you all!"

"Treat her wounds. You know what to do."

The five beings surged upon her, looming over her like shadows, and started to roughly treat her wounds. The Assassin's screams and roars of agony filled the medical team with terrible, gut-wrenching guilt. They were meant to save lives and relieve suffering, but under orders or not, they were intentionally letting another being suffer and suffer in the worst possible way. They breathed a sigh of relief when, finally, she passed out from pain and exhaustion. Just for a moment, she was free from the torture.

She awoke with no idea how long she'd been unconscious. The agony came over her in waves. Her old friend pain was back in an instant, and she certainly hadn't missed it. She groaned and instinctively tried to move. She couldn't. She felt a presence nearby, and a couple of seconds later, a face appeared above hers.

"How are you feeling?" Parvis asked.

"Terrible!" she growled.

"I'll give you something for the pain," he promised.

"What? I thought you people like torture?"

"I don't." He half smiled. "I can't say the same for those above me. I'm sorry about them and what they did to you."

He administered the pain killer, and in moments she was feeling slightly better.

"Why can't I move?"

"You're in a light barrier. They say you're dangerous and you're an assassin. Is it true?"

"I don't want to talk. Just do what you must and leave me be," she demanded angrily.

"I truly am sorry. It wasn't anything to do with me. I'm just here to treat you and look after you and get you fixed."

"You... you were in the room with that girl. Who was she?"

"Just a friend... Well, a patient of mine, really."

"You know her then?"

"Yeah, kind of. I mean, not really."

"Do you or not?" Her tone was rasping and threatening.

Parvis was getting too familiar, and he knew it. Unfortunately for him, the watchful eyes of Hardak knew it, too.

"Parvis, get out of there now. Stop talking to her. She is a prisoner, not a guest!"

"I gotta go," Parvis stammered. "I'll come back and see you if they let me. Just tell them what they want to know. It'll be far easier on you."

She said nothing, just chuckled in defiance. It was clear that this warrior would never talk. She would rather die.

"I like you, kid." The words were kind, but her tone was not. "Your name's Parvis, right?"

"Erm, yeah, Parvis." He wasn't all together sure he should tell a deadly assassin, if that was indeed what she was, his name, but Hardak had already done so.

"Right, Parvis, because I like you, when I escape, I'll kill you quickly. Just snap your neck, eh." Her tone was cold with not so much as a quiver. She stared through him like fire, like she wanted to consume his soul. He shuddered with fear. He could tell she meant to keep her word.

"This will make you sleep for a while." He administered the drug before she even had a chance to object. Once she slipped out of consciousness, he left the room.

"What did she say, Parvis?" Isha asked anxiously as soon as he returned.

"Nothing really. Nothing at all. She's certainly not the chatty type."

"Oh, come on. She must have said something?"

"Yeah, she said she liked me and is gonna snap my neck when she escapes." He gulped on the words, remembering the deadly stare in her yellow eyes.

"Ooh, looks like she got to you." Isha was almost teasing him, but he was obviously rattled.

"Well, would you want someone who clearly loves killing people to threaten to kill you quickly and snap your neck like they're doing you a favour?"

Isha stopped teasing. She could see he was distressed. "No, I wouldn't. She's terrifying. You have to remember she's been captured and tortured. That's enough to make anyone angry. I should imagine not everyone would survive the things she's been through."

"They kept armed guards outside her room. Eight of them. But now that she's in a light shield and unconscious, they've been reassigned. The drugs and the shield will keep her scrambled. Hardak knows if she ever gets loose, she'll tear the place apart. None of us will be safe."

"I saw a hundred souls flash in her eyes, and a trail of destruction behind her. I saw her pain, fear, and anguish."

"She didn't look very scared to me."

"She hides it well, but like anyone, she is afraid. She may never talk, but she doesn't want to be tortured. Part of her longs for the pain to stop, for death to come for her."

"See, telepath," he joked.

"No, I'm not, and no, you're still not doing any weird experiments on me."

With a chuckle he said, "Look, Isha, I've got to go. I've got to go and report to Hardak again. He hates me, and now he's gonna get mad because I was talking to her."

Isha put a hand on his arm before he left. He looked at her.

"I am sorry. I know you were only talking to her for me."

He smiled. "Don't worry. It's been fun to have you around for the last week. You'll be able to leave in a couple more days."

"Leave?"

"Yes, go home, wherever you came from."

"Back out there." She pointed in no particular direction.

"Yes, Isha, back out there." He hung his head. "I'll see you later."

Isha wasted no time setting her mind to work. She simply couldn't be back on the outside. If the explosions and death weren't enough to put her off, the child she sought was within those walls. She had no choice. She simply had to escape, and she would need to convince Parvis to help her.

The Fuzz

"I'm lost. Is anyone there?" Liam asked silently. He was trapped in a weird, endless dream.

There was no answer.

The Fleck, it seemed, had abandoned him and, with that, any chance of Liam's comprehension. He tried to feel, to sense its presence, but all he found was emptiness. Despair started to fill him. It seemed he was lost and alone in the fearful unknown. Soon, even the memory of The Fleck became hazy, then faded to nothing.

His senses were numbed and silent. All at once, he felt abject fear. Fear that he was stuck in the nothing or even in between realities. He tried to remember where he was and what he was doing, but everything was a fuzzy blank. Was he lost in a dreamworld? Was he dead? Was this what death felt like?

He'd thought death would be empty, that there would be only darkness, but here, there was fuzz and consciousness. It was as though static electricity surrounded his form and his mind, even though he was not of form or mind.

He couldn't connect his thoughts together. They lingered but had no meaning. Then he felt a great sadness, like a cloud of depression had consumed his soul. He felt the nothing around him, the hopelessness, and the endless loneliness. There was fear and jumbled thoughts. There was pain and desperation, but mostly there was nothing. Liam felt a great need to escape from this, his mind's prison.

It was harrowing. He fought the need to wail, but wailing was something of which he was not capable, or surely he would have. Now he struggled to remember who he even was. Was he slowly being erased from existence? He silently said his name over and over so he could stay, just so he could exist a little longer. He preciously clung to the essence of his existence, yet still it drifted away from him.

His mind raced to nowhere in particular, bouncing around randomly. He saw pictures, but ones that were unclear. Sometimes he could almost recognise something, other times it was as if he never knew anything at all. He was like an empty vessel rocking violently upon the stormy ocean. He had no destination mapped out, and no starting point.

Once again, he tried searching for The Fleck, but he didn't even know that was what he sought. Liam couldn't even remember what The Fleck was. He felt as though there was a sentence on the tip of his tongue that simply wouldn't escape, or he'd wandered into his mind's kitchen and forgotten what he'd come for.

Then, it was as though he had no thoughts, like he was a spirit. Pure emotion trapped in the fuzzy prison within. He grew desperate to free himself from the place that held nothing but fear and loneliness. His humanity wanted to crumble. After all, what are humans without a body? What are humans without thought but a vessel of emotion and instinct? If he could cry, he would have. To let out a scream was all he longed to do, but it was trapped inside him. He felt locked in a tiny, dark room with no way of escaping. He felt like he was suffocating but without breath. He panicked, alone and in silence, probing all the time with his jumbled mind. Searching for answers or for a reason, neither of which seemed to exist. He longed for a past forgotten or even a future uncertain. He yearned to escape, and his desperation burned. He wished he could remember who he was, or where he was going, but all there was for Liam was the fuzz.

Powers of Persuasion

Parvis entered the medical room and wished Isha good morning with a false smile as he perched on the bed. The enhanced tissue growth had nearly finished putting her back together.

He knew that she would be going back out into a warzone, and she probably wouldn't survive long out there no matter how resourceful and brave she was. He liked her and admired her spirit, and he hated to think anything terrible could happen to her. He dreaded that, indeed, it would.

She could feel his apprehension, and with it, she felt that the news he was bringing her would not be good. He fidgeted uncomfortably for a while, prompting Isha to start the conversation.

"You're acting all weird. What's going on?"

"Oh, you're not going to like this. I don't really know how to say it," he bumbled.

"Open your mouth and say it." Isha smiled half-heartedly to make him feel a little more comfortable.

"Okay, here goes. Your leg is better, and Hardak wants you out of here."

The news immediately brought a pained expression to her face. She flung her head back with a loud sigh and held out her arms. She couldn't hide her disappointment. "What?"

"I don't really know what you want me to do, Isha, I have no sway around here. You already know this. I wish I could do something, but I can't."

She sat, staring out to nowhere in particular, her leg jiggling. She was visibly anxious and annoyed. She didn't even bother hiding it.

"Hey, maybe I can run tests on your telepathy. If I say that you show signs, he'll happily let me run the tests."

"Yeah, right! He'll keep me locked up in here. I don't trust him. He'll sell me to the highest bidder or put me in a zoo or something."

"Look, I totally understand why you don't want to go out there, but this may just give you a few more weeks here. I kind of like having you around."

Her thoughts were a million miles ahead of his, and she hardly listened. She sat there another few seconds, then just blurted it out like she was about to burst. "I have to get out of this medical centre. I came here to find someone. They're here somewhere. I have to find them. Can you help me, Parvis? Please?"

He instantly grew uncomfortable. "You know I can't…"

"Come on. You know you're my only friend here. I need to find a child. They'll be able to stop this crazy war. That's how important it is."

"What are you talking about?"

"I haven't got time to explain. I just need to do what I need to do, and nothing is going to stop me. It's that simple. With or without you."

"You're wasting your time, Isha. He will not do it willingly. He's a coward."

"What are we going to do then?"

"Just focus."

Isha didn't know what she was supposed to focus on, but soon waves of energy went through her, as if it was inside her very soul. In her mind's eye, she wandered through memories and thoughts, most of which were her own while the occasional one was not. She remembered places she'd never been and people she'd never seen, and it wasn't long before she realised they were the thoughts and memories of the young man in the room with her.

She stared at him intensely. He awkwardly averted his gaze from hers.

A warm fuzz started to fill Isha's host's head and build up until it felt like it was boiling. Now Parvis stared blankly ahead, unmoving, lifeless, vacant. She felt the connection between their minds, and then from within her, Flick whispered words to him. Isha knew Flick had spoken, but the words she could not hear. Suddenly the connection between them was broken, and Parvis shook his head awake.

"*What did you do to him?*" Isha demanded to know.

"*I suggested he helps us.*"

"*You're trying to control him, aren't you?*" She was angry.

"*I had no other choice. We must succeed. We must do whatever it takes.*"

"*But he's my friend, Flick!*"

"*Yes, I know, Isha. I'm sorry. I like the one known as Parvis, too, but he is the only chance we have of finding the child.*"

Isha felt a great sense of hopelessness, but she knew Flick was right, and they had no choice. "*Let's at least not get him killed or anything, though.*"

"*Don't fear. He will not be harmed. He is still him. He just wants to, and must, do something, but doesn't know why. It was something deep down he must have wanted to do or there'd be no way he could be persuaded. He wants to help you but is afraid of what it will mean for him. Often, humans feel unsafe with the unknown. This will be his sliding doors moment. Where he'll break free from this Hardak and live for himself. He will never be the same again.*"

"Isha, what happened?" Parvis snapped out of his weird dream.

"Erm, you said you felt light-headed. Are you okay now?" Isha deceived him.

"Yeah, I'm fine. Right, are you ready?"

"Ready for?"

"We're going to get you out of here."

The smile beamed across her face. "Yeah, I'm ready."

Parvis sprang into action, dialling in the code that unlocked the door and leading Isha out of the medical room.

"It won't be long until they pick up our movement in the cameras and send guards to bring us back. We're unauthorised wherever we go now. They're going to come after us. We're going to have to be quick. Let's go."

Isha's leg was still a little stiff, but it was moving fine as they rushed down corridors and through sliding doors.

"We'll cut through here. This is where the armed guards were earlier, but now they're gone. We should be able to get out of the medical centre unseen. I hope."

They ran through the doors and down the long corridor and that was when, through the windows, Isha saw her again. The Assassin. She stopped.

Parvis grabbed her by the wrist. "Come on. We've got to keep going."

She shook her arm free and gazed in through the glass for a few seconds before something called to her. Whether it was an idea or a feeling, she didn't know. "Parvis, open the door."

"Isha, this is bad," Flick warned her.

"I know what I'm doing. Trust me."

"What do you mean?" Parvis asked. "She's crazy. She already told me she'd kill me. Come on, Isha, we have to go!"

"No. Open the door. She can help us escape. She'll help because you know the way, and she'll be desperate to escape anyway. It'll work."

"She's fully awake now and almost healed. Please, Isha. She said she was gonna kill me. I really don't think…"

"Look, do you wanna take on a hundred armed guards with no weapons or experience alone? Just trust me. Open the door."

He let out a sigh of indignation, knowing he wouldn't change her mind. The door hissed as it opened.

Isha approached the fearsome muscular figure on the bench and looked down into her yellow eyes. "Do you want to get out of here?"

"Of course," the Assassin hissed.

"We need some help, and I figure you could use some yourself."

"Let me out then."

"Isha, she said she'd kill me," Parvis interjected.

"We'll let you out if you give your word that you'll help us and not kill Parvis."

"I can make no promises."

"We can't let you out then. Simple."

"Okay, I give my word. I won't kill the kid, though I was kind of looking forward to it." This was her idea of humour which sent chills through Parvis.

"Let her out."

"Are you sure?"

"Let her out, Parvis."

Parvis dropped the light barrier, and at last, the warrior was free.

The alarm began to wail.

Isha took a step back as the Assassin approached her. She towered high over her, deadly and rumbling, angry, itching for a fight.

"Follow my lead." The warrior went out the door and into the corridor. "They'll be here soon."

Isha felt the body she was within filling with fear, although she couldn't be sure if it was the body or her that was more afraid at that moment. She had never been much of a fighter and Parvis certainly hadn't either, yet here they were, about to step into the heat of battle.

The Assassin put her finger to her lips to tell the others to be quiet. Isha and Parvis stayed silent.

The Assassin moved like a viper, deadly and wild as the guards burst through the doors and into the corridor. Bolts of plasma flew and lit up all around them. Isha and Parvis dropped to the floor, covering their heads. The Assassin evaded the blasts, and with fury, she tore into them, using her bare hands, claws, and teeth. Flesh and blood rained down as each guard was quickly overcome by their deadly opponent. She took up their weapons and ushered her companions to do the same.

They headed to the door and opened it. Explosions and a hail of plasma met them. They ducked down low and put their backs tightly against the wall to stay out of harm's way. Each spark and crack made Isha and Parvis jump in their skin.

"If it had just been us, we would have got out of here quietly. Now we're in for a full-on war!" Parvis complained, loud enough to be heard above the explosions.

"Without me, by now you would both be dead," the Assassin rasped with a scowl. The fear that consumed Isha and Parvis showed no sign of itself upon her.

"Follow my lead. I think I know how to get us to the tunnels. Of course, it may not work, and we'll all be blown to bits, but what else is new?"

She took Parvis's weapon and strapped it to her back, grabbing him and pressing her weapon hard against his head.

He grimaced. "Hey!"

"Shut up, kid." She looked at Isha. "You, follow close behind me."

Isha was in no position to refuse, so she followed, clutching her weapon, knowing this wild creature was her best and probably only hope of survival. She simply had to survive to find the child.

The Assassin yelled at the top of her lungs, "Hold your fire! We're coming out."

The order was repeated a few times among the rebel guards, and slowly, the explosions stopped.

"Don't twitch, or we're dead. Are you ready?" The Assassin didn't wait for an answer. She surged forward, one arm holding Parvis firmly around the neck, the other forcing her weapon against his head.

There was silence as they came through the door.

"Hold your fire or the boy's dead!" she warned.

Isha stayed tight behind her, pointing her weapon towards the guards. She tried to hide her trembling hands and look mean, but she feared it wasn't working. They crept slowly, eyes alert, through the silent guards. Some were down on their level, others above them, lining the gangways, each poised to take them down, but they were not willing to risk one of their own.

If the three of them could reach the tunnels, the guards could only approach from one direction through a narrow opening. If they tried to storm them there, it would be near suicide. The matter of minutes it took to walk through the gauntlet of angry stares and itchy trigger fingers felt like forever. The tension was thick in the atmosphere. All that were present knew with one twitch, all hell would break lose.

The tunnel entrance was close. There was a nagging temptation to run those last few steps, but they needed to stay composed and together or they'd be sitting ducks.

The Assassin's voice filled the room. "If you follow us, you will die. Ask your friends back where we came from. They'll tell you how it goes. Oh wait, no, they won't. They can't."

The three of them finally disappeared into the tunnel, and in an instant, the darkness consumed them.

Behind them was a rumble of activity as the guards came down from the gangways and lined the entrance of the tunnel, but they were not about to chase after them. They knew all too well, at the expense of their brethren's blood, how dangerous this Assassin was.

Back in the darkness, the Assassin was in her element once again. Her injuries almost healed, her anger far from tamed, and her mission a long way from complete.

"Where are we even going?" Isha asked the Assassin, breathless from running.

"I must find someone."

The Child

The child huddled, trembling in the corner of the room. They were scared witless, their eyes wide with fear darting all around. The alarm was still screaming over and over and seemed to have been forever. The child looked almost human but was certainly something different. They could sense that something was coming for them.

The door opened and standing there was the stern-faced woman. "Get out of the corner, and stand up, you little coward!" she snapped in the alien language.

The child was silent as they stood and stared up at her.

"It will be over soon. You will not be harmed."

The woman sounded sure, but she did not know the things that the child did. That child had never known comfort. They had been passed around from place to place, never belonging, never finding a home, leaving a deep sadness clear in their eyes. They were nothing but an orphan from an unknown world whose life had been on the line for as long as they could remember. A child that had never known safety, only fear. Inside of them dwelled a deep emptiness, the emptiness of never knowing love. The child knew no different. They couldn't possibly miss a life they had never known.

The woman looked down at the child, angry and impatient. "Fine. Come out here with us if you want."

The child shook their head. They would find no comfort from these monsters who had stolen them. They were called "adopted parents," but they had no love for the child and certainly were not parents. They knew the child was a telepath, and the scientists would pay a handsome price for the opportunity to test one. To the child, this was their harrowing life. To their captors, nothing but a quick profit.

"Suit yourself, you little wretch!" The woman slammed and locked the door, and once again, the child was alone.

In the dark of the tunnel, the Assassin ran free, blending into every shadow, moving stealthily like a predator on the hunt. Her senses were alert. She was quick and never seemed to grow tired. Isha and Parvis, full of fear, followed behind, desperately trying to keep up. The Assassin was now their only chance of survival.

Twice the guards had tried to come up the tunnel, weapons blazing, in an attempt to rush them. That had proved to be a huge mistake, one that had cost them their lives. Soldiers came and inevitably fell in seconds to the deadly Assassin. Isha and Parvis had done little to aid her. Mostly, they stood gawping, watching on in a mixture of awe and terror. Her speed and ferocity were such, that they hadn't so much as had to fire their weapons up to that point.

The Assassin stopped and listened. "There are guards up ahead." She looked at Parvis. "What is this place? Where are we?"

"This is close to the living quarters. There's always guards at either end of the tunnels. They will have set an ambush for us, no doubt. We'll be walking into a wall of fire."

"Then we are close. Stealth will be our weapon." She stared ahead into the darkness, listening, sniffing the air. "I want you two to draw their fire. I'll do the rest."

"What do you mean 'draw their fire?'" Isha asked nervously.

"Find a place where they can't hit you and fire your weapons at them. Fear not, they will quickly be dead."

They continued, but now only walking in complete silence. The anticipation was building up through Isha and Parvis. Their hearts were pounding, and they did their best to still their trembling hands. Anxiety tied them in knots as they got ever nearer to the end of the tunnel, to where the battle awaited them.

"Here is the place," the Assassin whispered.

The inexperienced pair looked around with blank faces, and then looked at each other. The Assassin said nothing, just pointed upwards. There was a narrow ledge high up on the rocky wall. It wouldn't be easy to climb, but if they could get up there, they could creep along the ledge to the very end, stay low, and they should be safe from the return fire.

Isha nodded. She knew what they had to do. She shouldered her weapon, as did Parvis, and she ushered him in front of her.

"Give me a leg up," she whispered into his ear.

He lifted her ungraciously, and she pulled herself up. She reached down, and with her pulling and him scrabbling upwards, finally, they were both safely on the ledge. The Assassin watched on, shaking her head, smirking in amusement as they started to creep their way forward.

Isha was trembling as the surges of fear and adrenalin rushed through her. The anticipation of the battle ahead loomed ever larger. The heart in her borrowed chest thundered through her entire body. She could hardly believe what she was about to do, and judging by the look on Parvis's face, of him she could say the same. Isha poked her head out over the ledge to let the Assassin know that they were nearly there.

From below, the Assassin moved like a lizard, she slinked expertly up the rocky wall, along the ceiling, and hung upside down in the shadows. Even though Isha knew where she was, it was as if she had vanished into thin air.

They crawled all the way to the end of the ledge. There, they could poke their heads over and look down to see the guards taking cover and waiting below. Isha readied her weapon and glanced at Parvis, searching for some moral support, but he offered none. He was terrified. Isha reached out a hand and touched his trembling arm. He looked at her. She stared into his eyes, half-smiling. He nervously did the same.

"It'll be okay, my friend. I promise," she whispered gently so as not to be heard.

His half-smile grew to a three-quarter-smile when he realised that she had called him her friend. He nodded awkwardly and swallowed hard.

With weapons poised and staying as low as they could, they poked their guns over the ledge and, without even looking, fired down towards the guards. A second later, a volley of plasma fire smashed into the rocks below their hiding place, shaking the walls with blinding, flying sparks.

They lay flat and covered their heads. With such fire power, they realised that the tunnel could collapse around them, or the ledge could crumble beneath them. They would quickly be torn from their hiding place or trapped there permanently.

They screamed loud as the explosions came one after the other. Smoke poured around them and sent jagged cracks through the rocks. The ledge below them shook. They needed to get out of there, but they were pinned down.

"Where is she?" Isha yelled, referring to the Assassin.

The plasma fire stopped for a second, leaving the rocky walls cracked, glowing, and smoking.

Isha took a breath. "We're not just going to die like this." She poked her weapon back over the ledge. Staying on her belly, she fired again towards the guards. Another return barrage sizzled and crackled all over the rocks around them as rubble and chunks crashed to the ground. The terrified pair huddled low, covering their heads with their arms. The cracks forked out, growing bigger all the time in the deafening rumble. The ledge below them was starting to give way.

Terrified eyes met, and instinctively they reached out a hand for each other. They locked their fingers together and held on tight. The realisation that their time would soon to come to an end clanged down around them.

All at once, the explosions around the pair stopped, and the guards' fire was redirected. In no more than twenty seconds, all the fighting below ceased. Soon after, the confirmation that they would, in fact, live at least a little longer set in and showed itself on their smiling faces.

They quickly peered over the edge. The sight below was horrific. Blood and death littered the scene with one figure standing tall and powerful amongst the carnage—the Assassin.

Isha and Parvis ungracefully climbed back down the rock wall and dropped to the ground. It was far easier on the way down aided by gravity. They scurried quickly towards the Assassin. They stepped over the death, slipping in blood, weaving between the bodies until they reached her.

"You're wounded! Let me help you." Isha saw blood oozing between the Assassin's fingers.

"I'm fine," she growled.

Isha didn't probe further. There was little point as the Assassin didn't seem to even care. The pain seemed to drive her on; perhaps she even liked it.

The Assassin marched forward as if nothing was wrong. All the while, the blood trail behind her told an entirely different story.

"The residences are just here," Parvis announced as the three of them approached.

There were round metal doors lining both sides of the corridor, each cut from the rock. The Assassin stopped and was silent, the blood still trickling. The mighty warrior looked from side to side and walked up and down the corridor. She moved randomly, zig zagging her way back and forth. She was clearly sensing, searching for her prey.

The Assassin stopped. "In here. I need to get in this one. That's where the target is."

"But those doors are sealed. You'll never break through—" Parvis didn't even finish his sentence. The Assassin fired a volley of plasma from her weapon, lighting up the tunnel and exploding all over the door. It left little more than a scorch mark.

"You." The Assassin pointed her still-smoking weapon at Parvis. "Open this door. I have to get inside."

"I... I..." he stammered in fear. "I can't. It's locked from the inside. The whole facility will be locked down anyway. It's part of our emergency procedure."

The Assassin roared. Her wild anger echoed through the tunnels, striking fear into all who heard it.

Isha slowly and quietly approached the door. Something inside called to her. She stood facing it, but she wasn't staring at it; she was staring beyond it, within her mind.

"The child is inside, Isha," Flick spoke from within.

"I know. I can feel them. They are calling to me."

"You're wrong," Isha told the Assassin. "The one you want isn't in there. There is no one in there but a small child."

The Assassin said nothing. Isha shouldered her weapon and closed her eyes. She felt a build-up of energy filling her body with tingles like electricity.

"Flick, what are you doing?"

"Nothing. It's the child."

With a grinding and cracking noise, metal crunched, and the thick doors folded in on themselves like they were made of paper. Standing there within the wreckage was the child. Inside and out of sight, the child's adoptive parents were dead.

Isha grabbed the child by the hand. "Let's go."

From inside the Assassin, a voice echoed around her being: *"Kill the child!"*

It was the hissing voice of The Fleck. It spoke to Liam, and Liam, in turn, spoke to his host. Controlling her actions, forcing her hand. Free from the light shield, the fuzz had long since lifted and he was firmly back in control. So long he had waited, patiently, hidden deep in the recesses of the Assassin's mind. The warrior, his mighty host, had hardly needed his guidance up until that moment. But now was his time. He twitched and bristled, filled with excitement when, finally, he saw his target.

"Stop!" the Assassin demanded. "The child must die!"

Isha froze and closed her eyes, awaiting the deadly blow. A shot exploded out. Bright light from the plasma burned through her eyelids, but still she stood. She opened them. The Assassin lay unmoving and smoking on the tunnel floor. Standing behind her with wide eyes, consumed by shock, was Parvis. The weapon smoked in his trembling hands. He stood panting, mouth agape.

Isha gazed towards him in amazement. The awkward Parvis had saved her life and, most importantly of all, the child's.

"Come on, Parvis. Snap out of it! Let's go," she urged. "As soon as the guards realise she isn't with us anymore, they'll rip us apart. Which way?"

"Th...Th...That way." His mind was somewhere else, back in the moment he had pulled the trigger and killed the fearsome Assassin who had saved their lives on numerous occasions. Isha grabbed him by the arm with one hand, the child's hand in her other, and dragged them both down the corridor.

Hand-in-hand, suddenly, the child stopped dead. Isha halted with a jerk. She yanked back to get the child moving again, but they were like a dead weight that refused to budge. Then, with eyes pearly and unnatural, the child let out a gasp, then a scream, and pointed up ahead.

"What is it?" Isha asked. They didn't speak, but Isha knew what the child was telling her.

"Come on," Parvis said, knowing at any moment the guards could come rushing up on them.

"No, wait, there's guards ahead. Around that corner." She nodded to show the direction.

"How can you possibly know that?"

"Telepathic, remember?" She winked and smirked.

"Isha, what are we going to do?"

"I don't know. Come on."

The child started moving once again.

"Flick, what is going on? Where are you?"

"I'm here, Isha. I am always here."

"Yeah, could you be a bit more here, a bit more often? I don't know what the hell I'm doing."

"You are doing fine. Allow the child to guide you. They have great powers. I must..."

"Flick... Flick?" But Flick was gone. Flick was still there somewhere inside, Isha could feel it, but they were distant or somehow distracted.

The child pulled on Isha's hand. She fought back, but the child dragged her forward with great strength far beyond their size. Her feet slid along the ground. They rushed forward until they'd nearly reached the next corner, and there, the child took to the shadows, out of sight, dragging Isha with them. Isha wanted to ask what was happening but knew then was not the time. She could hear the guards moving up ahead.

The child started to vibrate, like energy was building up within them. Then Isha's host's body started to vibrate as well. A strange feeling rushed over her, and Isha's vision faded in and out, unfocused and confused. The vibration built ever more, flowing from the child into the host body, and finally, into Isha's presence. They both screamed loudly as they released a wave of energy from within themselves. It flowed out like a tidal wave, powerful, yet invisible.

It lasted only a second. Isha felt instantly normal again and then panicked. Having heard their screams, she was sure the guards would be coming, but there was not a sound from ahead. An ominous feeling fell over her, and telling the others to wait, she was compelled to step forward and round the corner.

Parvis tried to stop her, but she had already gone. He scrunched his face up as he expected his friend to meet her demise right then, but at that moment, she would meet something far more horrific than her end.

She looked around with her mouth wide and shuddered to her soul. Tears immediately welled in her eyes, and a tingle ran down her spine. What had she done? What had she been a part of? Every single guard was dead, their eyes pearly white, their skin grey, and their lips blue, like the very life had been sucked out of them.

Isha couldn't take it. She dropped to her knees and bitterly howled. She never wanted to kill anyone, only save lives, yet here she had killed countless guards.

"It was the child. It was not you, Isha." Flick tried in vain to sooth her.

"No, Flick. I killed them."

"Let it go, Isha. This is battle. This is the cost. I know it hurts, but it is right. This is how it has to be. They would have cut you in half."

"I'll be okay. I just need a moment."

"There are no moments remaining. You must move now and feel later."

She swallowed her pain and went back to get the others. She carried the child through the maze of bodies, covering their eyes so they couldn't see the results of their work. That was pain she wanted to spare them. They tiptoed between corpses, shuddering all the way.

A silent Parvis, horrified in the realisation of what his companions had done, followed behind. He didn't understand what had happened, only that it was their doing. Once the death was out of view, he got his thoughts straight. There was no time for questions, guilt, remorse, or grief; they had to get out of there.

"We need to get to the main tunnels and find an escape hatch. That is the only chance we've got of escaping. Now if they catch us, we're dead." Parvis rushed.

They headed on with footsteps echoing off the rocky walls of the tunnels as they went. Always the constant fear drained them, weakening their will, but somehow, they needed to be stronger than they had ever been.

Far behind them, in the distance, the unmistakable sound of weapon fire could be heard. There was only one reason a gun battle could possibly be happening at that moment—the Assassin was still alive. Isha's gut dropped with the realisation that now the fearsome angel of death was coming for their souls.

They ran faster. They had to try and get out of there and hope the guards would take her down. Having seen her in battle, Isha considered it unlikely, even though the Assassin must have been badly wounded.

"The main tunnel is just ahead. There's a hatch above a ladder. If we can get through that and into one of the escape transports, we can get off the planet, then we're home free."

Parvis's words brought Isha at least some hope that they could make it out alive.

They kept on running as fast as they could, but their bodies were tiring and failing. Their lungs were burning, muscles were straining, and the constant fear drained them more all the time.

Behind them, the Assassin ran limping, staggering, dragging her injured body towards them, ignoring the pain. She was one-minded in her goal—with her last breath, she would be the bringer of death upon the child. She was driven on, beyond her normal capabilities, by Liam and The Fleck inside her. She roared out, echoing up the tunnel, carrying fear upon the cry directly into her prey's ears.

The group ahead tore around the corner and out into a bigger tunnel. Parvis pointed towards a tall ladder that went from floor to ceiling and up to a manhole. They ran until they reached the very limit of what their bodies could endure. No matter how hard they tried, all the time the Assassin was gaining on them. Injured she may have been, but with Liam and The Fleck fuelling her along, she was a different creature all together. She cared not about pain or fear or fatigue; all she cared about was the target.

Their legs were like jelly as they finally reached the ladder.

"Go first, Parvis." Isha ushered him forward.

He grabbed the ladder and started to climb.

With a boom, a shot fired with a blinding spark followed by a deafening explosion. The bottom part of the ladder was now broken and skewed, the jagged metal twisted while Parvis dangled there, hanging on. He desperately looked around for the others.

Isha's foresight had saved them, and they had moved quickly out of the brunt of the blast. Nevertheless, Isha and the child were sent flying with the explosion. Isha dragged herself up, picked up her weapon, and felt a surging pain. Her recently healed leg was wounded once again by shards of splintered metal. She growled, took aim, and fired at the Assassin almost without thought. She pumped her finger on the trigger over and over. The Assassin moved, expertly avoiding the blasts. It seemed that even in her current condition, clearly Isha was no match for her.

From behind her, the child let out an ear-splitting scream, and the Assassin clutched her head. The scream rang out long and shrill, and eventually, the Assassin fell in a heap, writhing in pain.

She roared out wildly, and Isha knew that this was their chance. She took the child in her arms and limped back to the ladder. Parvis was now standing on the upper rungs. She held the child high, and Parvis reached down as far as he could, looping his arm around under their armpits. His skinny frame struggled as he hung onto the ladder with one hand and lifted the child over his head with the other. They clamped tightly and safely to the rungs above him.

"Go, kid," Parvis urged. "Isha, grab my hand."

She reached up a hand for his, then her heart sank as a growl came from behind her. The Assassin was back on her feet, staggering forward.

Isha turned and looked at the menacing figure hobbling towards her, then she took one desperate look up. "Go, Parvis, go. The child has to survive. Get them out of here."

"Isha, no!"

"Don't worry. I'll catch up. Get going."

He looked upwards, took another desperate look down, and knew she was right—the child had to survive. In that split second, he made the hardest decision he had ever made in his life and started to climb.

A shot flashed and boomed, and then another, and finally one more, then there was the sound of weapons hitting the floor one after another.

Parvis stopped and looked down with his heart ready to break at what he saw.

Below, Isha was sitting on her backside, the weapon out of her reach. The Assassin loomed over her, unarmed. She could have easily picked up Isha's weapon and finished the job.

"Why don't you just shoot me?" Isha croaked the words. She was hurt. Her skin was blackened and blistered, and blood was pumping from the wound in her leg.

"Because I'm going to rip you apart and then...them." She said it in a tone as cold as ice, pointing to the ladder above. As she neared, the wild stare of anger was burning in her yellow eyes.

Isha scrabbled to her feet and threw a clumsy punch as she did. The Assassin watched it sail harmlessly by with only the slightest of movements. Isha stumbled forward, off balance and on her way down anyway, but her foe delivered a swooping strike, dealt with the back of her enormous hand. Isha flew off her feet and landed hard on her front. The savage impact knocked the wind out her lungs.

She wanted to lay there and give up. Her body was beaten and broken, but inside, Flick gave her strength. She grew to the moment, and groaning and huffing as she got back to her unsteady feet. She had to somehow win this fight.

She turned her head just in time to see two massive hands reaching for her. The Assassin grabbed her, lifted her off her feet, and threw her towards the shattered ladder. Isha's head crashed into the twisted metal, and she slumped to the ground. In an instant, she felt the warm trickle of blood running down the back of her neck. Her eyes went blurry. She lay back, stricken, on the very brink of death. The Assassin mounted her with one knee on either side of her torso and clasped her hands around her throat.

Above, the noise of tearing metal rang out and then came an enormous *clunk*. The Assassin fell forward, limp, as the weight of the manhole cover struck her. Isha lay dazed, covered in her own blood and the Assassin's, the dead weight of her enemy's lifeless body slumped on top of her.

One more time, Flick gave her strength. One more thrust of energy. With a grunt, she pushed the body off her. She looked upwards and there were Parvis and the child looking back at her, the manhole above them open. She smiled up at them.

"Grab my hand, Isha. I'll come and get you," Parvis yelled down.

Isha struggled to her feet and reached up as he climbed down the last few rungs. Then she was hit by a bolt like lightning. The Assassin was laying there with the smoking gun in her hand. With a chilling, smirk the Assassin rolled over, overcome by her injuries, dead.

Isha was too far gone to even feel pain. Her eyes flickered and grew heavy. She took one last look towards Parvis, though she couldn't really see him. She smiled and croaked her final word. "Go."

The blurry light faded to grey and then, finally, to nothing.

The Worms

The phone rang again for the umpteenth time before Liam snapped out of his trance. He sat up and reached over for it. He cleared his throat in an attempt not to croak, but he croaked nevertheless. "Hello?"

"Liam, are you still in bed?"

A smile fell across his lips at the sound of Penny's voice. "Yeah. I'm getting up now. I swear it."

"Well, hurry up. You're super late again."

"All right, I'm coming, I'm coming. See ya soon." He hung up the phone and flopped down onto his back. He rubbed his eyes and stared up at the ceiling.

The ceiling that he'd stared at for so many hours through insomnia meant the greying and flaking paint and the cracks were all familiar to him. For a moment, his thoughts rushed by, clouded. Then he caught movement in his peripheral vision. Quickly his eyes flicked towards it, and sure enough, something was moving. In one of the cracks along the cornice, something small and maggot-like was wriggling. He furrowed his brow in disbelief. He tried to focus, staring intensely, but his vision swirled and then faded from the physical to another plain.

Soon, flashes of the past rushed through his mind. Images churned of strange events that he had seen or lived, but not within his body, within his being. Nothing seemed real, and yet it *felt* so real that it had to *be* real.

He may well have been going completely insane, hallucinating, or both, but as Liam regained focus, at that moment, there was something physical wriggling through the ceiling.

It moved along the cornice, pulsating, squeezed in the crack that ran all the way along the edge. Soon it was over his head. It dropped down onto his pillow. With a shudder, he sat up and scrabbled around, grabbed the pillow, and in one motion flicked the worm, propelling it arcing upwards until it hit the wall and then landed on the floor. He peered over the edge of the bed. There it was—a small, green worm writhing on the carpet.

A strange high-pitched squeak hit his ears, one that seemed to come from the worm. He turned his eyes upwards when he heard another squeak, this time coming from above him. Two more of the worms were coming through the crack. They squeezed through and dropped down onto his bed. He jumped up, rushing to the other side of the room while more of the creatures squirmed through.

The ceiling above him creaked and started to bow with a great weight pressing down upon it. The crack widened and countless more worms fell down. They landed all over the carpet and bed. The ceiling wobbled, and the crack widened while the worms, squeaking and squelching, oozed out and rained from above. The shrill squeaks rang out, now jumbled and confusing, one blending into the other, at the sheer number of them. Soon, they looked like a writhing blanket all over the bed and floor.

As they dropped down on Liam, he turned to get out of the room, desperately trying to escape the disgusting things. His skin crawled as he felt them hitting him like droplets of rain, splashing into his hair and onto his shoulders. He needed a moment, just to move, just to get out of there, but like a bomb had exploded, the ceiling burst open and thousands of the worms poured through. They lay quivering all over his room, ankle deep and rising fast. He patted himself down, frantically brushing them from him and struggling to reach the door. They streamed upon him through the ceiling like a waterfall.

He stood in the corner with shock etched on his face. Soon, they were a foot high on the floor and still coming.

Liam had to get out of the room to call the exterminator. He had no idea what they were, but one thing was certain, he had a serious infestation. With each step his feet sank into the mass until they were above his ankles.

On his tip toes, he made a dash for the door, but his foot caught on something. He half stumbled but managed to stay upright. He looked down. The worms had twisted themselves together like strands of rope and looped themselves around his foot. He kicked desperately to free it, but his foot was trapped. The worms twisted and morphed and started to rise up in a conjoined mass. They snaked around his lower limbs, getting heavier all the time as more worms joined the strands. He fought, trying to brush the worms from his thighs, but it was useless. They were one solid muscle, flexible and strong like an eel. He yelped as his legs gave way under the weight, and he fell onto the floor. Quickly, he was completely consumed beneath a pulsating mass of worms.

The creatures swarmed upon him, leaving him blinded as they covered his face. He tried to scream, but worms poured into his mouth. They squirmed inside his nose and his ears. He tried desperately to free himself, kicking and swinging his arms, but the weight on top of him and the strength of the worms combined was too much. His worst nightmares were realised when he felt them wriggling inside his body.

Waves of horror and disgust ran through him. He was stilled, overcome, helpless beneath the mass. His senses were gone, only pure panic remained. He couldn't breathe or move. He couldn't even throw up.

The mass of worms contracted, and like he weighed nothing, they lifted him onto his feet. They started to reach out like tangled octopus' arms. Liam was suspended, useless, as the strands of connected creatures spanned out, grabbing each corner of the room.

Something firmly grasped the back of his head. A second later, his head was ripped back forcefully. Instinct told him to scream, but as he opened his mouth, more and more worms fell inside him until he could feel them wriggling down his throat and all through his body. They were inside his stomach, inside his head. He could even feel them wriggling in his veins.

His heart thundered and raced out of control, skipping beats as it did. He was powerless against the creatures. They swayed him side to side with his head pulled back as far as it could possibly go without bones snapping. Then the voices came. At first, like a million separate ones talking into his mind, but in time, they became one voice, high-pitched and invasive.

"We have you now, human. You are ours!"

Liam fought one last time, trying with all his might, kicking his arms and legs. The muscles contracted, but he couldn't move at all. Then the worms ripped his eyes open against his will. They were pearly and glazed, void of colour, maybe even void of life. All that remained was darkness.

"Liam, what the hell are you doing?"

Liam opened his eyelids, let out a yelp, and sat bolt upright, eyes wide in fear. Pushing his legs, he scrabbled across the carpet on his backside. He hit the wall and pressed his back tight up against it. His eyes flittered, searching the room for the worms, panting.

"Liam... Liam, easy. What's going on? Hey... Hey."

He stared into the middle distance, drained from fear, confused. A cloud in his mind blurred his vision. He slumped, exhausted. His head hung heavy, and he teetered on the brink of consciousness.

Penny rushed over to him, crouched in front of him, and took his hand in hers. It was freezing. Through half-opened eyes, he looked at her face. He knew it was her even though he couldn't really hear her, and she was just a blur to him, but he could feel her presence. He smiled weakly as his eyes rolled in his head. Blackness overcame him once more.

He awoke again, a moment later, cradled in Penny's arms.

"I'm going to call an ambulance," she whispered.

"Don't. I'll be fine. It's just the nightmares," he croaked faintly.

"Nightmares? You look terrible. Can you stand? We'll get you into bed."

He nodded and pushed himself up against the wall with Penny helping him get to his feet. He put his arm around her shoulders. She steadied him and braced herself for the weight. It was only a few steps to the bed, but Liam was heavy, and Penny was small. She let out a huge breath as he finally flopped down onto the bed. She gently put the covers over him.

"Penny, what are you doing here?"

"I called you three hours ago, and you said you were coming into college. When you didn't show, I got worried."

"I'm fine. I just had another one of those super real dreams. They're so weird."

"I don't think dreams leave you in this state. Well, at least, they never leave *me* in this state. What's going on? Is there something troubling you? I'm here for you, my friend, always."

"I know you are. Thank you. There is something wrong, though." Liam stared up thoughtfully at the ceiling, which just hours before had worms pouring through it. He probed every inch with his eyes, searching for any sign of the damage. He didn't find any, which further confirmed his suspicion that he was indeed going crazy.

"Are you sick?"

"No. Well, maybe. Maybe inside my mind. So many things are happening that I don't understand."

"Please tell me what's going on. You do trust me, don't you?"

"Yeah." He looked at her. "Yes, of course I trust you. Never let me down yet. I just don't know what to say to you. I can't understand it myself."

"You're not making much sense. Is it boy stuff or something?" she asked.

"What? No," he laughed. "It's weird stuff, like the dreams and my life are connected or like I'm living two lives. One here with you, and one out there somewhere. One where I'm driven, where I have a mission. I may see inside someone else's mind or something else." He shrugged the best he could while lying flat on his back and sighed deeply.

Constantly trying to make sense of the senseless was pushing him to the edge. Was there a limit to the amount of fear and confusion one human could endure? If there was, Liam was close to that limit.

He couldn't understand. Almost all of the time, The Fleck kept him confused, kept him cloudy, but at times it was clear. He remembered back to killing with the Assassin's hands. He remembered the joy he felt. Had some of her stayed inside him? He loved the power, the freedom, yet all the time, he was a slave, a slave to the force that lived inside him. That was when he remembered—the child had escaped!

"Remember now, do you, human?"

"Remember?"

"You failed. Weak-minded human!"

"I did," he confessed. *"Is all lost?"*

"No, but we can no longer..." The Fleck trailed off.

Liam opened his eyelids and stared up at the ceiling again. It appeared misty. He flashed his eyes to Penny, who was looking all around her. Soon it became clear it was tiny particles of dust falling down. The thicker it got, the more it became mixed with a smoky haze.. It drifted and settled on their skin and hair.

"What is that stuff?" Penny asked, brushing the dust off her clothes.

"I don't know. It's dust. But where's it coming from?"

"I don't know, but it's getting thicker."

They sat watching on as the dust fell and settled all over the room. It rained down from above. It tasted bitter and chemical; there was no way they couldn't breathe in some of it. Thick like sparkling snow, it sat all over the room. When everything was covered, it finally stopped falling.

The pair stood, patting themselves down and sending puffs of the strange dust floorward and airwards. There was an enormous spark that flashed bright. A breeze blew across them, stirring the powder from the surfaces.

Liam reached out his hand for Penny's, knowing all too well that something was about to happen, and in his recent experience, it could be literally anything. She gripped it tight, and her frightened eyes met his.

"What's happening to you?"

"Nothing, but I think something *could* happen. It feels weird."

"Liam, look at your hand!"

He looked down to where her hand met his. It looked normal for a second, then it went slowly transparent. It became solid again, and like cold waves through his body, it disappeared and reappeared over and over. Penny's face was etched in fear as she tightly clung to his hand. She, too, seemed to be fading in and out of existence. The cold waves went through them both, time and again, leaving them hazy and confused. Another flash sparked through the dust making it glow blue, then both of them vanished completely.

Power to Fear

Isha fell through the sky, wrapped tightly within the misty dream. Her stomach turned upside down, and she screamed out, shrill and loud. The ground rushed towards her. She closed her eyes and braced for impact. The impact never came. She opened them again, and there she was, staring in the mirror. She jumped in surprise at seeing her own face staring back at her. She rubbed her eyes and looked deeper still into her reflection.

After all she had been through, she expected to see someone else standing there, in some other place. Haunted whispers echoed through her mind, quiet and lingering, words that were indistinguishable. They could have been muffled English or a strange alien language. It was impossible to tell. She had long since given up guessing and was starting to accept that she was a mere passenger on this wild journey.

The whispers swirled and repeated, over and over, like they were speaking to her in words that she couldn't quite hear. She grew frustrated. Maybe it was a message. Maybe the voices had the answers she needed. Soon she was desperate to hear what they were saying. The voices came, not from with out but from within, taunting her. She screamed out and put her hands over her ears while her body burned in anger, trying to either hear the words or block out the sound, but still, those incoherent whispers came.

"The child!" she screamed.

"*The child is safe,*" came the voice from within.

"*What happened? I died!*" She let out a whimper and hugged her body with her arms as she remembered her last breath. "*The Assassin!*"

"*Do not fear, Isha. You saved the child and slayed the Assassin.*"

She half laughed and half cried and blew out of her lungs in relief. "*So, we won? We did it?*"

"This battle is far from won. They will come again. Time is running out. The Fleck was inside her, and it becomes more powerful with each passing moment. They sent the Assassin... who will they send next? They are certain to be of even greater power. Now Dark Space has learned to infiltrate host bodies. This is bad. Now our enemy could be anyone or anywhere."

A furrow instantly appeared on Isha's brow and her hands went to her head. The Fleck, working with the dark forces... against her, Flick, and the child. *"More powerful than her, even!?"*

"She was obviously not powerful enough. The more powerful the host, the harder they are to control, but now, they must risk losing control completely. Time is short. Our enemy is strong. There is still much work to do."

"I can't think now. Can't I eat and get some sleep, Flick? This is crazy. I'm worn out." She huffed in exhaustion and frustration.

"Yes, Isha, sleep now. The hardest part of our mission is yet to come."

"Oh great! I can't wait." The sarcasm was clear in her inner voice. Isha needed a moment to herself, and before she'd even formed the thought, all of a sudden, just like that, Flick was gone. She could no longer feel her presence. For the first time in as long as she could remember, inside her body, she was alone.

She flopped down and sat on the bed, bouncing onto her back to stare up at the ceiling. The thoughts ran through her mind. She wondered what on earth was happening. It was a mission that made no sense to her. Her enemy was sending fearsome and almost invincible assassins, and their side only had, well, her. She couldn't fathom how she was even a part of this cosmic battle let alone how she could ever win it. She shuddered at the thought, unable to even imagine who or what could be more powerful than the Assassin was.

She scanned her mind, trying to learn lessons from her experiences. The memories were there, but they were flashes, like parts of a dream from which she'd just awoken. Her whole life had been like that recently.

Her mother's voice called her down for dinner. She struggled up from her bed and made her way downstairs. Questions that received short answers were asked and a few voicings of concern expressed, to which Isha just said she was tired. She ate quickly, helped with the washing up, and made her way back upstairs. Finally, sustained, yet still with cloudy memories churning over in her mind, she drifted off to sleep.

Reflections

"Where am I?" Liam asked as he opened his eyes. There was no answer. He squeezed his fingers and felt the comfort of Penny's grasp in his. A second later, he was trying to focus, but this was a world upon which eyes like his could not focus. Everything was strange and blurry. This was a world the likes of which he had never known. He looked around. The colours warped and blurred as ripples like water waved over them.

He looked over at Penny and dropped her hand in shock. She was no longer Penny at all. She was a strange creature that exuded green from round her edges like a badly painted picture, sneaking colour beyond the outlines with a yellow glow in the heart of it.

She spoke, but in a bizarre language, yet somehow still, Liam understood. "Liam, where are you?"

"Here," he said, looking down at his own body for the first time. It looked like a reflection on a puddle. He moved his arm, if indeed that's what it was. It moved, but in the opposite direction it should have, like it was a mirror image.

"What's happening?" Penny's voice, though speaking in an alien tongue, sounded fearful and panicked.

"I don't know, but I'm here. Just take my hand."

He reached out his hand and she reached out hers at the same time, yet they both moved away from each other. Confusion swirled and their bodies felt cold. Liam moved his arm the wrong way this time, and it moved towards Penny or, at least, whatever strange entity had taken her place. She may not have looked like his friend, but in his heart, Liam could feel her presence with him. He knew the warmth and love of his best friend. He had felt a deep connection to her from the moment they met, and now he had never been so grateful for it. It took the edge off the loneliness and fear that had surrounded him for what seemed like forever. It may have been selfish, but for once, he felt some comfort that he wasn't completely alone.

Maybe now she would believe him when he tried explaining. Maybe she would understand a little better, though he had a great sympathy that now she was wrapped in confusion and fear, just as he had been all along. He didn't want her to go through what he had, but that was beyond his choosing because here she was.

Their hands connected, although they couldn't feel each other's fingers or anything solid. It was just warmth and weight, but that still somehow brought them both comfort. There they swirled, not a solid body, but not liquid either. The pair floated in the strange place, moving in mirrors like reflections.

"Where are we?" Penny asked again.

"I don't know. I just have no answers."

The Fleck entered his mind. *"You must move. You must find it."*

"Find what?" Liam asked silently.

"The window. Only the window has the answers."

"What—" He was cut off.

"No more questions. Just move."

"Penny, we have to go." He pushed himself towards her, which in this strange world felt like pulling.

Confused and discombobulated, they were lost. Colours flowed and lapped the edges of their vision like waves against the shore, but unlike the ocean, it wasn't calm and relaxing. It was terrifying. Nothing around them was ever truly in sight but never completely gone either. Images hung on the periphery, elusive and unclear.

Awkwardly, they floated through a hazy soup, reversing their way to who knows where. Their world a muddle, they lingered, floating like a leaf being pushed across a puddle by the wind.

They hardly spoke as they went. Only occasional words of reassurance from Liam to calm Penny while he pulled her gently behind him. He guided her, and in turn, The Fleck silently guided him.

Through the misty rainbow dream they wandered blindly and slowly. Bit by bit they went from fear to awe. The colours were beautiful, and soon, an unnatural calm washed over them.

In that place, there was no gravity weighing them down. Here they floated effortlessly, like a seed on the breeze. There was no straining of muscles or effort to breathe. The light was never too bright or too dark; no straining of eyes. Just existence. They dreamed not of the future or the past as they were locked firmly in the present.

The floating colours all at once surged like a river's mighty current, dragging Liam and Penny helplessly forward. They went like that for a time, still holding onto each other, then slowed and, finally, stopped.

They hung for a moment, still, and time stopped with them, until they were smashed by what seemed a tsunami of colours ripping their hands apart. They both called out to the other in anguish. The comfort in each other's presence was stolen and replaced with the deepest fear.

The strange forces gripped them and dragged them powerfully round in a sweeping circle. They were pulled further and further from each other as the blurry colours stole the form of the other from view. They called again, but now they were too far apart to hear each other.

Like a curtain falling, darkness came clanging down around them, then the forces were gone. Hanging in complete silence, in the darkness of nothingness, the two strange forms floated side by side.

At least they were close together again, which brought the slightest sense of relief. Neither of them wanted to be there together; alone would be far worse.

"Help me, Liam. I'm scared! I don't know what's going on."

He wished he could reassure Penny with his answers. He wished he could tell her what was happening, but he had no idea himself. Once again, his life was like a dream. It had seemed nothing but a dream forever.

He pulled his form towards her and took her hand again. "I don't know. I can't explain. Just stay with me, and we'll get through this. Together."

They floated without saying another word; words at that moment were useless. The dark around them was menacing and vast, holding them there in the nothing. They were prisoners to forces far beyond their control, and soon those mysterious forces were at work again.

The blackness below them ripped apart and made way for bright and beautiful light. Like they had been dropped from a mountain, they were jerked downwards. They started to spin, slowly at first but then fast and out of control. They free-fell into the light. They dropped like stones, through the brightness, hand in hand, for what felt like forever, and then flopped down onto a solid surface. It wasn't with a bump; they landed as if they had always belonged there. They blended with the surface like they had done nothing more than taken a simple step.

For the first time, they felt something. The ground below them was cold and smooth. The darkness was gone, the colours were gone, and all around them was a box of mirrors. In it, they could see their own reflections, countless times in all directions. Before confusion even met them, there was a flash of blue light and blurry images slowly appeared around them.

A flash of pink lightning lit the backdrop, and from nothing, a landscape became clear. Fiery orange clouds ripped fast across the sky. The watery sky was pink from the strange red sunlight while a storm raged. Thunder crashed but louder and more ferocious than they'd ever known. Wild wind whipped up orange sand and howled away far stronger than any wind on Earth.

"*The child is there,*" the Fleck hissed.

"*Where?*" Liam asked silently, but there was no answer.

Clutching each other tightly, they started to spin. The force dragged them up, like they were falling in the wrong direction. The landscape grew ever-smaller below as they fell upwards through a haze and then, once again, into nothing.

Present

Liam and Penny awoke, if that's what it was, on the floor in Liam's apartment, still hand in hand. Though somehow it didn't seem they had woken up at all but more that, suddenly, they were present, slipping from nothing but the haze to the real world with a bump. Penny looked over at Liam. Her eyes were wide, her brow furrowed. She tried uselessly to make sense of what had happened. They clutched hands as tightly as ever, staring at each other for a few lingering seconds.

They pulled themselves into a seated position and stared blankly at the wall. The conversation had to begin at some point, but for a few moments, neither of them had any idea where to start. Penny's eyes darted back and forth around the room, running the crazy images through her mind, seeing things behind her eyes.

"Was it real?" she whispered, staring right through Liam.

"I don't know. I just don't know. Were you really there?"

"I was there. You know I was."

"I don't know anything. Nothing for sure. I felt you there."

"I was there."

"So, now you've seen. This is exactly the kind of thing that's been happening to me lately."

"*This* keeps happening to you?!"

"Yeah. Well, not this exact thing, but loads of weird things. It's like being in strange places, inside other bodies."

"Please, tell me what you can. I'm so confused." Tears welled and then rolled down her cheeks; tears of shock, tears of fear and some tears of relief that she was back. Her mind swirled, just as Liam's had been for all this time.

He reached across and took her in his arms and pulled her close. His gesture was not just for her benefit; he needed the hug as much as she did. He was lost in the embrace for a moment before his friend gently pushed herself from the hug.

"Okay, start at the beginning," she said, her eyes red from tears and exhaustion.

"Penny, I can't truly explain. None of it makes sense, but I'll try. Basically—man, I sound so mental—basically, there's this voice inside my head or… one that lives inside me."

Penny gasped. "I heard it! In the dream—the reflection world—the voice spoke to you."

"You heard it?!"

"Yeah. It was faint, like it was far in the distance, but it was there."

"This is… The voice is inside my mind. Inside me. How could you hear it?"

"I thought it was real when I heard you talking to it. It's not your imagination."

"Oh, wow! That's such a relief. I can't possibly tell you."

"Who does the voice belong to?"

"They call themselves The Fleck. It's not a person. It's not solid. It's like a thought but inside my soul. It's there watching and manipulating things. I'm doing something important, but I don't know what. I don't know if I have any control or I'm just a slave." He sucked in a huge gulp of breath trying to hold back the tears that welled, but they came anyway. "I'm just so afraid. I feel invaded. It's watching us now. I can feel it here."

Tears rolled down his stubbled cheeks and clung to the short hairs. He turned away from his friend and balled his fists. He clenched his jaw, and his anger burned. It surged through him like waves as he fought for control.

In the end, he exploded. "Why me?! What do you want from me?! Get out of my head. Get out of my head!" He grabbed the sides of his head and slumped forward, wailing, losing all control of his emotions. All his confusion and fear poured out of him as his body shook and he gasped in air.

Penny rubbed his back. She couldn't know what he was going through. Well, nobody ever could, but her experience in the reflection world and hearing The Fleck had at least given her some degree of understanding. If something as unimaginable had happened to her, how could she doubt a word he said?

Her friend sat before her, bent in two, rocking back and forth, gasping into his hands. He was in pieces. She didn't know what to do, but she knew she needed to do something.

She put her hands on his shoulders and placed her face tight against his back. He felt solid with tension. She rubbed the top of his arms gently just so he would know she was there. He stopped rocking, shuddered, and cried into his open hands.

Pulling her face away, Penny tugged on his shoulders to unfold him from the ball he was in. Reluctantly, Liam followed her guidance and sat up.

She turned him round to face her. "Hey... Hey. I'm here." She tugged at him to invite an embrace. He fell into her and wrapped his arms around her back, clinging tightly to her. It was his turn to sob. It took a number of minutes for him to recompose himself, until all the emotion he had been bottling up inside flowed out.

"I know it's coming. I will have to go again soon."

"Go where?"

"To kill." His eyes stared at her wildly, unnerving her. A frightening look that she had never seen before. "I've already killed so many in these dreams. I was an assassin more than once. I have to kill someone."

"Don't be silly. Who do you have to kill?"

"A child."

"You can't kill a child!"

"I must. The future depends upon it. There are things we do not understand. I don't understand any of it. I'm afraid. I don't want to, but I don't think I have any choice or control over it."

"You're not making any sense. You can't kill anyone and certainly not children. Snap out of it, mate, please. You're scaring me."

"That's what we saw in the window, Penny. In the mirror room. Where the child is. They'll put me inside another being to find and kill the child."

He stared into the distance, and his thoughts drifted. "It's too late. I've already killed so many. The child will be next... The child will be next."

"Please. You're really scaring me, Liam." She jumped up and grabbed his hands. She pulled him, and reluctantly, he went up onto his feet. "Come on." She smiled, not so much with her mouth but in her eyes. He felt her love for him, and he knew Penny would be there for him no matter what happened.

"Right, let's just forget the freaky child killing thing for a minute," she joked. "You go grab a shower, and I'll shoot home and get some clothes. I'm gonna be staying with you for a bit."

"Don't go." He held her hands tighter to hold her back.

"Listen, mate, I have to. I'll be back in half an hour, and then I won't leave your side, okay? I've only got these clothes. You don't want me to start tramping it up and being all stinky like you, do ya, bachelor boy?"

He couldn't help but roll his eyes playfully and let out a little chuckle. "Guess not, girlfriend."

"Look, I'll be back before you even finish in the shower. I know your beauty regime is a proper long-winded one."

"Well, it's hard when you're as butt ugly as me." He laughed.

"Yeah, you fell out the ugly tree and hit every branch on the way down."

"Well, we can't all be the belle of the ball like you, can we?"

"Hey, bro, you're beautiful." She cheekily jabbed his arm. "I'll see you in thirty. And I've got the keys, so I can get back in."

"Okay, tiger. See you later."

The Tournament

The mist rose, and stepping forward, the warm water hit Liam, enticing goose bumps from his skin. He hadn't realised how cold and drained he was until that instant. The steaming flow massaged his aching muscles. Even though he hadn't, he felt like he'd run a marathon.

He put his head beneath the water and closed his eyes. The warmth trickled, sending shivers down his back. He breathed out, making the steam swirl, adding more moisture to the air.

Liam washed his face and opened his eyes. All around him, the shower's mist gathered thick as it darkened from steamy white to grey. It began to obscure his vison, becoming less like mist, more like smoke. It filled the shower cubical until he could hardly see a thing. The air changed, like it had been replaced by something thicker.

Breathing became hard. He drew deep breaths, trying to capture the escaping oxygen, but now it was nearly impossible. He wanted to scream, but he felt like he was drowning.

Even when he stepped out of the shower's flow, he could feel the damp warmth around him. The air glooped and bubbled, and he grew desperate to catch a breath. He started to panic, ripping back the shower curtain and stepping out into the bathroom.

The entire room was full of the smoke, and his lungs burned for a breath. Liam had a sinking feeling. He was suffocating and powerless. It was like he was trying to breathe in slime. His heart raced and then fluttered, and from the smoky greyness, Liam slipped into darkness and out of consciousness.

The strange colours surrounded him as he flew free of his body and out through the misty cosmos to another place. He floated for an age and then, like always, snapped from the journey. He zoomed towards a dome, flying at first, then falling.

The dome was surrounded by a metal frame and a ruby, crystal-like outer shell. It sparkled strange with flecks of orange and yellow reflecting the light.

Falling towards a certain clash, he screamed out. There was no impact, just the feeling of going from nothing to being. His consciousness again entered another body.

Liam scanned his surroundings. All around the colours glowed electric pinks and fiery reds. A mighty roar screamed out, the roar of thousands of beings rammed tightly on sloping banks, high up to the roof of the dome. Their voices called out as one, angry and blood thirsty voices, primal roars, calling for death. He flashed a glance around him and then down at himself. In his hand was what he knew was a weapon, though he had no idea what it was or how to use it.

An orb glowed blue. It flashed and hurtled towards him. Where he got the ability to move the way he did, or even recognise he needed to, he did not know, yet he moved anyway.

He leaned and arched his back and the orb zipped past his head. He sprang back upright and readied his weapon. There was a glowing hoop in each of his almost-reptilian hands with a sparkling, fizzing chord between them.

A silver being swooped into sight. It was like chrome with no seams upon it. Flowing almost like liquid, each move connected it in perfect choreography to the next. Though it was huge and heavy, it was swift.

All at once, Liam knew—of these two beings, only one of them was walking away from that battle.

Liam sneered and growled like a wild beast. He puffed his chest out large. The thirst for blood flowed through him. The fire in his body burned. Flashes of the Assassin before brought him comfort. No longer was he a stranger to being the dealer of death. No longer would his fear hold him back; a part of him wanted the blood.

Instinctively, he released one of the hoops from his grasp and flung it round in a series of loops above his head then criss-crossed it around his body. He lunged forward and grabbed the second loop again. There, he menaced with his weapon ready. There, he dared the silver being to challenge him. The instinct took control without thought or emotion, just the yearning for battle—the place his host was at home.

Liam's opponent looked down upon him with disdain, a smirk on its cold face. The pathetic show of force would never intimidate this being.

The metal being lifted its hand and another orb shot out of its palm. Liam moved quickly like a viper. He jumped in the air doing a full summersault, avoiding the orb, and flinging out one of the loops from his weapon as he did. The loop flew through the air, flashed like lightning, and exploded on the silver being's hand. The hand was gone, leaving the stump pumping out blood.

With wild rage, it flew at Liam, shaking the very ground with each mighty step. It reached out its remaining hand for the strike, but Liam flung his weapon behind his back, spun around in a complete circle, and, in one movement, let the weapon swoop out.

The silver being flew past Liam and stood, panting, facing away from him. It stumbled. Its head dropped from its neck, and it fell forward like a tree, hitting the arena floor with a thud.

A mighty cheer roared out from the crowd. With his momentary thirst for blood satisfied, Liam reached his hands aloft, holding his weapon like a trophy, and screamed his brutal war cry to the sky. The crowd gasped, stunned to silence for every second his blood-chilling scream lasted. Then, as it faded out and echoed round the dome, they exploded into rapturous applause.

There he stood, in the circle of red sand, surrounded on all sides by the baying crowd. A feeling rose in Liam, a frightening one that was out of character as he milked them for all they were worth. He bathed in the adulation and basked in his own glory.

The ground in front of him opened, and a figure floated up from below. The figure raised its hands high in the air and spoke aggressively in a strange alien tongue. The words meant nothing to Liam, yet still, he understood.

"Rakid from Kwelasoin is the victor! He progresses to the grand final tomorrow. One step closer to winning the coveted halithstord."

The crowd went wild again.

Liam, or as it seemed, Rakid, went down an elevator through the floor and off into a dingy hallway. At last, he was alone. *"Hey, you. The Fleck. What the hell's going on?"*

It said nothing.

"Oh, I see. You choose to invade my mind when it's convenient, never when I need help. Right, got it!"

"I speak when I need to speak, not because you demand it, human. I speak when I feel. I am The Fleck. You are nothing."

"Let me stop you there, pal," Liam angrily burst. *"You clearly need me more than I need you. I was fine, having a cool life and everything with one awkward friend and just about scraping by at uni. No part of you or this did I need!"*

An electric shock jolted through his body. His muscles contracted, and he fell screaming to his knees. The Fleck's voice entered his mind as ever, but so much colder than before. It made the pain worse.

"You are here because you are needed. You are necessary to our cause, but fight against us, and you will know pain like never before! All around you will crumble, and you, you will be last. You will watch them fall, all of those that you love."

Liam, still on his knees, was grimacing and panting in pain. *"So, I'm your slave?"*

"You are no slave. You do not have to do The Fleck's bidding. It depends how much you like your mother or how much you like Penny. If you'd like to see them screaming in pain while the flesh is removed from their bones, go right ahead, human, resist!"

An image flashed through him. It lasted no longer than the blink of an eye, but it was one that would be etched upon his soul forever. The faces of the two people he loved the most, tortured and screaming. It broke him. He screamed inside, in pain and fear, the image harrowing and traumatising. He could never let anything happen to them. He was helpless. Any thought of resistance or defiance still alive within Liam was extinguished right there.

"Okay, I have no choice. Okay. I'll have to do it, won't I?"

"I can't hear you," The Fleck taunted.

"I'll do it!" he shouted, this time out loud.

The Fleck faded back into another part of his being. It slunk into the background, to the dark places within, the shadows in which it was at home.

How Liam hated The Fleck. He seethed and despised it within his soul. He cursed that this should ever have happened to him, how his life had been turned upside-down against his will, and now he had no control at all. The bitterness consumed him, and the rage burned through him, and The Fleck basked in it like glorious sunshine.

Liam finally returned to his feet and went along unguided in a place he'd never been, yet somehow knew the way. He went all the way down the hallway to a room he knew was his. He sat on a stone bench that jutted out of the wall and doubled as a bed. Now was the first time he looked down to properly examine himself and the strange new form he took.

His hands were huge and a milky yellow colour. Thick and scaley fingers stretched out three times as long as his human hands. There were purple flecks spread up his long thick arms. His body was huge and muscular and covered in black armour. His legs were also huge, rippling with muscles, and his feet were inside massive boots. His strange weapon, no longer fizzing, was looped around his body.

Only then did The Fleck return to him. Liam's anger surged again. Resentful and wishing to be left alone, he huffed.

"You must fight. You must win. They will call you soon."

"Fight what? Who?"

"It matters not who you fight. You must slay them. You must win."

Liam rolled his eyes in frustration. Here he was, trapped in another being's skin, having to fight a mortal battle in which he could not fail, a slave to the biddings of a powerful force, and The Fleck gave him as little information as it could.

No matter how frustrated he was with his lack of knowledge of what lay ahead, he simply had to do what he needed to do to survive. Anticipation began to swirl. The only way to survive was to fight and to kill.

The crowd again burst into bloodthirsty cheers as Liam stepped out into the strange ruby light of the dome. He entered the circle of sand, and his heart started to race with exhilaration. The warrior within was coming alive.

He raised his hands aloft and screamed his mighty war cry, but this time, one of challenge, not of victory. The crowd went wild then silenced to a murmur as they awaited in anticipation for his opponent.

From the other side of the arena stepped the huge and intimidating figure. The ground shook with every step beneath its mighty frame. Glowing, electric blue power sparked around its exoskeleton, and its fiery blue eyes stared down. The Machine stood huge, fierce, and ready.

Liam looked upon his foe. It was impossible not to be intimidated, but his host bristled around him. This was the place where Rakid belonged. The place he loved, amongst the battles, amongst the blood, amongst the carnage of combat. This was where he thrived.

The Machine crossed its arms, making fists with its huge hands. It dramatically thrust them skyward, and the baying crowd roared once more, the loudest yet. It screamed a wild scream, one that would strike fear into the hearts of most. Thankfully, Liam's host was not one of that number. He stared upon his enemy, twitching for the battle, fists clenched, itching to get at the warrior before him.

The crowd quietened to an excited hiss, then the horn loudly sounded. That sound meant one thing—it was time to fight. The crowd roared like wild animals, waiting for the carnage to begin, howling, baying for the first crunching clash between the pair.

The warriors stepped forward, eyeballing each other. It was Liam's host or his opponent who would walk out of the arena. For the other, it would become their resting place.

Forward they surged as Liam pulled his weapon from round his body, and it sparked into fizzing life. The distance quickly closed between them. They ran headlong for each other.

The Machine threw out a punch that was a blur with its powerful arm. Despite it looking like it was too far away to land, the arm kept extending. Liam was confused for a split second. The Machine was not close enough to reach him, but in a flash, it had struck him in the centre of his chest with a crushing blow. It buckled his armour, and the air immediately left his lungs. He flew backwards, taken right off his feet, and rolled over as he crashed into the sand, releasing his weapon as he did.

The pain came, surging through him, but he was too winded to scream or groan. He turned his body, and the bones in his shattered chest crunched. He coughed, and thick green blood bubbled up from his elongated mouth. He was stricken, gasping for air.

His eyes were barely open, but he saw the ruby dome above him sparkle. A shadow slowly loomed over him. The Machine raised its foot high, it hung there for a second, then came crashing down. Rakid, the mighty warrior, was dead in the sand, and the tournament was lost.

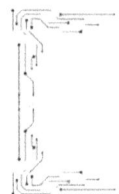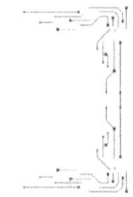

Questions of Sanity

"Liam, I'm back," Penny called, shutting the front door behind her. She was greeted by silence. She walked through the front room and towards the bedroom. "Liam?" She peered round the doorway, but his bedroom was empty. That meant he must still be in the bathroom. She was worried since she had left some forty-five minutes ago. She knocked on the door. "Liam, you in there?"

"Yes." His reply was croaky and strained. She could only just hear him.

"Is it locked? Are you decent?"

"It's locked. Give me a second, and I'll be out."

"You've got five minutes, mate, or I'll have to smash that door down."

Three minutes had passed before Liam stumbled out of the bathroom fully clothed. He looked terrible as he slumped down into the armchair.

"The shower was supposed to sort you out. You look awful. Are you okay? Did something else happen?"

He sat blankly staring at the wall, playing the visions through his mind. Seeing the hazy, incomplete memories that by now were so familiar to him, yet never making sense, always confusing and disconnected. With each awakening, more memories remained than the time before.

To start with, only split seconds of each journey stayed, but now more came flooding back. They were jumbled like a story with huge chunks of the narrative missing. The trauma and fear always kept him on the edge, like treading on eggshells. The fear of the entity haunted him, cruel and abusive, but abuse he could not escape from for his abuser lived within him. It could hurt him and manipulate him, torture and control him. That thing, dark and lurking, watched everything he did, every move he made, maybe even invaded every thought he had. It ate away at him, keeping him guessing, wallowing constantly in uncertainty. He could slip away any second, never a clue as to who he would be or what he would face.

Liam was a million miles away yet there, locked inside his skin prison. His thoughts jerked from scene to scene and then stopped. That was when the cold realisation dawned heavily upon him—he had failed again.

Now fear surged. The Fleck would be scornful and cruel. It may even hurt him again for his failure. Not only had he lost the battle, he'd also lost the entire war. He awaited the pain, like at any second he could burst into flames. Nervously twitching, knowing all the time The Fleck waited, torturing him with uncertainty.

"Liam, do you wanna answer my question?" Penny waved sarcastically to catch his attention.

"Oh, what? Sorry, yeah, I'm here." He shook his head and snapped out of his dream, focused on his friend. "I'm okay, I think. I just skipped again." He sighed deeply, slumping his shoulders in exasperation.

"Skipped... is that what it is?"

"I don't know what else to call it. We skipped somewhere else, right?"

"I don't know. I don't remember clearly. Something happened, but it could have been a hallucination or a dream or something. I can't really see it now, like it wasn't real."

"Penny, we wouldn't have the same hallucination or dream at the same time. That just doesn't happen. If it was a figment of our imagination, how could we have been there together?"

She knew he was right, but none of it made any sense to her. "Look, I don't know what the hell's happening to you, or what happened to me, but maybe we should get you to a doctor. What do you reckon?"

"You think I'm crazy then?" He was slightly agitated by her comment.

"I don't think you're crazy, my friend, but I do think you're going through something that we don't understand. We need to find the answers. You're talking about killing people and children, of all things, and it's scary. Please, get some help."

His frustration burned. "I'm not lying, and I'm not crazy! I know it doesn't make sense, but this much I do know—I am involved in something important, in something that means so much more than this." He looked around the room with disdain, a half scowl across his face. "This means more than you can ever know. It's more important than my life, or your life, or any of this."

"Okay, I don't know what you are talking about. Like, do me a fave, yeah. Let me take you to the doctors tomorrow? Of course I trust you, and I believe you. At least, I believe it's very real to you, but I wanna get my brother from another mother back." She stared deeply into his eyes and he stared back.

He saw the twinkle in her eye, and he couldn't be frustrated. She, as always, just wanted the best for him. He reluctantly conceded that he would go, if for nothing else than to appease his sister from another mister.

They sat and chatted until, with a rumble of her stomach, Penny offered to make dinner. She went off into the kitchen, and for a few moments, Liam was alone.

"*I failed. It got me.*" He said in his mind. He'd hidden it well, but the whole time he'd been terrified of the pain The Fleck may inflict upon him. He felt like the entity was now gaining more and more control over him, even over his intent.

Liam could think of nothing worse than killing, but when he was them, he felt the pleasure that surged through their bodies. He felt the glory of the kill. He felt powerful and savage, and even though he was a slave to a force, when he was them, he was free.

The jumble in his cloudy mind fell silent for a moment.

"*Yes, you failed,*" the voice growled from his core.

"*I'm sorry,*" he silently whimpered in abject fear, awaiting the pain.

"*Yes, human, you failed, but this was a test. All is not lost. Yet.*"

"A test?"

"Now we have found our host," the Fleck hissed. "Now things are the way they need to be."

Intelligence

"Okay, I'm awake!" Isha was grumpy and groggy.

Her mother stood in the doorway and called her for the sixth time that morning. She sat up and glared at her. Her mother said nothing and walked away, happy in knowledge that at last her daughter was going to get out of bed. Isha dropped down onto her back, picking up a pillow and burying her face in it. The thought of a mundane school day irrationally irritated her that morning.

She huffed and squashed her face deep into the pillow, pulling it round the sides of her head. She lingered in the muffled darkness, breathing in her own morning breath, trying to hold off reality for just a few moments longer. Then, as she fought to stave off her grumpiness and conjure some motivation, the world around her felt like it was spinning. Slowly at first, but then faster until dizziness overcame her. Dreading what she may see, she slowly removed the pillow from her face.

Everything was spinning apart from her and her bed. Soon she started to feel nauseous as the world sped round fast until it was nothing but a blur. Isha felt faint and longed for a way off that sickening ride.

With a mighty rumble, louder than thunder, the walls that surrounded her crumbled and floated away. Her bed, her house, the whole planet was gone, and the familiar form of her bedroom gave way to the darkness of the endless cosmos.

Strange colours swirled again as she was sucked away on her journey. Through tunnels, she floated free, out into the great beyond, into the mysterious depths of the universe, and onward towards a new adventure. Her heart raced with the sudden feeling of falling, and that told her, very soon, she would be inside the restraints of another body.

Isha opened her eyes with a jolt that almost made her heart stop. Two creatures stood before her, both of them alien and strange. They were tall and lean and green-skinned. They didn't wear any clothes apart from thick belts with unrecognisable items hanging from them. They looked semi-reptilian but bipedal, with tiny fine scales that reflected the light, ever changing their tones. Their eyes were huge and yellow, taking up most of their elongated face. Their arms were thin with delicate clawed fingers on their hands, but their legs were muscular and powerful with huge feet and long toes stretching outward.

To Isha, the colours around her looked strange, but whether that was the place or her host's eyes, she could not tell.

The taller of the two creatures spoke urgently in bird-like tones, an incomprehensible language, but as always, Isha understood. It wanted her to follow it. It turned, revealing for the first time a long tail with a spiney, bony crest that ran all the way down the centre and swept round to the tip. It set off running like an ostrich, light on its feet and quick. Its tail jutted out straight, giving the creature perfect balance.

Isha instinctively started to run. Her heart raced with excitement as she did. Never had she run so fast and so freely. She skipped over the cold floor, hardly even planting her feet, zooming along with her new companions. They were headed down a badly lit corridor with walls that towered high over them, dingy and grey. Struggling to keep up, she followed the two creatures until up ahead was a high vertical wall that looked like a dead end.

"Quickly, quickly," came the chirping voice from the creature in the lead. The voice was filled with urgency. It was clear they were on an important mission.

All around a shrill whistle rang out and hummed a constant tone in the background. The creatures leapt and gripped the surface of the wall, shooting upwards like geckos.

Isha had no choice but to attempt the same thing. Never had she jumped so far or so high as she reached out her limbs and clung to the surface. She pushed, and almost as quickly as she ran along the ground, now she ran vertically. She zipped over the surface, higher and higher.

The creature in front reached a square opening at the top of the wall and disappeared through it as the second followed. Isha closed in on it, but with her inexperience, her toes slipped beneath her. She reached up a desperate arm to grab the bottom of the opening and dangled for a moment. The second creature turned around and came to her aid. It climbed down below her and pushed Isha up through the gap. She got her feet and headed into the darkness, tearing after the creature in the lead. The whistling stopped.

There was a bright flash followed by a pop. Isha turned to look, but all she could see was the tail of the creature that was behind her. It was smoking and blackened; the rest of it was gone. She gasped in shock and started heading back the way she'd come from to see if there was anything she could do, even though she knew it was hopeless.

"Stop!" She was grabbed on the shoulder. "He's gone. Let's go. We don't have much time."

She turned and faced the creature, took one look back, and together they moved on. They went tearing through a long straight rectangular tube. It was dark inside, but Isha's host could see everything. The tube went on and on until finally they reached a huge metal grate at the end. It looked like some kind of ventilation grate, but this one was massive, towering high over them. They squeezed through the narrow holes, and the darkness made way for bright light. They dropped down onto the floor on the other side.

Out of nowhere, a huge shadow loomed menacingly over them. Her companion moved swiftly, pushing her violently out of the way. An instant later, an enormous boot thudded down next to her, quickly followed by a second. In comparison to whomever those boots belonged, she was as small as an insect. The feet continued on their way as the tiny Isha got swiftly back to hers.

They scuttled fast across the busy hallway, avoiding the stream of hustling feet, in constant danger of being crushed. They pressed tightly against the skirting to get away from the main flow of the giant beings clumping down the hallway. Finally, they reached a door, and following her companion's lead, Isha squeezed underneath it. Inside, the atmosphere was very different to the hall. It was warm and close, unlike the airiness of the open corridor.

She heard the muffled sound of an urgently spoken alien dialect that she did not understand. Eight enormous beings sat round a table. From the floor, at her angle, she couldn't see their faces, just huge legs beneath the table and the back of the one nearest to her.

The tiny creature by her side fumbled around its belt, and a clear bubble seemed to materialise in its hand. It swished its fragile finger across the surface and released it. The bubble floated up and hovered on the edge of the ceiling.

"What's happening, Flick?" Isha asked silently.

"You must get the information out of here. It's inside the bubble. The enemy knows where the child is, so we must learn for ourselves and beat them there. They will send a fearsome warrior. If they get there first, the consequences will be devastating."

"Okay, got it."

"You have to get to the array and release the bubble into it. That's the only way a message can get above this atmosphere."

"Where is the array?"

"Enough now. I'll tell you only what you need to know, when you need to know it. It's very important for you to be present. Just do one task at a time and think not of the next, and your task right now is to follow this creature and get out of here with that bubble. Concentrate. We cannot fail. Do you understand?"

"I understand."

Before the alien meeting had even finished, slowly and gently the bubble floated back down and landed in the other creature's hand. "The word has been said. Now we must go." The voice was so small, the other beings in the room couldn't have possibly heard it. The creature placed the bubble back in a box on its belt. "Follow," the creature said and shot under the door, out of sight.

Isha quickly followed out into the brightly lit hallway. They ran as fast as they could, swerving the gauntlet of enormous boots that shook the ground all around them. They tore tight in the corner, down the long hall. Isha's body burned hotter and hotter, but as her temperature rose, the faster she ran, the more alive she felt.

Soon they came to another grate sitting low in the hallway. They expertly scrabbled up the wall and through the gaps. Now they were inside a tube. It was drenched with darkness, and warm and humid. Isha felt her body heating up all the time. They tore further through the narrow tube until they approached a T-junction at the end.

"Left here," the creature squealed.

As they rounded the corner, her companion stopped dead with an enormous jolt, leaving Isha skidding and nearly falling over to avoid it. It looked desperately down at its feet and back up at her.

"Stay back!" it screamed out, pointing down to its feet. It was trapped ankle deep in a jelly-like substance. "Take this and get out of here. You know what to do." The creature threw her the box with the bubble inside. Isha caught it.

That was when countless burning green eyes flashed from the shadows and quickly swarmed forward.

"Go!" the creature shouted once more.

Isha didn't think. She took a huge step, leapt, placed one foot on the wall of the tube, and sprang up high, jumping clear of the jelly. She landed softly on her nimble toes on the other side and ran.

A scream rang out, blood curdling and terror-filled, haunting her mind, forcing her to stop and look. Instantly she regretted it. She was hit by a wave of horror as shock filled her body and pain nagged away in her soul.

Her companion was being stripped to the bone by swarms of tiny creatures. They were ferocious. They swam through the jelly like octopuses, spindly arms reaching out, wrapping round the creature, and then feasting on its flesh.

Isha turned her back; she could watch no more. Her companion was lost and now it was up to her. She set off again, leaving the screams of agony behind her.

"What do I do, Flick?"

"Get to the array."

"Where is it?"

"Just keep going. I'll guide you."

Isha did as Flick instructed and now the being inside guided her, but not with words, with pictures. She showed Isha and drove her like it was instinct, like she knew where she was going, yet Isha was still a mere passenger on the journey.

She was drawn by Flick's guidance to a tiny pipe that, even at her small size, she could only just squeeze inside. It was such a tight space she had to crawl. The temperature increased again when she entered the pipe and grew hotter as she went. She reached the end of the pipe that finished in a small opening. With the tiny box still in her hand, she squeezed out and dropped down onto the dusty ground of the strange planet's surface.

Now the heat was scorching. Her feet started to burn the instant she touched the ground. Isha was driven forward, the pain stinging her limbs, surging through her feet as blisters bubbled up all over them. She ran with everything she had, trying not to touch the planet's surface, taking huge bounds, and screaming in agony each time she landed. She could hardly see a thing through the thick yellow haze that surrounded her, but there were lights glowing up ahead, brightly piercing the haze. Skipping on her flaming feet across the hostile planet, it became clear the lights were attached to a tower.

She screamed ever more as her legs started to flame. Fighting the pain, she got closer and jumped with all her might. In the strange atmosphere she went up higher and higher, like there was hardly any gravity holding her down. Her body and face were starting to blister as she was ravaged by roaring heat. She flew upwards.

She fumbled with the box, opened it, took the bubble in her flaming hand, and threw it as hard as she could. It flew out of her hand like a rocket, whooshing and sparkling through the air. It entered a hole in the top of the tower, and Isha half smiled.

Flying upwards still, higher now than the tower, she screamed once more. The flames licked and blackened her entire body, then burst savagely through her skin, cooking her from the inside out.

The Machine

"What did she say?" Penny asked when Liam finally emerged from the doctor's office.

"She just said I'm showing signs of high stress and anxiety, and my blood pressure is high. That was it. Apart from that, there's nothing wrong with me. She signed me off for a few days and gave me some sleeping pills that we'll have to grab on the way back. I just need to chill out and get some sleep. I don't feel like I've slept for a year."

"Come on then, mate. We'll get the pills, then I'll take you home and cook you some dinner."

Penny placed the plate down in front of him. He thanked her and added an appreciative smile. He was glad he had her to look after him. He always tried to put on a brave face, but he wasn't sure he would have been able to cope without her. She had been the one consistent thing in his life since he'd moved away from home. He was lucky to have her, and he made sure she knew what she meant to him as often as he could.

"What do you think then?" Penny chewed slowly, thoughtfully looking at him.

"It's a bit dry, but tastes awesome," he replied.

Penny tutted. "No... I meant about the doctor and stuff, but thanks all the same for your observation."

"Oh, sorry." They both laughed at the misunderstanding. "Thanks for cooking for me, again. I really do appreciate it."

"Well, you're cooking tomorrow, and you better not poison me."

"Oh, my speciality, spaghetti bolognese." He put down the knife and fork and rubbed his hands together.

"Ha! That's the only thing you can cook, isn't it?"

"Actually, I resemble that remark," he joked. "I make a badass cheese toastie, too."

She nodded well over enthusiastically. "Yep, it's true. Culinary skills are obviously your forte, so now, I humbly delegate all cooking duties to you."

"But Penny... I want you to live." He massively overacted, bringing a laugh from both of them.

Penny quickly went back to the subject at hand. "What do you think? And no, not my dry cooking this time."

"Well, my beautiful friend, I see it like this... all I can do is try and chill and sleep and live my life, and just hope I don't skip again. I mean, I will. I know I will, but there's nothing else I can do. They're not done with me yet."

"And then?"

"Then I just have to complete the mission, do what they want me to, and hope they leave me be once I do."

"I wish I could do something to help. I hate this."

"Penny, you do everything to help. Absolutely everything. You are everything to me. Thank you."

"Aw, shucks!" she said in a bad American accent. "Same, bro, same."

They finished their meal having a fake argument over who would do the dishes and enjoyed a fun evening for once. Still, always there, nagging away in the background, was the knowledge that sooner or later Liam would skip again. He knew his mission was nowhere near complete and the time would come. In the end, the doctor had only succeeded in making him even more unsure of himself. In so many ways, it would be easier if there was something wrong with him. If he was crazy, at least then this wouldn't be real. Unfortunately for Liam, it was real.

It wasn't until he had left Penny snoring on the sofa and climbed into bed that, once again, he was sucked involuntarily out of his body and sent off zooming into the cosmos. Through colours and tunnels and a hazy dream, he fell through nothing and into darkness, then back into light. He snapped into being and once again awoke behind another's eyes.

The two shadows surged towards it, huge and menacing. It didn't even have a split second to react, yet somehow, it reacted all the same. Its hands glowed with an electric blue light and a bubble of energy formed around its body. The attacker's weapons bounced harmlessly off the force field with a fizz and a spark. Two fists on extended arms flew out like a blur. Its enemies scattered, flying, from the bone crunching and devastating impact.

They stood no chance against the fearsome and mighty machine. It stood victorious, looking down upon its fallen attackers. Those once mighty warriors were now nothing but lifeless bodies in the sand.

The Machine's eyes were sharp and alert, wild and ready. It looked down at its own form, and immediately, Liam knew he was inside the mechanical warrior that had defeated him under the ruby dome.

"What the hell?" Liam asked from within the Machine. "I'm in this thing. Why didn't you just skip me into this one in the first place? Wait, I'm not really inside this thing, am I?"

"The prize you fought for, the halithstord, is a powerful symbiote. This creature is a machine. We cannot enter a computerised entity. We're inside the symbiote."

"You rigged the battle? I was meant to lose?"

"Yes, it was our will. Rakid was a fine warrior, and possibly could have beaten this machine, but where we're going, flesh and blood won't be a good thing."

"Let me get this straight then...we're inside the creature, that's inside the Machine?" Liam asked silently, but there was no answer. "Man, this just keeps getting weirder!"

"We cannot control the actions of the Machine, only those of the symbiote. This will be difficult. You need to concentrate and do what The Fleck asks. If you do this, we shall succeed."

Liam silently agreed. He had no choice.

High up on the cliffs, the Machine looked around. It gazed out to the distance, but there was nothing out there. A baron planet with a jagged rocky landscape and a hazy atmosphere. There was nothing but inhospitable terrain stretched out before it. The sky glowed fiery red, the wind howled wild, and the mission once again called. It was time to get moving.

Liam didn't know where he was going, but whether he was guided by The Fleck, the symbiote, or the Machine itself, they headed off together. The robot warrior made its way effortlessly down the sheer cliff face and sprinted out into the nothingness.

For hours and hours, it ran, never slowing, never showing signs of fatigue, relentlessly it went. It skipped over rocks that littered the path almost as though they weren't there. Those pesky obstacles hardly slowed its progress at all as the Machine leapt over them in a single bound.

Somewhere within, Liam admired this machine. It was perfect for its task. It was clear why it had been chosen for the mission ahead. Though his plight looked hopeless and the planet appeared arid and lifeless, the battle on the cliff gave him hope that, somewhere, he could find a settlement and a way of getting off that planet.

The Warrior

"It's too hard, Flick. I can't keep doing this." Waves of emotion overflowed, leaving Isha sobbing into her hands. The confusion had clouded her mind forever. The fear that hung around her, hounding her, never giving her a moment's peace had all grown too much.

She had bravely faced everything, but for a moment or two, she needed to be human. She was traumatised beyond measure, seeing her dying moment over and over, and seeing the deaths of so many others before her eyes. Each of the moments haunted her soul, taunted her thoughts, and invaded her memories.

She lived and breathed their final moment, not with them, but through them. She felt the pain and fear of life slipping away, just as they did at that last moment. She was left with the memories, the fear and grief that they were free of, and somewhere she envied them for that.

She had to carry it with her. She could not be free as they were. The visions and the pain were like an echo within her soul. Those remarkable beings, those that she had felt and lived within, those that she had loved were those that had become a part of her. Each of those beautiful entities in which she had connected, lost to a moment. All that remained were the whispers of the lost souls inside Isha.

"Why do I have to keep dying over and over? I feel it, every bit of it, and I remember it, like it was me. It's too hard, Flick. I'm scared. I'm exhausted. What if I fail? What if I can't do this?"

"I do not understand human emotion, Isha. The Fleck has no concept of what your mortality feels like. I can't understand any more than you understand what we are, but I can tell you this—you are capable of doing this. You can handle the pressure. That is why you were picked. You are not alone. I am with you every second to give you guidance and strength. Please do not fear, Isha. You are

very special. You were chosen for a great many reasons, all of which you have proven enough so far. I believe in you."

The words made her grow in strength. If one as powerful as Flick believed in her, just maybe she could do this after all. She slowly stopped crying and blew her nose. "It's just so confusing, not knowing if I'll be me or someone else from one moment to the next."

"In which case, I will inform you of what is going to happen, if that will make it easier to cope."

"Yes, I think it will."

"You will skip very soon. Time is short. Dark forces are already working against us. You must go tonight. That is when the hardest part of our mission will begin."

Isha's heart sank a little. She had hoped she'd at least have a little time to get used to the idea. She was powerless to stop it, so get used to the idea she must. The anticipation ran around her. If what was coming next was the hardest part of the mission, after all the challenges she'd already faced, she couldn't even imagine how bad it would be. Uneasily, she floated into the evening.

Her eyes were closed then open, and once again, she knew she had skipped. Before she had even focused through her new eyes, she could feel the other being's emotions and thoughts muddled and jumbled in with her own.

Her host's image was shown in sparkling ice that was all around her. She jumped at the reflection that stared back at her.

It was a woman, considerably older than Isha. If it hadn't been for the huge size of her dazzling blue almond-shaped eyes, she would have almost been convinced she was human.

Isha rubbed her pretty face and examined the numerous scars upon it as she dragged her fingers through the short white hair on her head. She was tall and rippling and muscular as Isha looked down upon the body.

"Well, at least I'm hot," she joked to herself, and then felt a little weird for having done so.

It was clear that this host had faced many battles; the scars told their own story. Isha felt powerful. There was no doubt that within this form she could more than handle herself in battle, and many coming battles were the only certainty she had.

She gazed at herself one more time before the steam from her breath misted up the reflection in the ice. Isha's host shivered a little from the cold. Wrapped snuggly around her body was an all-in-one suit that seemed to move with her, not like clothing, but like a second skin. It warmed on the inside just as she'd started to notice the cold, and within seconds, her body was the perfect temperature.

"Time to move, Isha. Let's go."

With those words, the mission called to her. She knew immediately that she was in search of something, but this time she sensed it was not the child. It was something else.

"What are we doing here?"

"You are currently inside the mind of the hybrid warrior assassin known as Daze, unbeknownst to her. She is powerful, very powerful, but we will need a halithstord."

"A what?"

"It is a symbiote, and a mighty weapon and ally. Our enemy already has one. We must find one also to even have a chance of stopping them. They are nearby, but make no mistake, this mission will be fraught with countless dangers. The halithstord will not be captured easily."

Within Daze's body, Isha set off running through the icy caves. The cave floor was slippery and treacherous, but she gripped it easily. Her remarkable suit covered her feet and gave her perfect traction. Even in the frozen air, it regulated her body temperature.

On either side of her, unclimbable, sheer icy walls jutted up, sparkling in the small amount of light that made its way inside. The pathway between them was narrow and dark, but her huge eyes could see clearly.

She moved silently, gliding over the slippery surface, skipping effortlessly through the darkness. On and on the warrior went, never seeming to tire or slow. Soon she reached the end of the pathway where the cave floor made way for a huge underground cavern. It fell away before her to a sheer drop, deep and dark, still with shimmering ice lining the walls. There she stopped. Silently, she crouched and listened.

Flick, just as promised, gave Isha more information. "*Down below is the halithstord nest, protected on all sides by the Keepers. Each has a symbiote inside them, and they are fearsome enough without one. In a battle with them, we will lose quickly. We must get lower.*"

Daze didn't wait for the discussion to end. She flicked her eyes across the cavern, up and down, side to side, and instantly the route she was to take appeared like a map in her mind.

The fearless warrior leapt headfirst off the ledge and free fell towards what would be a certain death. She opened her arms, and from the sleeves of her suit where before there was nothing, a small disk appeared in the palms of her hands. She flipped her body over in a summersault and reached out for the wall.

Though Isha had no idea how, the disks gripped the icy rock, and she clung to it like a spider. Now more disks appeared on her knees and gripped the wall every bit as effectively.

She shuffled down the wall and then across to a small ledge on the other side. There she blended into the shadows and crouched silently. Daze's eyes and ears saw and heard far better than Isha's ever could, so through them, she observed the scene below.

There was a wide space with a brown pillar in each corner, each with a huge, rounded top like a mushroom. In the centre was a rolling mass of green flame.

"*They are the Keepers.*" Flick was referring to the mushroom-like pillars. "*And within the green flames is the halithstord nest.*"

"*They are the Keepers? It looks like they can't even move.*"

"*Don't be fooled, Isha. They can move like lightning.*"

Isha didn't argue. Nothing had made sense in her life for so long that what looked like inanimate pillars that were, in fact, deadly seemed not only reasonable, but a likely thing.

"Well, how are we going to get one if we can't defeat the Keepers?"

"There is only one chance, and even that is a long shot. We'll have to draw them out of their stasis to defend the chamber and somehow make a dash for the nest. If we get a symbiote inside, they will no longer see us as a threat. We may just get through without being destroyed by their weapons or their tricks, but there is certainly no guarantee of success."

Daze stood tall and screamed loud. It echoed round the chamber. If the Keepers didn't know she was there before, they certainly did now.

The Keepers scanned their foe and used their first line of defence. With a mighty hiss, yellow gas started pouring out of the top of the pillars. Spraying in jets, it filled the entire cavern in seconds.

Daze's suit came into its own, stretching and morphing to cover her nose and mouth, neutralising the effect of the gas and helping her breathe.

Isha thought quickly and silently relayed her intent to Daze. Daze stood bolt upright upon the ledge in plain view, and like she had been poisoned, she grabbed her throat and collapsed over the side, plummeting like a stone. The seconds passed. In silence, the mighty warrior fell, unmoving, downwards.

It worked. The Keepers were fooled into thinking their gas had poisoned and killed the intruder. Now she only had to hope the landing would be a soft one. Down and down, gathering speed she went, until she disappeared into the fiery glow.

The flames engulfed her, and sparks rose out of the pit. The strange flames, not burning but warm, softened her fall as she slipped deeper into them. She sank down through the glowing green light and into a brighter yellow core beneath. There, she hit a solid surface.

The occupants of the nest immediately squirmed and writhed around her, hungry to make their bond. The symbiote wrapped around her neck, long and thin, and then snaked its way into her ear. Daze screamed out, though muffled in the nest, while blood came from her ear and trickled down her cheek.

The creature burrowed violently inside her head, gnashing and chomping as it did. Her body convulsed with horrendous pain, like the symbiote was eating her from the inside out.

She clutched the sides of her head and every muscle in her body contracted. All there was at that moment was pain. Hellish seconds passed, seconds filled with writhing agony, then Daze felt something pop and crunch inside her head.

Immediately, energy surged through her, heating her body from within. Her blood burned like fire, her heart raced, and immense strength bubbled inside her.

Daze, growling and rippling, crawled out from amongst the flames and stood tall and mighty in the chamber. She felt a great power surge within her, a power that she felt had always belonged. For the first time in her life, Daze felt complete. She stood, arms aloft, letting out her warning to all who would oppose her, her fearsome war cry.

Captive

The Machine bounded on, endlessly searching for any sign of life. Time was growing short and all around it was wilderness. Nothing but rock and sand stretched from horizon to horizon.

Despite how fast the Machine could travel, it was no closer to finding a destination. It didn't care nor could it; this metallic warrior had none of the weaknesses of humanity to hold it back. It never felt panicked or tired, never exasperated or scared. All the Machine had, fuelled by forces it did not know, was the task at hand.

Unfortunately for Liam within it, he was not free of the weaknesses of humanity and was filled with anxiety. The mission weighed heavily upon him. Everything that he knew and loved was relying on him, this machine, and the halithstord, which fed off an AI brain just as easily as it could an organic one. They rumbled along, always scanning the horizon, but with each passing hour, Liam feared evermore that their plight was hopeless.

Days had passed on the run. How far the Machine had travelled Liam could not tell, but at last, in the far distance, they saw a tall tower jutting skywards on the side of a rugged valley. It was huge and stretched up higher than even the mountains behind it, its top covered by copper-tinted clouds that rolled across the sky.

Even though the tower was miles away, the Machine could see everything. It zoomed its vision in and observed. In short order, several transports took off from the higher levels of the tower, bursting through the clouds and heading up into space. Liam silently rejoiced. This was what they had been looking for.

The Machine did not rejoice; it was incapable. All it saw was a target.

It took many hours to cross the treacherous valley. Rocks fell from the rugged landscape as they were dislodged under the Machine's enormous weight. It was a journey an entire team of humans would find impossible, but this fearsome warrior met each obstacle, overcame it, and continued to the next, never losing sight of its goal. Never was it impatient for the future or dwelling in the past. It was present, unfeeling, persistent, and focused. With the scaling of a crumbling dusty cliff, finally, the Machine was beneath the tower.

The transports took off from a platform at the top just below the cloud line. It would be easier to climb the tower from outside than to try and fight its way through every level inside. One thing was clear—they certainly wouldn't let the Machine merely walk in and help itself to a transport. Being the only sign of civilisation around, the security was sure to be tight.

The Machine stepped towards the outer wall of the tower and, with a clunk, climbing hooks came out the end of its fingers. It readied itself to leap and climb, but the ground below it exploded open, and it fell out of sight through the sand, down into darkness. It slid out of control down a narrow tube. Trying to slow itself, it quickly found the climbing hooks couldn't grip the smooth sides. Then, with a mighty clank, it landed on its feet contained within the tube. There was a hiss and woosh, and a lid slid quickly across the top, sealing it from above.

Although it was dark within, the robotic eyes could see perfectly. It scanned its surroundings. Strange, small purple figures, wide-eyed and excited, danced around the Machine's jar-like prison. They looked through the glass, whooping and hollering, hardly able to contain their joy. They laughed and pointed at their new prize.

Inside the tube there was no room to move. The Machine was trapped. Its captors tormented and goaded it. While a machine couldn't care, Liam boiled with rage, and the halithstord yearned for blood. They would not be stopped by such pathetic and small beings.

The Machine flung out an arm with hardly any room to move, yet still it generated an incredible amount of power. The blow thudded off the glasslike surrounds of the tube and bounced off harmlessly. The creatures outside jumped up and down with delight. Their prison was too strong. They rejoiced in the fact the Machine had tried and failed to escape.

It seemed the more torment those creatures caused, the higher they became, the wilder the celebrations, the louder the laugher and goading. The tube was sealed tight, and striking it again would be pointless, so the Machine stood frozen.

Deep inside the symbiote, Liam's apprehension grew. Little could they afford to be trapped. Time was running out and here he was, stuck, taken captive by these beings that the Machine could rip to pieces in seconds. At that moment, the future was in jeopardy. Surely, it couldn't end like this, defeated by such a weak and foolish foe. They laughed and pointed, enjoying what would be if he failed in his mission and with the destruction that would follow their own demise.

The weird creatures never took their eyes off the Machine. Instead, they salivated at the riches such a thing could bring.

"Scavengers! They plan to sell the Machine, for its metal and its core. They haven't trapped us here just to stare at us like zoo animals. As soon as they make any move, we'll rip through them and break free. All we need is patience." The Fleck hissed the words like it couldn't wait, like it yearned for death, twisted and dark, awaiting its moment.

It wanted so badly to spill blood, and Liam could feel it. He felt it so deeply that he started to lose touch with whether he or The Fleck wanted the blood most.

Patience is something you can have with the luxury of time, but time he could not afford. He was annoyed that he had been captured. The taunting from the small creatures made him wild with frustration, but the thing that angered him most was that his host, the Machine, didn't care. It waited with no sense of urgency or desperation while the whole time, inside, Liam wanted to scream. No matter how much he needed to continue his mission,

Liam couldn't do anything. All that was left was to sit in silence and await their moment.

Welcome Committee

She stayed low as the explosions rang out. Debris rained down upon her. Her back was pressed up against the rocks, and an endless barrage of weapon fire cracked and fizzed, sending blue sparks raging into the sky. In a situation where most would tremble in fear or run and hide, Daze had no intention of doing either.

She rolled forward, and with a flick of her hand, countless darts flew from the sleeve of her suit. They sailed silently through the air, and as quickly as the weapon fire had started, it stopped. Her three attackers fell limp to the ground.

She rose back to her feet. Her eyes flicked left then right. The compound was up ahead of her in the distance, and that was where she was headed. In each of the corners were guard towers surrounded by huge metal walls.

She was over a mile away, and she had already met resistance; now they knew she was there. It was clear stealth would only get her so far. She would have to fight her way to the compound and then inside. There could be thousands of guards within—she had no idea—but fear and failure were not options.

The landscape was rocky, and a cold wind whipped across her face bringing tears to her eyes. The warrior's suit protected her from the harsh elements. Part clothing, part armour, and part weapon, it morphed seamlessly from one to the other or even all three at once.

She stepped forward, heading right for the building and staying tight behind the boulders as she went. There could be snipers nearby. She reached each boulder, looked around, and chose her moment to move on to the next. She was all too aware that at any time a stream of guards could come out to confront her.

She crept along, senses alert, checking constantly for traps or mines, knowing that this compound was clearly designed so no one could get inside without an invitation. Daze wouldn't wait for the invitation. She was going to crash the party and bring bloody fury upon those within.

Above the wind Daze heard commotion up ahead. "The welcome committee," she growled to herself in a strange alien dialect with a half-smirk on her face. Most would be frozen in fear, but not this warrior. This was her world. Where the majority would crumble, she would thrive.

Moments later, the sky was ablaze with sparks and explosions as countless guards unleashed their fire towards the warrior. She huddled tight against a rock while the weapon fire crashed into and around it. The explosions from the powerful weapons slowly chipped lumps off her cover and sent chunks of rock skyward.

When there was a break in the attack, even for just a split second, Daze had darts ready. Each time she caught so much as a glimpse of one of her attackers, she took them down instantly. The darts sliced through the air, passing through armour, bone, and flesh like they weren't even there, leaving sealed smoking holes and lifeless bodies behind.

There she huddled, silent and waiting, but she could little afford to wait for long. Two triangular drones zipped overhead, and next came the fearsome crack and mighty explosion. Daze ran, and with a dive and a roll managed to avoid the worst of the blast, but now she had left her cover.

All hell broke loose. She ran powerfully, ducking, jumping, rolling, and diving while weapon fire exploded around her until she reached the momentary safety of another rock.

Above, the drones circled. She flung darts from her sleeves, and a split second later, the drones fell crashing to the ground, sparking and useless.

She pressed her back tight up against the rock, drew a breath, and ran out once again, flinging darts in all directions as she did. She was lightning fast and deadly accurate. She rolled and jumped and avoided the volley coming back in her direction.

More and more of the guards fell to her lethal weapons and devasting aim. She crouched low behind another rock, calculating that the guards' numbers had been greatly depleted.

Another silent drone swooped in. She launched her darts and moved. Again, a crack and then an explosion boomed out. This time she wedged herself between the rocks but stayed behind her cover. The rocks took most of the blast and her suit protected her from the rest.

Sand and rock came falling down, as did the drone—Daze never missed. The guards ahead were sure to think she was wounded or killed in the explosion. They would have to come and check sooner or later.

She waited.

It wasn't long until she heard footsteps coming towards her. They were the unlucky ones who drew the short straw. She crouched low, muscles coiled and ready to explode. A moment later, a crowd of twelve guards burst around the edge of the rock from either side. Even with their fingers poised on the triggers, Daze was too quick for them.

In a blink of an eye, she flung her darts from her sleeves, dropping five of the guards before they could even get a shot off. In the same motion, she swooped, grabbing the nearest lifeless guard and catching him before he fell, holding his limp body out in front of her like a shield. The weapons went off and cracked into him, but his body armour protected her. The dead guard was huge, but Daze, with her great strength, held him up in one hand. She let the corpse take the brunt of a few more shots and then kicked it powerfully forward, scattering the surviving guards.

Instantly she flung her darts again before the body had even found its target. Three more foes hit the ground limp. Four wide-eyed figures were left standing. They knew they could not win this fight.

She charged towards them, flying through the air and kicking the first in the side of the head, knocking him immediately unconscious. In the same movement, she wrapped her arm tight around the neck of the second, and with a twist of her body and a fearsome crack, the guard's neck was broken. Now only two remained. She growled.

One dropped their weapon and ran back towards the compound. The last unloaded their weapon. It exploded with fury where Daze had been standing, but she was high in the air above his head in a mighty leap. Two blades morphed from her suit into her hands and flashed silver. As she landed, she brought them swooping down and then violently across. She stood looking at the guard whose eyes were wide with shock. Slowly, as she watched on with a fearful smirk upon her face, the guard's head rolled off his neck and his stomach opened wide. She smiled with blood-thirsty pride, but Daze was far from done yet.

She leapt into the air again, her deadly darts dropping the remaining fleeing guard. She landed safely behind her cover. "Fancy, bringing a gun to a dart fight."

That had taken care of the scouting party, but still, amongst the rocks, many guards remained. They opened fire and slowly made their way towards her. She waited just a moment, then breathed and spun out from her cover. Through her sleeve came a handful of little silver balls. She threw them in the air, and as they dropped, they scattered amongst the guards. Daze was back behind the rock in the blink of an eye. The barrage of fire raged towards her but never found its target.

"Three, two, one," she said out loud with a wicked smile etched on her lips. Then there was a blinding flash and a rumbling explosion. A wave of light ripped through the guards, tearing off limbs, scattering them everywhere. Silence fell. Even the wind seemed to stop howling for a lingering second, then the screams and moans of dismembered and dying men became clear.

The weapons fired once more, but now they were scattered and few. They stood their ground and fought with brave hearts, even though deep down they knew their plight was hopeless. The warrior, deadly and quick, had delivered the fatal blow to no fewer than fifty men in mere moments. The eighteen left didn't stand a chance.

Daze burst out from behind the rock again. She moved fast, head ducked low, avoiding the blasts. She skidded on her knees and rolled down onto her side, taking cover behind another rock. She sat up quickly, poking her head up, and released another barrage of darts. Once again, weapons followed by lifeless bodies thudded down onto the strange planet's surface.

Now she ran towards the compound, almost gliding as she went. She got closer by the moment, keeping her head low, her huge eyes bright, awake, and ready.

Streams of burning white light flashed through the sky and cracked against the rocks or into the ground, exploding and leaving scorch marks. There were snipers in the towers. Daze tore towards the building, desperate to get tight to the bottom of the formidable compound walls. Once she was there, she was out of the sight of the snipers. She bristled with a lust for blood, a taste that would soon be satisfied.

She worked her way along towards the entrance. It was fortified and packed full of guards and static weapons that would soon be ablaze when they saw her. The warning alarm wailed out. The task before her seemed suicidal, but this warrior knew too much was at stake to turn back or fail.

Moments later, the fire started, pouring out from the building, from both above and below. They were robotic sentries, six huge weapons raining out sparks. Daze couldn't get past those weapons without being torn to pieces. The symbiote inside her bristled and reacted with a will of its own. She felt a charge building up inside her, then like a flash, a pulsating electromagnetic wave left her body and flowed out like ripples in a pond. The guns stopped. Their electronics were fried.

She rushed towards the fortified entrance as weapon fire came at her like a constant stream of glowing flame. She jumped high and released the exploding balls, this time from each hand, and flung them. They made their way inside the entrance. She took cover, and three seconds later, the flash and shockwave rushed out. She waited a few moments, took a breath, and carefully came out from her cover.

The micro-grenades had done their job, leaving the fortified structure blackened and bodies strewn about the place. Some were recognisable, some were not. She finished any remaining stragglers and started to make her way into the compound.

It was dark. The smoke from the guns and explosions still lingered thick in the air as she pushed through. She could sense that it wouldn't be long before she faced more resistance. She slipped silently through the building, tight against the wall, staying in the shadows.

From behind her, there was a crack and a flash, and the fearsome warrior was stunned and blinded. An instant later, she was lost to darkness.

Blood Lust

The Machine watched on silently, unmoving, as the pulsating bands of light fixed tightly round its body and buzzed loudly with great energy. They wrapped its arms and clamped them tight to the sides of its body and legs, strapping them together. It struggled momentarily to test them but quickly knew it did not have the physical strength to break the bonds. The struggle would be pointless.

The Machine's tube prison lifted upwards and flipped horizontally down onto a floating platform. With a hiss, the seal above it broke, the tube lifted to an angle, and the robotic being slid down and flopped onto its back, landing with a clank. The purple creatures that had been watching on were cheering and dancing excitedly by its sides.

With a whir, the shelf below started to move. They jumped up and down, taunting the stricken machine as they did.

One of the purple creatures jumped and skipped, laughing near the Machine's feet. In less than a second, its arm extended like a telescope and grabbed the creature tight, gripping it firmly around the body. With a mighty squeeze, the creature's ribs crackled as they were crushed in the mechanical grip, on the verge of snapping.

It screamed loud and struggled wildly, but the Machine squeezed tighter still, and soon the creature knew, fighting was hopeless. The Machine's mighty strength left that purple creature in no doubt of who was in charge of this situation.

The other creatures screamed and jumped up and down, but now in frantic panic, not celebration. Many drew weapons and pointed them towards their prize, though none dared fire due to the risk of hitting their stricken comrade.

The Machine spoke in a strange language. "Release me!"

"No, we need you." The scavenger chief came hopping forward.

The Machine squeezed a little harder. The creature in its grasp couldn't even breath as its ribcage compressed beneath the strength of the vice-like grip. "Release me or he will die!"

"Okay, okay, we'll release you. Just, please, don't kill him."

"Stop! You're killing me!" The creature in the hand struggled to rasp out the words from depleted lungs.

The Machine squeezed tighter for a second, and then released its grip, but only to the point the creature could speak. It panted, trying to catch breath. Its eyes watered in pain. "Release me," it gasped.

"Only once you remove my bonds."

The chief panicked. "Release the prisoner!"

The command was greeted with murmurs of refusal from the baying crowd. They were reluctant to lose their prize in such a place where prizes didn't come along too often.

"Release me or when I escape, and I *will* escape, I will kill every single one of you. Your prize will not be worth the destruction I will bring upon you. It will be a prize you shall not live to receive. Release me now, and I will leave this place with none of you coming to any harm."

"Undo the restraints!" the creature cried desperately. It could feel how much they underestimated this enemy that could easily crush them like a bug. "It will kill us all!"

Moments later the buzzing noise of the restrains stopped and the glow disappeared. The Machine at last was free. It flipped up onto its feet with a thud and held the purple creature helplessly dangling.

"Now release me!" it screamed.

The Machine saw no use for words. It tightened its grip evermore and crushed the creature within its hand. There was a crunch, and the Machine threw the corpse amongst the screaming crowd. Some creatures tried to fight, and they were finished first by crushing blows. The others scattered as destruction rained down upon them. Bodies flew everywhere, and death was all around, dealt swiftly from fists and feet. In moments, all that remained were dead bodies and the screams of the ones who were not dead yet.

Inside the symbiote, Liam screamed in terror. *"No! How could we? No!"*

"We cannot control the Machine. It has will of its own. It decided this."

Through the horror he had witnessed, Liam would have sobbed. He would have dropped to his knees or curled into a ball and wished the sight away, but he could do none of these things. He was the helpless audience of the horrific scene. Those that were still alive soon were not. The Machine went forward, leaving destruction and blood in its wake.

"It is the sacrifice of battle. It is a price we must pay. You must focus," The Fleck hissed.

"Okay, okay!" Liam silently yelled. He was appalled by what he had seen. He was a good man, and this was going too far. To kill for the mission, he could explain to himself. To kill to survive, was pure nature. But to kill just to kill... he would never wrap his mind around that.

No matter how much he wanted it to stop, he was out at sea, drifting helplessly on the tide, useless. If he couldn't affect the will of the Machine or the symbiote, he couldn't even understand what he was doing there at all. He was completely and utterly useless.

The Machine raged through the building until it found a way out of the basement in which it was trapped, destroying all who dared oppose it. Ripping flesh and stealing souls everywhere it went. It moved up each level of the tower, leaving carnage behind. Hundreds of guards lay fallen by the time it reached the top, but at last, the Machine, with a stolen rifle now in each hand, had found what it was searching for—transport.

The guards opened fire the moment it entered the transport bay. The Machine returned fire, plasma ripping through the guards like a knife through butter. Not only did it destroy its enemies but also all the transports apart from one.

Only when every guard was slain and every transport smoking did the Machine climb inside its own craft. Slowly it lifted from the platform, made its way out of the tower, and burst through the clouds and out towards the coldness of space.

The Escape

Daze awoke with her head pounding, groggy and blurry eyed. She struggled from her back to a seated position. Around her was a crowd of guards, all with their weapons fixed upon her. They were twitchy and nervous, itching for an excuse to kill her. She rubbed her eyes.

"Don't move!" one of the guards demanded.

Daze had no intention of moving at that moment.

Roughly, they put restraints on her wrists and closed them tight behind her back.

"Not this again." She rolled her eyes. She'd been captured many times, so this was nothing new to her. She had been captured, but she'd also escaped, so she already eagerly awaited her opportunity. She smirked knowing her suit was a weapon that could never be taken from her.

"Take her to the cells."

Two of the guards grabbed her under the armpits and pulled her to her feet. For a second, her legs buckled. Whatever they'd hit her with, she was still feeling the effects.

The guards held her up and slowly started to march down a corridor towards the cells. The crowd surrounded her as they went. Never for even a second was she out of the weapons' sights. There was obviously no chance of escape right then, not in her weakened state, not with so many weapons on her. She would have to wait for another opportunity.

Daze heard weapons firing in the distance over the alarm. Her heart skipped a beat, and her warrior instincts took over. Could this be the opportunity she needed? After receiving the order, the guards in front of her turned back and ran towards the commotion.

The two warriors swarmed at their enemies. One with her light sword buzzing and the other with her energy whip fizzing and cracking with wild fury. Together this formidable team ran through the narrow halls. They finished their foes, savagely cutting down guards where they stood. Their fury was wild. Both of them were drenched in the blood of their enemies.

They raged on, fearless and determined, ripping apart all that stood in their path. These guards had no chance against them. They searched, desperate to reach their goal. They had come for blood, and they left it like rivers in their deadly wake. This fearsome pair were locked on, relentless, and they had come for Daze.

With her hands bound behind her back, Daze took cover as a huge explosion rocked the compound. A bright light shone through the corridor; a burning bright light that sent guards scattering while skin was ripped from bones. The ones directly in the path of the blast were blown to pieces, the others maimed. Daze wouldn't get a better opportunity than this.

She released a palmful of micro-grenades and pushed off her weakened legs then rolled out of the way. Even with her hands bound, as the blast ripped the guards apart, she moved like lightning to avoid the brunt of the fireball.

Ahead were guards in their plenty, awaiting Daze, yet they were distracted by the battle raging behind them. Daze rounded the corner, and the guards opened fire. All she could do for the moment was take cover.

That was when, above the weapon fire, she heard the fizzing and crackling of the light sword, followed by the crack of the whip, extending long, exploding, and removing flesh from bones with each deadly flick. The guards all turned to fire upon the attackers. They couldn't keep eyes on Daze and these other wild warriors at the same time. The pair roared on, removing heads and limbs, revelling in the bloody carnage.

Daze crouched low, waiting for the last of the guards to be taken out, and swiftly, they were.

There was a streak of light and a crack that exploded, hitting the centre of the restraints that held her. They fell clanging to the ground. She was free. She turned and faced two mighty figures— one with a light sword menacingly in hand, the other whirling her whip, marching boldly towards her.

"Ladies," she nodded. "What took you so long?"

Two entities lingered in the background, dwelling deep inside Daze's being. One of them was content with the mission's progress. The other was confused and endlessly afraid.

Emotions bubbled in Isha's human consciousness. It grabbed a hold of her, the fear backed by the whirling confusion flipping around in her soul. The grief she felt for those who had fallen, maybe not by her hand, but at times, her will, consumed her.

She thought of Vaz and Parvis. She thought of all the things that had come before. What really ate away at her, what tested her very moral fibre, was for fleeting moments, she felt the pleasure. She absorbed the warrior's lust for blood, and it haunted her. Guilt hung over her while logic told her it was not a choice; it was the only one there was.

Maybe if she was capable, she would have cried a million tears, but crying, lost in that semi-reality, wasn't an option. She missed the gravity pulling her down in her bed, the knowing as she lay there that the only journey she would be off on would be one to the land of dreams.

Yes, Isha was strong. She'd had to be from a young age just to get by, but now she was spiralling and edging relentlessly towards the breaking point. It felt like it was all too much, but she was chosen for this task for good reason. She was selected from countless entities drifting through the cosmos. She was chosen because she was strong and dynamic, for her telepathic abilities, and most importantly, she was possibly the only person in the universe who was capable of such a task.

"Why is this happening, Flick?" Isha needed answers or at least encouragement. She had been an observer for so long.

"It just is, Isha. The why means nothing,"

"Then how can I ever understand? Why does the Dark Space hate us so much?"

"What makes you think it hates you?"

"It wants to destroy us."

"It doesn't hate. It is a higher being. It has a way of understanding that an insignificant human could never grasp." Flick's tone was mocking, harsh, and cold.

Isha raged at the lack of empathy or emotion, although raging was futile. "Why don't you try me?" She tried to contain her frustration but failed.

"Isha, you must not grow angry. I can sense your anger, and in this form, you could destroy so much. You are wielding great power, and you must control yourself to stand any chance of controlling it."

"Like I have any control." Her response was sarcastic and snappy.

"You feel it when she kills. You feel the power. You feel alive. She feels your will, too. Your anger left uninhibited will make her rage out of control. With the symbiote feeding her, there's no telling what could happen."

Silence lingered for moments.

"Humans are confusing and difficult," Flick stated.

"Maybe because we're insignificant." Isha admired her own quick-witted sass for a second.

"The why means nothing, but because of your irrationality, I will attempt to inform. This changes not the task or what will happen or where your focus should be, but I will tell you, to put your mind at rest. If it will help you control yourself."

"Sure. You'll probably crush me in a nanosecond or something if I don't anyway." This time, Isha's remark was delivered with an edge of humour, but the best jokes often make a point.

"The Dark Space doesn't hate. It feeds off matter, off stars and planets and life. It hates you no less than you hate a head of lettuce.

It simply has to feed, and everything you know to be true is food. It is coming, and it will not stop. The only thing between us and that is the child. At this point, nothing else matters."

"How can we destroy it? If I've learned anything in science class, energy can't be destroyed. It doesn't vanish; it just takes another form."

"Exactly."

"How can the child stop it, though?"

"I cannot know the answer. I just know it is so. Many things that are happening now must come together at the perfect moment. Things are in motion that are beyond our control. All we can do is the task before us. But, Isha, we must not fail."

"Wait, that sounds like you are working with others. Are you?"

"No, Isha. I am working with you and only you."

Isha could feel affection in her words. They made her glow and brought her comfort.

"Now, Isha, concentrate. We have work to do."

The Sisterhood

The three warriors marched fearlessly through the long and winding hallways within the structure. There was scattered resistance along the way, but most of the guards had retreated. The ones who hadn't were dead.

If Daze was fearsome enough alone, then together they were terrifying. Those sisters in battle that had seen so much together, that had grown up on the streets and fought every day for survival, were fighting shoulder to shoulder again. Individually they were orphans of war. Together, they were a family.

They annihilated highly trained and well-equipped guards like they were little more than an annoyance. Daze was quicker and more deadly than the others with the symbiote giving her greater power. Jax was an expert with her light blade, removing heads from bodies or mowing down enemies from a distance with the weapon at her hip. Nik's whip sparked, which cut and removed the flesh from her foes, or she blew them to pieces with the cannon attached to her wrist. They were a mighty force to be reckoned with, and though the guards had retreated, the sisterhood knew, somewhere they would be lying in wait.

Inside Daze, Isha's presence had a flash of images, and she knew all at once that what she saw was another part of the compound. Hundreds of guards awaited her host and her friends inside the transport bay. Without even relaying the message, through Isha, Daze saw the images, too.

"There's a little surprise waiting for us." Daze uttered the words, and within them, the excitement grew. The thought of battle ahead never failed to set the blood in their veins on fire.

"Wait... how can you tell that?" Nik looked a little confused.

"I don't know. Just trust me." It was like Isha's visions were her own instinct. She didn't even have a shred of doubt that what she had seen was true.

"Oh, I love surprises!" Jax's eyes danced at the thought.

"The hangar is up ahead," Daze explained. "There's going to be plenty of resistance inside. All we gotta do is bust down the door, go in, and crack some skulls. I swear, we're gonna party hard after this one."

"Easy." Jax nodded with confidence and looked dotingly down at the blade in her hand.

"This ain't my first rodeo." Nik rolled her eyes.

For a moment, they laughed at Nik's favourite catchphrase, not as warriors the moment before battle but as friends on an adventure. They marched on side by side towards the deadly fight that lay ahead.

There was no longer any sign of movement or life within the corridors apart from robotic flying sentries which were soon destroyed. They rushed through the compound until they reached the huge metal doorway of the hanger.

"How are we going to get through that thing?" Nik asked, looking over to Daze who seemed to have all the answers.

"I think I may have just the thing." Jax removed the backpack from her shoulders and took out a disk-shaped object about the size of a dinner plate. She started to fiddle with her arm unit.

"Woah! You've had that the whole time?" Nik exclaimed. "In your bag?"

"Yeah, sure."

"Yeah, the contents of Jax's bag: Tissues, mirror, hairbrush…magnetic limpet bomb. I thought everyone knew that," Daze joked.

"Oh, you know me so well."

"What if someone had shot the bag in the battle, though?" Nik asked.

"Well, kinda like a click-kaboom! sort of energy."

"Yeah, that's a comforting thought."

There were a series of beeps as Jax set the timer on the bomb. "I'll set it for two minutes. We don't wanna be anywhere near this thing when it goes off."

"Yeah, but you carry it around in your bag and hang around next to me. Right, got it." Nik laughed.

A moment later, the bomb was set on the door and the warriors ran down the corridor to find some cover. They knew as soon as the explosion detonated, they had to rush inside the hanger. If they didn't, any element of surprise would be lost, and that was an advantage they needed in this situation.

"Three... Two... One." Jax counted it down on her arm unit. A split second later, there was a blinding flash, and the explosion rocked the walls.

The thick metal door was ripped to pieces, sending shards of metal into the room. The three warriors rushed towards the door and burst through the wall of smoke to launch their savage attack upon the stunned guards within. Many had already met their end from the explosion.

Daze rushed forward, zig zagging, constantly moving. Guards were slaughtered mercilessly while they were still stunned from the boom or the light that had blinded them. She drew her two blades and slashed and ripped with fury.

Nik ran screaming, her eyes wild, her arm cannon blasting and whip cracking, removing heads or limbs from bodies with perfect precision. Spinning around like a tornado, she tore a path right through the guards.

Jax twirled her sword with artistic wonder as the light glowing from its blade hung momentarily behind it. The bright white glow was only invisible as it passed effortlessly through the armour, flesh, and bone of her enemies.

In a matter of minutes, many were dead or dying, and the three warriors had not a scratch on them. It was then the order was given. The surviving guards put their weapons on the ground and surrendered. They would rather be with their loved ones again than die in a hanger protecting a transport.

Tears fell from eyes at their fallen kin and their failure. Their job was to protect the compound with their lives, but in the end, a building could never be worth it.

They went around the hanger disabling every transport but one, then the warriors climbed aboard.

"So, can you fly this thing, Jax?" Daze asked.

"Course. I'm a five-hundred-year-old cave witch. I can do anything," she joked bringing about a laugh from the others. "I'll need a code to take off, though."

"Can't you just hack the computer?"

"Of course I can, but it'll take a while."

"I'll get you the code." Nik smirked. She didn't even wait for a response. She jumped catlike down the ramp and back into the hanger. Not more than five minutes later, she was back inside the craft with all information at hand.

"What did you do?" Jax asked.

"No, no, he willingly volunteered the information." That smirk was back on her face, and the others knew it was sometimes best not to know. It wasn't important now. Well, it wasn't important to anyone but the pilot from whom she had prised the code. He was in tears and trembling on his knees in the hanger. The transport and her deadly passengers were at last on their way.

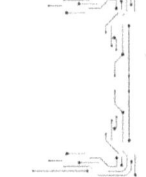

Internal Massacre

The transport travelled gently through space with the hours and days passing, yet still many more remained until they were anywhere near their destination.

Amongst the music and singing that so often accompanied their trips, at times there were serious moments. Moments when they planned ahead or discussed what had come before.

"I thought they would have come after us by now," Daze said. "They must be able to track this thing."

"It depends if they think one transport is worth it. Oh, and I blocked the tracker before we left." Jax said.

"Of course, you did." Daze smiled.

"I'm not just a pretty face, you know," she laughed.

"Well, let's just hope we make it without any unwanted interactions. These transports aren't exactly designed for battles. If we meet any military craft, we'll be blown to bits."

Two hours passed and Daze and Jax were happily arguing about who killed the most guards back in the hanger.

"Wait a sec," Nik interjected. "What is that?"

Jax turned her attention back to the screen. "Hang on. Let me zoom in on it." The image they had dreaded became clear. "Erm, it's a bunch of military craft by the looks of it."

"Why did I speak? Damn, Daze. You don't always have to say it," she castigated herself.

Jax nodded slowly. "It's pretty simple really. We have to surrender and let them take us on board. At least we can fight it out there. Out here, we've got no chance."

"What if they try and take my whip, though?" Nik pulled a look of fake concern.

"Good luck to them, I say. That's probably gonna hurt." They laughed again. Humour got them through the dark times, the times when blood and fear reigned supreme.

"*Transport seventy-four A, surrender to our tractor beam now, or we shall use deadly force. Repeat, we will use deadly force,*" the voice came through the intercom.

"Ooh, scary! What a badass." Nik laughed, doing an exaggerated tremble. "Just ignore him for a moment. It'll be funny."

Jax opened the communication channel and drew her sword, waving it side to side, sending back nothing but buzzing static. They all giggled.

"I bet you the first round of drinks when all this is over, next it'll be a warning shot," Nik offered.

"But what if they blow us out of space? How will I get paid then?" Jax probed.

"Nah, they won't. Don't worry. Watch. I served on one of them things once."

"You were never in the military. You're so full of it." Jax shook her head.

"Excuse me? I never claimed I was in the military. I was the entertainment."

"I bet they go for a kill shot after what we did," Daze said. "I'm not sure we should risk it for a bet."

"That is no fun at all. I'm sticking with warning shot. Whichever move they make, we'll call it in after."

A warning shot flew across their bow. "*Transport seventy-four A, this is your final warning. Surrender to our tractor beam now, or we shall use deadly force.*"

"Boom! No buying drinks for me. Told you I served." They laughed again.

"Right." Jax put her business head on. "Enough games now. I'm calling it in because the next one *will* be a kill shot."

Moments later, they were being dragged helplessly towards the craft which dwarfed the transport. It was hundreds of times bigger, and that was only one of twelve craft that surrounded and bullied the tiny transport. If those on the military craft thought for one moment that these warriors would be taken easily, however, they couldn't have been more wrong.

"Isha, now it is your time to shine. They will not survive a battle. They are outnumbered by thousands."

"What can I do, Flick?" She was surprised by the request.

"You know what to do. Drift, Isha. Drift, and you will know."

"Drift. Right." Isha wasn't altogether sure what Flick was talking about.

"Just drift…"

All at once, Isha slipped into another state as her consciousness drifted away. She saw visions of colour, of stars and planets. Each flashed through her mind's eye, if indeed she had a mind at all. The visions slowed, and all at once she felt the cosmos' energy flow through her, like it was inside her, or a part of her.

Then, like pins in a map, she saw them. Each glowing brightly in her vision, the minds of all the beings around the ship. Her telepathy was being amplified by the powerful symbiote that was with her. She felt a surge of power, and was then connected one by one to all the heavily armed guards that surrounded the transport as it docked.

"Daze. Daze?" Jax nudged her. She was stood staring into space. "Daze, wake up. We need a plan."

"Just wait," she responded, looking right through Jax like her mind was lost in a dream.

"Wait, she says. Wait! Like, there's only a million guards that are gonna tear us to pieces out there. This is a great time for waiting."

Inside Daze and then, in turn, the symbiote, Isha's thoughts connected to the minds of all the guards. She had to persuade them to let them through or at least stop them from ripping her host and her friends to shreds. Unfortunately, the blood-thirsty symbiote's intention was very different from hers.

A shrill noise rang within the guards' heads then grew louder until it rattled their teeth and their eyes started watering. Each trembled violently like they'd lost control of their bodies. They screamed and wailed and dropped their weapons. Seconds later, they were clutching the sides of their heads and falling to the floor.

"Go, now," Daze whispered, lost inside her trance.

Jax and Nik drew their weapons and readied themselves. They were not going to be captured and tortured. They were prepared for a battle that they knew they would surely lose.

"I think you should go first, Daze," Nik suggested. "Seeing as you're the one acting all weird and stuff and telling us to trust you."

She nodded and pushed the button that opened the exit ramp.

Inside her, Isha and the symbiote were gripping all the guards' minds, holding them helpless, making them roll on the floor, stricken, crying out in pain and fear.

Daze led them down the ramp where Jax and Nik expected to be greeted by armed escorts. All they heard were the sounds of pain from every single enemy in sight, who were down on the ground, howling with the pain burning in between their ears.

"What's up with them lot?" Nik looked at Jax, who returned nothing more than a vacant expression and a shrug.

Inside, Isha was straining to keep control of all the minds at once, like she was hanging from a cliff and her strength was running out. She knew if she released them, it would be certain imprisonment or death for the warriors. Worst of all, the mission would fail.

Isha struggled and concentrated and tried with everything she had to keep her grip on the minds, but her energy was waning fast. The grip started to loosen, but the symbiote had ideas of its own, ones that were far more sinister. Exhausted by the effort, she tried to break the connection, but the symbiote gripped harder, magnifying her power.

The noise inside them grew ever shriller, leaving guards writhing and convulsing. They screamed loud, and with the sounds of pain, the symbiote turned up the pressure further, greedily feeding off Isha's power and, in turn, their enemies' pain and misery.

She tried to fight back momentarily, but the feeling warmed her. The energy, fuelled by the symbiote and the cosmos beyond, excited Isha.

Together they pushed harder with the guards' screams one at a time falling silent as they passed out. In moments, they had all stopped writhing, and dark blood trickled out their ears. They lay, eyes glazed, faces etched with the abject horror of their final moment. None of the guards within the hanger had survived.

"Oh, no! What have I done? What have I done? I've killed them all!" Isha screamed silently.

"They had to die. They would have died one way or the other. This way, they died without a risk to the warriors' lives." Flick's words were cold. *"They were in our way. You know the mission is more important. Their lives are insignificant. It was not you who killed them. It was the halithstord."*

Isha took the words and tried to swallow them. She tried desperately to believe and accept them, but she knew that she had felt joy from the power that surged through her. She had wanted to hurt them, and somewhere, it pleased her.

"Let it go, Isha. Let it go. You did what had to be done. You did all that could be done. You could not hold them forever."

"Let it go, Flick? Are you twisted? Murdering people? How can I just let that go?"

"You did what was needed. You did what had to be done. You do not have to like it, but you had to do it. Your emotions are pointless. They are only harming you and the mission. Let it go."

She told herself she would let it go. She tried to justify her actions to herself. She fought her pain with logic and reason by convincing herself there was no other choice. Still, there was never anyone with even the slightest shred of humanity who could just let such a terrible thing go.

She was responsible for the deaths of hundreds of beings, no matter what her intention was. Her anguish and pain weren't going to get her anywhere. It had long been established she was just a passenger on this journey. She quietly blamed it on the symbiote, though deep down inside, she knew that was not the truth.

"Wow! What the hell happened to them?" Nik turned to Daze, who was still not quite there.

"I… I don't know." She shook her head and snapped out of her trance.

"They probably just died of old age. That tractor beam was so slow," Jax joked.

"What happened doesn't really matter now. All that matters is we are free to move through the ship. Now we make our way to the upper levels and the bridge and take over this craft. We've got somewhere to be and no time to lose."

"I don't suppose they're just going to hand it over." Nik smirked wide, knowing she would surely get another chance to use her considerable powers of persuasion. At least that's what she called them.

The warriors readied themselves for the battles that lay ahead, and then started to make their way through the enormous craft.

Highjacked

"So, when we meet resistance, do we get to carve them up now, or are you going to go into a weird trance and make their heads explode again?" Nik's eyes danced at the thought of battle.

"You're free to carve away…" Daze smirked for a second, then her face was deadpan straight. "I… I don't know what's happening to me. I don't even know what we're doing. I just know that you're gonna have to trust me on this one." She stopped and met their eyes with an unusual seriousness.

"We do trust you. That's why we're here. We're with you until the end. Always." Jax looked to Nik who offered a nod of confirmation.

"Thank you." Daze's smile was one of gratitude, she knew she wouldn't have made it so far alone, and her friends would never leave her. They would fight and die right beside her.

"Besides, this isn't the first time we've come with you on a suicidal mission without knowing what the hell is going on." Nik broke the serious moment.

"True," she said with a giggle. "Now let's get our game face on. I've got a feeling this could be challenging."

"Well, I personally love a challenge." Jax grinned.

They went through the transport bay and opened the huge doors. Outside, all around were the ship's personnel, unmoving and unbreathing. They were not even soldiers, just regular people, maintenance staff, or the ship's crew. They had been as indiscriminately slaughtered as the guards who meant to do them harm.

Isha screamed out silently again. The pain nagged away at her humanity. The symbiote was beyond brutal, and she could feel how much it loved the savagery, how the suffering brought it joy, how the power made it yearn for more. She could feel its desire for blood. With the use of her telepathic abilities as well as Daze's warriorship, they were a terrifying combination, one that Isha didn't want to explore any further, of that she was certain.

Of whom was controlling who, of what they were truly capable, or how much more damage they could do, she couldn't have been more uncertain. Her wish to curl into a ball and pretend it had never happened and the need to sob her heart out were both things that she simply could not do.

She was trapped. She had to cope somehow. She had to grow cold and thicker skinned. She had to defy her humanity for the very sake of humanity. She had to find strength that she never knew she had just to make it through.

How Isha wished she could go back to her normal life. She would have even loved to argue with her mother about things that really didn't matter, and with that, she saw in her being the vision of hope. The love she felt for her mother burned inside her. She was no longer fighting for the fate of all beings, but fighting for love, knowing she had to succeed. She shook out the pain and horror and dreamt of home for just a few moments longer.

Even though they would never admit it, the three warriors each felt a prang of guilt and sorrow for the lost innocents that lay sprawled all around, pools of blood around their heads, unmoving. The beings caught in the crossfire as spoils of war were one thing, but those who would have never engaged in a fight was hard on them all. Unlike Isha, however, they had become numb to such things as just a way of life to the warriors. They shrugged off their negative thoughts and feelings and focused fully on the task at hand.

"Someone's still alive on this thing or the ship would be slipping out of formation by now. Someone is still controlling it. Keep your wits about you. There will be a fight yet," Daze warned.

"Good," Jax muttered under her breath.

"*Security protocol one-oh-seven-point-four-six,*" said a voice that came over the speaker system.

"Ooh, protocol one-oh-seven-point-four-six is my favourite!" Nik said sarcastically, obviously having no clue what it was.

Daze stood silently staring as Isha felt up ahead. She sensed what was in front of them. She saw the way through the enormous craft. She could see security rushing to the bridge. Her mind trick had completely decimated the ship, leaving minimal crew still alive and hundreds lost.

"It means all remaining security to the bridge," Daze said. "There'll be a welcome committee awaiting us. The element of surprise is lost. The bridge is on the top level, so we need to get in the elevator."

With Daze following her senses and Jax and Nik following her, they made their way to the elevator. They climbed inside and the doors closed.

"They're waiting for us at the top. They know we're coming. They'll try and tear us apart as soon as the doors open." Daze began to mentally prepare for the battle ahead.

"And how are we supposed to get through?" Nik questioned. It seemed purely suicidal.

"Stay behind me. My suit will protect me."

"Yeah, your suit may be awesome, but we all know it's not designed to take a direct barrage from what could be hundreds of weapons."

"I have a trick or two up my sleeve, pun intended, don't worry about that." That all too familiar smirk fell across Daze's face.

The symbiote bristled within the warrior, and even though she had no idea what she was going to do, it once again fuelled her with a mighty power. It was ready. It had led her this far and would do what needed to be done.

She trusted her newfound power like it had always been a part of her.

The guards awaited them, weapons trained as the elevator doors opened. Jax and Nik took cover behind Daze. The blinding explosions began with the weapons' fire. Darts flew as micro-grenades rolled from Daze's sleeves, and in seconds, the security by the door was taken down. The blasts exploded on Daze's body armour. She screamed, running forward, closely followed by her friends.

The whip cracked and the arm cannon boomed. The sword sliced through flesh, and the sidearm fired rapidly. In moments, all that lay around them was death.

Daze grimaced. Below the scorch marks on her suit, her skin was blistered and stinging.

"It looks like you nearly got cooked. You okay?" Jax looked concerned.

"Yeah, I'll be fine. A bit of pain never hurt anyone," she joked. The truth was she was fighting through it with gritted teeth. Nothing hurt like plasma burns.

Even though her miraculous suit could take some impact and the halithstord made her body more resilient, it couldn't prevent all the damage. She had no choice but to take it, no matter how much it hurt. Daze would never show the pain she was in.

"Here, let me get you a pain killer out my first aid kit. It'll help. I get the feeling I may have needed to pack more on this one."

They moved onward. Now the only thing between them and taking the ship was the heavily fortified door protecting the bridge.

"You know they're not just gonna open that thing for us, right?" Jax said.

"Yeah, that's what you're for." Daze patted her on the back. "I know you can hack that thing."

"You know I can hack anything, but this will take time, and when I finally get it open, they're gonna try and mow us down before we enter."

"Tut. Tut. Tut." Nik shook her head. "Don't they ever learn?"

"Hard to learn when you're dead." Daze chuckled. "I'm hungry. Nik, you wanna get food or watch Jax's back?"

"I'll go and find food. Hopefully I'll run into a few stragglers along the way. It'll be more fun than watching her hack a security door or listening to your lame stories." She walked away chuckling to herself, twirling her whip menacingly.

No less than forty-eight hours had passed before Jax's arm unit finally found the code. Bored though the three warriors may have been, well rested and fed made them more dangerous than ever.

"Right, get ready and open it," Daze announced. "Then follow me inside."

"Sure thing, but you nearly got frazzled last time. Let's try the hologram; that worked before."

"Okay, if you have one."

Jax looked at her arm unit. "I have enough power for seven seconds of hologram. That'll be enough."

"Jax, do the honours, and we'll take this thing."

"Sure. I'll set the timer for five seconds, and then it'll punch in the code. I'm going in first this time. I've been on my butt for two days. I need to move."

"Why don't we go together?" Nik suggested.

"Yeah, sure, but only after me." Jax made them laugh for a moment, but before long, the smiles made way for serious faces. The warriors once again readied for battle.

Jax tinkered with her arm unit, then it punched in the code. The door whooshed open. Like magic, an exact life-sized hologram of Jax left her arm unit and ran onto the bridge. There was a volley of fire as weapons went off, and flashes and smoke filled the entrance. Two seconds later, the warriors burst in, taking out the armed security guards. Their weapons and skills removed heads and limbs. Many of them were dead, others were alive and cowering.

Daze walked through the wall of smoke, muscles rippling, face with a scowl, and approached the captain. She pointed her arm towards him, darts ready, daring him to make the wrong move. Jax and Nik stood grinning ear to ear before the guards and crew on the bridge.

"Anyone else?" Nik growled.

Heads shook, and as one, they released their weapons. They clanged down onto the floor.

Daze, with her weapons still trained on the captain, announced, "I'm taking this ship. I'm relieving you of command."

"If I don't return the code, they'll know that the ship has been taken. They'll blow us to pieces."

"Well, I suggest you send the code then, Captain." She stared at him wildly.

"I can't... I would never... Do you know what they'll do to me if they knew?"

"Do you know what she'll do to you?" Daze pointed at Nik as she stood twirling her whip with a smirk upon her face.

"I can't. My duty is to go down with my ship. I cannot and will not let you take my ship!"

"Nik..."

There was a mighty crack. In an instant, her whip flew across the room, sparking as it went. For a few seconds the captain stood there stunned. Then the pain hit him. He grimaced and reached up to hold his stinging ear. Most of it was gone.

"So, about that code?" Daze's tone was menacing.

"I... I... I just can't!" he wailed.

The whip cracked again, and this time, he screamed out immediately. A sliver was expertly removed from his other ear.

"You should give it to her, Captain, sir." Nik's tone was mocking. She could see the fear in his eyes. "Or I'm gonna take you one slice at a time."

The trembling captain broke at that moment. "I'll send it. It'll be easier than trying to explain for you. Just, please, let my crew out of here in one piece. You've already killed hundreds!"

"Nice! Ladies, we have ourselves a ship."

"Now, are we gonna make them fly it for us?" Daze said pointing to the crew.

"We'll need them to help us, but there's no way anyone is flying this thing but me." Jax rubbed her hands together. "Do I get to blow some stuff up? It does have lots of cannons."

"Maybe because we've still got a massive problem. As soon as we leave formation, they're going to come after us. They'll pulverise us. It's eleven to one out there."

Diversion

How do I get out of this one? The thoughts ran through Daze's mind. They seemed once again to be in an impossible situation. But the answer to the conundrum didn't lie within her. This one was on Isha.

"You know what to do, Isha. It's only you who can get us through this."

"What? Explode everyone's brains in all the ships? Even if I thought that was the answer, I wouldn't possibly have the power to do that. I nearly blacked out last time."

"No, you don't need to get inside all the minds. Just ten."

"The navigators!"

"Yes!"

Flick's exclamation warmed Isha's heart. She felt like Flick was happy with her.

"All I need to do is slightly adjust the course they plot to chase us and make them crash into each other. I think I can do it, and then the one that's in front of us, Jax can blow up."

"Yes, well done! I know you can do it, Isha. I believe in the things you can do. That is why you are here with me. Not any other being. You. You're special to me."

Isha glowed again. Flick couldn't have timed the words better. Isha grew and swelled and slowly became more aware of the fearsome power she possessed. Without her, Daze wouldn't have the halithstord, and the child's fate would have long since been sealed.

"Right, get ready to leave," Daze announced.

"What?! Jax screamed. "They'll rip us in two!"

"I have a plan. Trust me." Once again, Daze asked for blind faith. "Target the ship in front of us with our cannons. We can squeeze past it, but they only have to move slightly to block us off. They haven't got their shields up. They're unprepared and think this ship's secure. We cut her in half, then we've got open space. Once locked on, we get moving."

"But they'll chase us down in moments!" Jax protested.

"They won't. Trust me. I got this."

"Well, okay. You've got us this far. But you're not going to do that head exploding thing again, are you? That freaked me right out."

They laughed. "Now, enough shenanigans. I need to concentrate."

"Here she goes again." Nik sighed.

Isha again let her consciousness drift, negating the space between entities, finding the connections, and locking onto the navigator on each of the ships. Silently, like a thief in the night, she snuck in, implanting her will inside them, making them believe that it was a choice of their own. They knew which coordinates to put in before anything had even happened. They would all meet at the same point in space.

Daze nodded to Jax.

"Woo hoo!" Jax cried out as the cannons on either side of their craft went off, booming in the hundreds. They smashed huge holes in the ship's hull, and with amazing skills, Jax had their ship speeding away in seconds. They were grazed by return fire, but their shields were up. On the rear-view screen, they saw the ten enormous craft crash carelessly into each other, and the one in front drifting apart and spinning out of control. Explosions boomed through the emptiness of space as the craft exploded, leaving countless souls lost.

Before the shockwave hit them, their ship was long gone, leaving behind a ring of debris which was now little more than a cosmic graveyard.

The Crash

The Machine had been flying for many days, never losing focus for a second. It needed not the humour or singing that the warriors did. It was always one-minded in its goal. The burdens of humanity didn't exist. It never wondered of its purpose, or the meaning of existence. It just did what it did, and that was what all it was meant to do.

The strange planet appeared before it. First it was a pink dot in the distance, but slowly, as the craft neared, it grew larger.

Though the Machine could never feel excitement or relief, locked inside the symbiote, Liam did. The mighty halithstord was yearning for battle, impatient for carnage, thirsting for blood. The symbiote loved the power the Machine gave it, this mighty warrior whose power it fuelled. Together, they were close to invincible.

The small transport neared the planet, and the computer started plotting its landing. Slowly, the craft reached the edge of the planet's atmosphere.

Daze stood before the monitor and, inside her, Isha sensed the presence of their enemy. She knew that feeling now. She had felt it before, when she had met the Assassin.

"Take it down. That is the enemy." Daze pointed at the screen.

Jax didn't even bother asking how she knew. Within seconds, she fired a single shot. The cannon went off in a flash and exploded against the side of the transport in a glancing blow.

"I nearly missed!" she huffed, disappointed.

"Well, those cannons aren't designed to hit something that small. I'd say it was a great shot. They'll be nothing but ash in seconds."

Flames burst out of the transport as it entered the atmosphere and quickly got pulled down by the planet's gravity. It free fell with hot flames licking its flanks. It was clear that the transport was going to crash.

The Machine knew that it had to survive, not for itself, but for the mission. It thrust its arms forward powerfully, denting the metal skeleton that surrounded the craft. It did it over and over until it finally burst right through the hull. The Machine pulled with its mighty strength and a huge metal panel came off in its hands.

Not a split second later, and the mechanical warrior was sucked out of the craft and free falling through the atmosphere. The transport fell apart and the burning debris rained towards the planet.

The Machine fell at terrifying speed towards the ground, fire sparking and glowing white over its body. Down and down it went, faster and faster until, blackened and glowing with heat, the flames made way for smoke. Soon it was falling through clouds. Mountains were stretched out far below. All around the terrain was rugged. The Machine would surely never survive the fall. Hurtling ever closer, it needed to slow itself.

The symbiote took control. A blue glow surrounded its host while massive power grew inside it. It plummeted out of the sky, below the mountains, and then, just before the crushing impact, a wave of blue light pulsed and powerfully left the Machine's body.

It hit the ground with a force that cracked the rocks. Enormous clouds of dust went flying skyward. Huge cracks ran jagged across the planet's surface.

The explosion echoed for miles around, sending great plumes up into the atmosphere, dimming the starlight. The Machine had hit the planet like a meteorite, and all that was left was a vast crater.

Tornados

"Wow! Look at the dust from that thing," Nik said as the warriors watched the crash from above. It was so huge it could be seen from their lofty position. "We don't want to get too close to that."

"I agree," Jax replied. "We'll avoid it, but we can't land a craft this size on the planet. Well, we can, but we won't ever be able to take off again. We need to take a shuttle down."

"We leave the ship, and they will blow us out of existence in minutes." Daze pointed around at the silent and miserable looking faces of the remaining crew.

"No problem. Give me one moment." Jax fiddled with her arm unit and then, in turn, the ship's computer. "Okay, done."

"What have you done?"

"Well, Captain Half Ears over here is gonna keep the ship in orbit for us while we pop down to the planet."

"Oh, do I get to persuade him?" Nik piped up.

"No, sorry," Jax replied with a titter of laughter.

Nik did an exaggerated huff.

"I've set a code on the ship that my arm unit will generate every two hours. If I don't send the code up to the ship, she goes boom boom, and we have pretty fireworks." She caught the nervous glances of the crew and smiled. "I'll know where they are the whole time. I can track the ship's position from the surface." Then she stared intensely at the captain, unnerving him to the core. "One slight deviation from the orbit I set, and kaboom!"

He jumped in his skin with her final exclamation.

"I think he's in, isn't that right, Mr Captain, sir?" Nik teased him.

He nodded enthusiastically. He knew they had him in their pockets, and at every second, his life and that of his crew was in danger. These fearsome warriors were truly something to behold.

Before long, they were in their shuttle craft, slowly making their way down to the planet's surface. Each of them was silent and deep in thought. Though none was even sure of her mission, they knew there was a huge chance they would not be coming back.

They watched on in awe as the planet came towards them. Beautiful auroras and pink lightning flashed beneath the hazy glow of the planet's atmosphere. As they descended, the enormous dust cloud from the crash made visibility almost impossible, but Daze, through Isha's telepathic abilities, saw the landscape.

The rugged mountainous terrain and the huge crater was below, but she was drawn towards an empty section of the desert. It was well away from the devastation. There were no buildings, no trees, no anything, but Isha, Daze, Flick, and the halithstord were drawn towards that place as one, in perfect union. There was no doubt in Daze's being that was where they needed to go.

The sand flew up from beneath the shuttle's boosters, and they landed gently on the planet's surface. Now all they had to do was find the child. It would be much easier now that their enemy was gone. Nothing could have survived such a mighty crash. They could search without the constant nagging threat that whatever it was, was trying to beat them to their goal.

Inside, Daze burned with an insatiable desperation to get there, to make sure they were safe, and to protect them, and it burned in Isha, Flick, and the symbiote every bit as much. They were separate entities that had become one, within one body. Just like all things in the cosmos that surrounded them, they were entities connected. While separate willed and separate minded, still they worked in perfect unison to create this mighty warrior.

That is not to mention the two others at her side. They were brave, intelligent, tough, and loyal. The three friends were an almost unstoppable force, and in the harsh reality of the situation they faced, they truly needed to be.

The shuttle's ramp dropped, and the warriors crept down onto the planet's surface. Jax and Nik with their glowing weapons in hand and Daze with her suit always ready. The warm wind blew dust across them, and the air was so thin, catching a breath was hard.

They were alert; they couldn't afford to let their guard down for even a second. They had no way to know exactly what lay ahead, but they knew it was a battle they could lose. Even though the surroundings seemed sparce and there was obviously nobody around, there was an uneasy feeling among the group.

From the sand, spiralling up, strange colours swirled around them. Tall towers like lollipops of light wrapped the warriors within a force. They fought back to free themselves with all their strength, but fighting was less then futile against it.

Sand whipped tornados around them, leaving them covering their eyes. Dust swirled fiercely and whipped at their faces. The forces around them grew stronger until they were dragged off their feet and up into the air.

They held their breath while collectively their hearts raced. It was clear they didn't have the power to stop it or escape; they were on this ride until the end.

They were violently tossed, helplessly above the ground. The forces were so strong, they screamed out in pain. It felt as though their bodies would be ripped apart. They could hardly hold their breath any longer. Their lungs were burning, but there was no sign it would stop any time soon.

While Daze's suit covered her mouth and nose helping her breathe, the two others burned for a breath, teetering on the brink of consciousness. The thought did not escape them that this could mean their demise, not in battle like they craved, but trapped by some strange force of nature against which they were powerless.

They struggled on and their minds started to fog. They had to breathe and breathe now. Just as they had accepted this was to be their fate, their final moment, the force stopped, dropping them unceremoniously from a great height. They crashed painfully down and desperately caught a breath.

Bruised, winded, and groaning, they lay stunned for a moment, breathing deeply, assessing whether or not they were injured. Jax got to her feet and offered Nik a hand to help her up, but Daze needed a little more time. The wounds from her encounter in the elevator still stung. She growled as she dragged herself to her feet. The three of them finally stood side by side and looked out to the distance.

They were at the top of a mountain. Red rocks hung over them and the gloomy hazy atmosphere was cloudy with dust. Behind them was the entrance of a cave. It almost called them inside.

It quickly dawned upon them that the strange tornadoes were, in fact, not a thing of nature but had deliberately brought them to that place. That meant someone or something was behind them, and if they had already demonstrated such immense power to create such a force, the warriors could be facing anything.

There was no way they could climb back down the huge mountain. That left only one option—to enter the cave. They looked once more over the strange landscape.

"Ready?" Daze looked at her friends.

"Sure thing." Nik nodded.

"Let's do it." Jax said.

They turned their back on the horizon, and the darkness swallowed them whole as they entered the cave.

The Feeling

The Machine went from blackness to light, its vision flickered, its brain was rattled. It was damaged, dented, and blackened, but for the Machine, pain was not a problem. It would surge on regardless. Within, there was no concept of how lucky it had been, or how close it had come to death.

Slowly, it fought its way from its hole in the ground and out of the rubble and dust that still rained down. It freed itself and got to its feet. The mechanical warrior stepped forward and fell to its side, kicking up dust and clanging down. Its right knee was displaced, leaving its leg unable to take its body weight.

It reached down and, with a grind of metal, twisted and jammed it back into place. With its crushing grasp, it squeezed the joint back together. Now it could hold its weight, but it left the Machine limping.

It started to climb out of the crater. Scrambling over rocks as the sand gave way beneath its weight, finally, it fought its way onto solid ground. Visibility was poor even for robotic eyes; the dust clouds were blowing fury all around it.

With a terrible limp, the Machine began to run. Its huge frame thudded across the ground, vibrating the rocks as it went. The dust explosion from the impact was spreading all the time; like a wave, it rolled out. To a living, breathing being, it would be their demise, but the mechanical warrior rumbled on.

With steps that were thunderous, it ran at amazing speeds, even with its damaged limb. Any enemies would feel the vibration of its thudding feet before the thumps could be heard, but the Machine relied not on stealth but on fearsome power. The enemies may be aware of its coming, but they could never be prepared for the cold, callous, bloody fury that would befall them at the Machine's hands. Death would rain down upon all who opposed it.

It had one mission, and it wouldn't allow anything to stop it. With The Fleck, Liam, and the symbiote on board, it was more determined than ever to complete its task.

"It draws me. I can feel it," Liam said silently.

"It draws us all," The Fleck responded. *"It is where we must go and what we must do."*

Again, fear built within Liam. Such destruction and death had already come from his will. Murder and chaos had become his existence. It hurt him deeply, yet somehow, still he craved more. He had a longing that could never be fulfilled, not until the child was dead.

It was the thought that tortured him to his core—the feeling, the longing for blood, but not just any blood—the blood of one who seemed so innocent. The conflict was tearing him apart. It probed endlessly at his conscience, right down to his soul. It was an unwelcome invasion, not something he ever wanted to think about, but here it was, nevertheless taunting him.

If, for moments, he could forget, soon the feeling inside of him would twist his thoughts back to the darkness he did not want to face. Though that darkness was the haunted truth.

On he went within the Machine's mighty body, drawn the whole time towards that feeling. Never did he have any knowledge of what he was doing or where they were going, just relentlessly following the pull, like fate itself guided them. It was a set pathway, a beacon in the inky nothingness, and that feeling dragged them towards it.

The Mist

The three warriors stepped cautiously into the cave. Each one of them was on guard and twitchy, walking blindly into what could be, and probably was, a trap.

They stepped slowly and carefully forward, heading into the unknown. The ends of each of the sleeves of Daze's suit glowed, creating flashlights. The light penetrated the darkness, but hardly.

The atmosphere inside was hazy with mist that lingered and swirled and hung around them with each step. Her lights could never cut all the way through it. As they went, the mist morphed and separated, snaked, twisted, and then hugged at their bodies again.

The rocky walls were slimy with moisture that clung to them, slowly dripping down.

The air was thick, making it difficult to breathe, but these warriors carried on regardless. Something awaited them within, they could feel it, they could sense the cold threat dwelling in the background, awaiting its moment to strike. Their hearts raced with adrenalin and anticipation.

They carried on, weapons always at the ready, breathing the atmosphere, trying their best to penetrate the gloom. They stuck close to each other; feeling the presence of their friends brought them all silent comfort.

As they pressed on, slowly the mist got denser. At first it became harder to breathe, and then it became harder to walk through. It was like they were walking in water. Fighting on, desperate to reach their destination, it became air as dense as honey.

One by one the warriors started to feel faint while their limbs struggled through the atmosphere. They fought for breath, but there was no air to be had.

Daze's suit produced her breathing apparatus, but it was too late. All three of them were overcome. Their bodies slumped to the ground, and deep darkness surrounded them.

Their minds were dark, but they were not asleep, or even unconscious. Inside, the warriors slipped through strange visions, though not in their eyes, or even in their minds, but inside their very essence. They relived moments of places they had been and battles they had won. They slipped back through the hard times, growing up on the streets as they had. Three orphans who were destined to be together.

They were bullied by the vagrants of their homeland, a land that was even further away than who they had since become, as it was in physical lightyears.

They had learned how to survive, then how to fight, and eventually how to kill. Being a mercenary or an assassin was far better than scrounging for food or stealing, and those were the only options.

In quiet times, they had grown bored and restless; that was when they travelled far and wide, to find new masters, ones that could hone their skills. They had trained for a lifetime to become the women they were, both famed and feared throughout the near galaxy.

The strange visions flashed from one place to the other, but these were not individual visions; these visions, somehow, they shared. They walked back through a million moments together, but soon Daze started seeing things that the others did not. They were memories of times past, but these memories crept in uninvited, memories that were not her own.

There was a room in a house on a strange planet that Daze did not recognise, but she felt it within her soul. It was like she had been there before, maybe in another life. She was huddled in the corner of the room with tears flowing from her eyes. She was filled deeply with a bitter emotion that she hardly recognised—fear.

A male voice was raised but not in a language that she understood. She couldn't know what was happening, but she was drained with emotion and tears. Daze cowered like she had never done, the feeling inside her breaking her silently.

The door nearest to her slammed, then as she covered her ears, there were raised, raging voices. Soon, another door slammed, and she removed her hands from her ears.

A car roared away from outside the house. Tears fell and moments passed.

A woman burst into the room. "Isha, we have to pack. Quickly now. We're going on a road trip." The voice was emotional yet fighting to sound calm. Then, all at once, the image faded.

Daze flashed back into her own past once again and joined the others on their strange dreamlike journey. There was no way of knowing how long they had been lost inside the visions before, finally, they awoke on the cave floor.

The warriors stirred with a haze hanging over them. They struggled to move their arms and their legs, but they sprang back into place like they were attached to elastic. They were being held in place by a sticky web-like substance wrapped around not just their limbs but their entire bodies.

The cave was nothing but shadow, but they could see strange creatures glowing electric blue, lurking in the darkness. They were hand-sized and insect-like with huge bulbous heads and large glowing eyes. They watched on from the shadows, crawling over each other.

"These things are gross. Are we prisoners or lunch?" Nik asked.

"If we were lunch, I think they would have eaten us, or at least marinated us, by now," Jax replied with a chuckle.

The creatures surged forward like a wave, swarming the warriors, crawling all over them. They fought to free themselves as they shuddered under the creepy crawlies, but their bonds held them uselessly in place.

Daze was lost. She didn't notice the creatures at all. Instead, she lay beneath the mass, haunted by the strange visions she had seen within her dream. Never before had she felt so helpless. Never before had she been so afraid.

She started to doubt herself. Those memories may not have been hers, but they felt like they belonged with her, or that they lived inside her. In a matter of seconds, she questioned everything she'd ever known.

Were those another's memories or her own from another life? She felt strange, like she was not alone. The symbiote was there, yes, but so was something else, something she did not understand.

She snapped out of her haze and back into the present. She shook the visions from her mind and, with them, the harrowing feeling from her soul.

The symbiote inside her burned with fury, and in a flash, she unsheathed her blades.

With a roar, she flexed and ripped herself free, slicing away the web and shaking the creatures from her body. She was on her feet and darts were flying, killing the creatures in her way. She swooped down, blades flashing, freeing her friends, and killing more of the alien insects as she did.

The warriors sprang to their feet, throwing and brushing the creatures from their bodies and stamping them flat underfoot.

Nik's cannon went off, splattering gunk from the inside of the creatures, but her whip was no longer in her hand. Jax rattled off round after round from her side arm, but her sword was nowhere to be seen.

In moments, the three warriors cleared the cave of the creatures. Some ran back to the shadows, but most were dead.

"Daze, any sign of our weapons?" Jax's eyes danced around the darkness of the cave.

Daze shone her lights down onto a pool of thick slime on the cave floor. "They're in there," she laughed.

"Oh, gross! I am *not* putting my hand in there."

"Hell, no! Neither am I." Nik shook her head.

They looked at each other. "Rock, paper, scissors," they said in unison.

Soon enough, amongst howls of anguish, Jax drew the short straw and had the slime-covered weapons in her slime-covered hands.

"I've gotta be honest, I didn't have being eaten by bugs on my likely demise list," Daze joked. "We need to get out of here and stay away from that mist. That's what messed us up."

"Look, though... this isn't where we passed out. They moved us," Nik pointed out. "There's not as much of that mist here. So how are we gonna know which way we came from?"

"Maybe there's not much mist, but there's plenty of slime." Jax pulled a gag face and did an exaggerated shudder.

"Come on. Knowing where you're going is boring. There's a breeze coming from that way. Let's follow that." Daze said it, but she truly followed a path that was already set for her—she followed the pull. She followed her fate.

The Roots

Running on and on, the Machine had travelled many hundreds of miles. Its enormous footsteps thundered. Still the dust swirled in the sky, blocking out the light, leaving an eerie orange glow. The whole way the landscape had been littered with rocks, but eventually, there was only sand. From a flat rolling desert, it sloped gently upwards into one mountainous dune.

The Machine was drawn, like choice was not its own, and began to run up the steep slope.

Its heavy feet slipped constantly on the sand that fell away beneath them and tumbled down the dune. The huge weight of its metal frame dug deep into the loose substrate, sometimes wading right up to its knees. Although its legs would never grow tired no matter how tough the going, its damaged leg was a constant burden. It took many hours, but finally, it reached the top. The Machine stood, trying to scan the horizon with its powerful eyes. Visibility was poor in the dust clouds, but for what it could see, there was only desert all around.

Nothing went through the Machine's computerised brain, but it was like an instinct. Something called, silent yet somehow irresistible, pulling on it. The feeling beat away rationality and caused the Machine to act.

With its huge hands, the robot started to dig into the loose, gritty surface. Its arms worked like powerful windmills almost in a blur, displacing tons by the minute. It never slowed, never grew bored or impatient. It dug through the day and the night until finally, with an enormous pile of sand behind it, the Machine struck rock.

Without thought, it jumped high and punched powerfully down on its extending arms, cracking the rocky surface with a mighty blow. Up and down it went, over and over until the ground crumbled beneath it. The Machine went crashing through and down into the blackness.

Out of the dust, despite the abject darkness, the Machine could see everything. There was in a tunnel with other tunnels jutting from it in different directions. It seemed there was an entire network beneath the sand.

The symbiote bristled with wild fury, for it knew that soon its thirst for blood would be met. Battle would be upon it.

The Machine went marching through the dark of the tunnels with the damp air surrounding it. It searched always, looking ahead for movement or anything that could be an enemy or a trap, but the tunnels were empty apart from the mechanical warrior and its clunking footsteps.

It lurched forward, and as its huge foot hit the tunnel floor, the ground beneath it burst open. Its foot went right through as the rocks fell away below it. For a lingering moment, the Machine tried to balance on its damaged leg, but with a rumble, the rest of the floor fell away, and its vast metal frame disappeared through it.

It fell into a deep pit of darkness, plummeting like a stone and landing hard on the jagged rocks below. If the Machine had been of flesh and blood, the fall certainly would have killed it, but the rocks did little more than scratch its outer shell and crumble beneath its crushing weight.

It looked up to see the walls that had been so void of life above were now crawling with movement. Pink roots burst through the rock and wormed their way towards the Machine. They were oozing white, frothing slime from bulbous sticky buds. Hundreds of them came from the ground and the walls, wrapping themselves around the Machine's arms and legs.

It fiercely pulled back, snapping the roots. More of the white foam poured from them and fizzed on the Machine's exoskeleton. Smoke came up from the metal as the acid-like sap started to burn and corrode its armour.

The Machine stood up, tearing through the vines that held onto it. More sap poured out, degrading the Machine's metal body. Roots twisted and snaked, grabbing a hold of its limbs, wrapping around its vast frame. Finally, the mighty warrior fell backwards with a thud.

The plants instantly wrapped and entangled it, the weird acid oozing, the muscular limbs constricting, until the mighty Machine was completely invisible beneath the roots.

The Hive

The warriors carried on through the darkness. Always at the ready, senses sharp, coiled like springs, they watched for the next foe or trap that surely awaited them. Edgy and twitching, they were getting the closest they had ever known to fear. The things that had happened, the deadly traps they'd fallen blindly into, were things they couldn't have even imagined, much less prepared for. They had fought countless battles against all manner of beings on different worlds, but in that place, it brought them little comfort. Those tunnels that drained them by the second, sapping their energy evermore, could be hiding anything at all.

They would have welcomed facing any battle in any place instead of the endless threat that dwelled there. It lurked in the background, watching them, willing them along into its jagged jaws, lying in wait in the haunted darkness.

They didn't speak; they dared not. Stealth was now their friend. Each was filled with apprehension knowing full well, sooner or later, they would once again have to fight. They had never backed down from a fight in their lives, so there was no chance they would back down from this, their most important battle of all. The mission was calling them on.

For what seemed an age, they silently crept along, the tunnels forever winding or crisscrossing. There were tunnels leading to tunnels. It was almost impossible to know where they were going and hard enough to know where they had already been. There were no landmarks or anything to recognise one tunnel from the next, with the little of each they could see at least. They went in haphazard directions, at one point heading one way and then the next, back on themselves. The only thing that gave them any sense of direction at all was the fact they were always going downwards, deeper into the mountain.

They grew even more nervous when the tunnel roof became lower in places, and the warriors had to stoop or crawl through, leaving them defenceless from an attack. At those times, no matter how powerful the three of them were, they were nothing but sitting ducks.

The only light they had came from Daze's sleeves and through the mist that now rolled like a carpet around their ankles. In the inky gloom, they could hardly see at all. It was always hiding anything that could emerge from its depths.

Finally, the silence was broken when they heard a scratching noise ahead of them. Daze shone her light towards it, jumping alert in an instant. There was a deep, dark hole in the tunnel wall. Carefully, with weapons ready, the warriors crept towards it. The scratching was coming from inside the hole. Using her torchlight, Daze peered inside, and a small, fat creature emerged. It had huge eyes, stubby short legs, and a round body with porcupine-like jagged spines all over its back.

"What is that thing?" Nik stared at it intensely.

"I don't know. I think it's quite cute, though," Jax replied.

The creature stopped and stared wide-eyed at the light.

"No. Move. Now!" Daze yelled out.

Immediately, they ran back up the tunnel the way they'd come. Seconds later, the creature exploded in a mighty flash, sending razor sharp spines in all directions.

Daze was taking up the rear and her suit took the brunt of the impact, yet the blast sent her hurtling forward and rolling along the ground. Jax and Nik were swept off their feet as the flash flew past them. They lay bruised, groaning, and reeling.

Daze was winded, but mostly she was annoyed. She grumbled as she lay on the ground for a moment, grimacing, clenching her teeth, the new pain adding to the injuries she'd already sustained. Her companions recovered more quickly than she did, but after giving her a moment, they helped Daze back to her feet.

Suddenly, the tunnels were alive with movement as more of the spikey creatures emerged from the darkness. The warriors rushed down the tunnel, running for all they were worth as an even bigger explosion set the darkness alight. They followed the path round a bend just as the shockwave hit, their speed and fortune narrowly saving them from the heat and spikey shrapnel.

After a moment, they slowed down to a walk, quietly contemplating what may lay ahead.

Daze broke the silence. "These aren't just tunnels into the mountain... this is a hive." There was a slight quiver in her voice.

The others looked at her in silence as they processed what that meant, and unfortunately for them, it meant the worst was yet to come.

"Flick, what is it? Where are we?" Isha asked buried away inside Daze's mind.

"We are in a nest, a nest of creatures that appear to be weapons. There will be many, many more. These are not natural, which means someone created them for protection. Daze will need to be on her guard."

"She's always on her guard."

"She is tired and wounded, and the worst is yet to come. This will be a tough task. She'll need all your help, Isha."

"That's how she knew it was a bomb—I told her. I don't know how, I just did. And she'll need all our help, Flick. We're in this together, right? All four of us."

Flick didn't answer. Flick didn't need to. All that needed to be said, had been.

The three warriors, battered and bruised, continued through the tunnel which narrowed and then opened out into a wider cavern at the end. Isha could sense danger all around them, and in turn, so could her host.

The symbiote fizzed within, and Daze stopped in her tracks. The others followed her lead, lighting up their weapons at the ready. There was a slight rumble around them that quickly stopped. The three of them stood still, listening, anticipating, then the rumble came again, though this time more violent, more fearsome.

The whole cavern shook. The floor vibrated, leaving the warriors stumbling, trying to keep their feet. Small chunks of rock started to tumble downwards from the stony walls above. They rushed to the centre of the cavern to avoid them.

Daze shone her light up to the ceiling and a flash of silver streaked through the beam. Above them, flying creatures emerged from the darkness, shimmering in the light with silvery, shining scales down their flanks. They moved like they were in water, pulling huge fan-like tails behind them and flapping wings that looked like fins. They were graceful and quick and darted effortlessly, flying in the thick, misty atmosphere of the cavern.

Momentarily stunned by their strange beauty, the warriors looked on, but soon, the beautiful floating creatures jagged and turned, rushing towards them. They swooped downwards and hissed. Small hot streams of plasma shot from their mouths like dragons.

The warriors moved in a flash, ducking away from the streaks of white-hot breath. With a crack, Nik's glowing whip flew through the air, Jax's light sword left streaks of light in its wake, and Daze's darts pierced the flesh of the deadly organic weapons. In mere seconds, many had fallen, yet for each one they killed, there were more pouring into the cavern. Soon, there were hundreds of them swirling overhead, spitting fiery fury from their mouths until the darkness was lit up like day. They zigzagged above and then swooped in for the kill, jerking and hissing with raging, deadly beauty.

The warriors screamed their fearsome war cries and tore through the creatures as if they were nothing. Their immense skills and almost perfect timing were on full display. Heads that were separated from bodies rained down as the warriors' expertly wielded weapons ripped easily through their flesh.

In moments, the entire cavern floor was covered in the dead creatures, but still even more poured in above them. Blinding and deadly bursts of plasma streaked all around. The creatures somehow expertly avoided each other like a flock of starlings.

"We need to move. We're overrun!" Daze drew her blades and started to cut her way through the swarm, doing all she could to avoid the waves of plasma.

Nik and Jax followed her lead and set to work tearing a path through the creatures, killing them in seconds while the plasma licked their bodies, scorching the flesh, becoming harder and harder to avoid. With a wild flurry, they found a way out of the cavern.

Daze turned and covered her friends, ushering them into a smaller tunnel. There was only enough room inside to crawl. Never for a second dropping her guard, Daze squeezed in the tunnel backwards, knowing full well the creatures would follow them through.

There she crouched low, her darts and blades ready, and a second later, the creatures began to swarm into the tunnel entrance. She flung her darts, followed by a palmful of micro-grenades, which rolled back into the cavern. She hacked the remaining creatures in the tunnel to pieces with her blades.

The grenades exploded with a blinding flash and a boom, ripping through the creatures that remained inside the cavern. The stragglers desperately flew at her, but bottle-necked inside the tunnel entrance, they were helpless against the deadly warrior. Slowly, she backed up the tunnel with not even enough room to turn around, taking out all of the remaining creatures that followed her within.

Finally, when she was certain they were all dead, her backside hit Nik at the other end of the tunnel. At last, there was enough room for her to stand up and turn around.

"Oh, cheeky!" Nik laughed. "But we've got a bit of a problem. I'm not sure there's a way out of here."

Daze shone her lights around the walls. They were tight. The three stood huddled closely together with hardly room to move. She shone the lights from side to side then worked her way up. The walls shot upwards, tall and narrow, like a rocky tube.

"So, the only way is up. We climb." Daze went first and shoved her back against the wall. She jumped from the ground, pushing her feet against the other wall, wedging herself against them. Slowly, she moved one foot and then the other, sliding her back up the rock as she did.

Jax followed suit after an invitation from Nik, and finally, she followed behind. Just as her feet lifted off the ground, five of the spikey exploding creatures trundled out from the tunnel entrance below them.

"Erm, more of those explodey things!" Nik called out desperately.

"Kill them!" Daze yelled.

"But what if they explode?"

"They'll explode anyway, and we'll be dead this close to them. Just do it!"

Nik gritted her teeth and flung her whip fizzing downwards, nervously awaiting the explosion that never came. The creature shrivelled up like a spider and died. She quickly cracked her whip four more times, back-to-back, killing the creatures instantly.

"This mission is gonna be the death of me." Nik shook her head as she resumed climbing.

They struggled and fought up the sheer walls until they were so high a fall would mean certain death. Eventually, like Daze had known it all along, they found a small tunnel cutting through the rock that they could get inside. They scrabbled in, and for a moment they were safe. Jax pulled some rations out of her bag, and the sore, beaten, and bruised warriors ate and took some rest.

Traps

The warriors sat huddled in the small tunnel, and even though they fought it, one at a time, they fell asleep. It was as though a wave of tiredness had swept over them all. Normally, they slept lightly with one eye open, and never would they all sleep at the same time, but here and now, it forced itself upon them and stole them from consciousness.

Daze dreamt in her sleep. It was, at least, what felt like a dream. The colours of the cosmos stretched out before her in tunnels of light that were so familiar yet, it was a place she had never seen. She swooped out of body through misty patterns and psychedelic colours. The journey was cosmic and wild and exciting. Her sleeping body's breath quickened, her heart raced with exhilaration, and she smiled.

She zoomed lightyears, and then, for a moment, she would stop to see some beautiful place, somewhere out there. A meadow of purple flowers, or mountains stretching tall, glistening in the star's rays that bathed each planet. Foreign landscapes of places no living thing could ever tread, but here, without her body, Daze could.

She felt it in her heart. These places were no visions of her mind, but real places of unrelenting beauty created from cosmic violence. The cosmos was a work of art, from the grand right down to the quantum, everything interlocked and connected. Never again could she look at the stars and feel small because now she knew, she was from them. She was part of them as much as they were part of her.

Isha went on the journey with her host, seeing all she saw and feeling all she felt. Now she understood how they could be connected, and for the first time, she saw the workings of the cosmos from another point of view. She no longer saw it outwardly like a human, but where her body didn't matter, and all that existed was consciousness and energy. The matter on which humans are fixated was only the froth on the waves in a vast cosmic ocean, the very depths of which are on a different frequency altogether.

Isha began talking to Daze in pictures, and for the first time, Daze spoke back. Finally, she accepted that she was there and that she had been for the whole journey. Together, the truth of what they were up against became clear.

The hive full of organic weapons was created by someone to protect themselves. That meant that the prize at the end of this suicidal journey would be a large one—the child. The goal burned inside them both.

To Daze, the reason was unclear, but the desperation to complete the task at hand was tugging away at her.

She awoke with a start, at first mad at herself for falling asleep, yet soon a calmness washed over her, the golden remnants of the beautiful dream.

She sat up and looked at her sleeping friends and smiled. She had brought her sisters-in-arms here to this deadly place, marched them into this trap, yet their loyalty and love for her meant that they followed gladly. They would fearlessly step into any battle with her. They would die for her, and as she thought about it for a moment, she glowed with gratitude and love for them.

They stirred with stiff muscles, aching from the battles they'd fought and the distance they'd travelled. Crammed inside the small tunnel, they groggily struggled to their feet.

"Woah! Super weird dreams." Nik yawned and her shoulders cracked as she did her best to stretch in the limited space.

"Yep, me too," Jax confirmed. "It's probably that trippy mist stuff again."

"Or maybe it's just a different type of journey." Daze stared into the middle distance thoughtfully.

There was a moment's silence.

"Well, that was pretty deep." Nik laughed.

"Yeah, I'm sticking with trippy mist theory myself." Jax turned to Daze with a cheeky glint in her eye. "But maybe you can hang up your suit and become a philosopher when we get out of here. Then all you'll have to do is sit there thinking all day."

Daze did an exaggerated rub of her chin. "I'll think about that. Hmmm. Is that how it's done?"

With a chuckle, they continued on their path. Through the darkness they went, and as they got deeper into the tunnel, the weird mist thinned out. At last, Daze's lights could penetrate the dark. Even though there was nothing to see, it brought them some comfort.

All around them were the rocky walls, the ceiling, and the floor of the tunnel. They went for hours, crawling at times through the lower parts. Though these warriors were fearless and formidable, in that place they couldn't help but feel vulnerable. In most situations they had an idea of who their enemy was, how many there were, and what their battlefield would look like, but here, in that alien underworld, anything could happen at any given moment.

The long periods of quiet amongst them were the most nerve-racking thing of all. They marched along, each in silent contemplation. It was draining on emotions and then, in turn, their minds and bodies.

At times the tunnels were so tight they were almost impossible to fight within, leaving them feeling like they were hunted or walking into a trap, at the mercy of the haunted darkness.

Isha inside was even more nervous. She had to concentrate more than any of them. She had to see the things that the others could not. She was the one who could sense the danger coming and that made her the first line of defence. Maybe she couldn't fight with the warriors, but her role was a vital one. She needed somehow to endlessly focus. She could little afford to let it slip for even a moment.

Soon Daze switched off her lights.

"What are you doing?" Nik asked.

"Ahead...there's a light. Be careful. This is probably a trap," Daze warned her companions.

"This whole place is a trap. What else is new?" Jax joked.

They crept, weapons drawn, towards the light. Each step slow and deliberate, each backed with anticipation. The tunnel ahead swooped round a bend, and then opened out.

Daze took the lead around it. She caught a flash in her peripheral vision, a burst of glowing blue flame sparking out of the rocks. She jumped back in an instant. The heat like a raging monster, forming a formidable wall, nearly wrapped around her body.

Carefully she backed away. "Go back, go back."

They took a few steps and, behind them, another inferno erupted from the rock. Nik lunged forward in a desperate effort to avoid being consumed within. The warriors were trapped between the hot raging flames in front and behind, furiously burning, leaving an impassable wall of heat.

"What are we going to do?" Nik asked.

Daze searched her mind for the answer, but it was Isha within who provided it. There was a reason Isha didn't sense the danger, and it didn't take her long to figure it out. The flames were an illusion. Even if they looked real, even if they could feel the heat, they were not a true danger to them. No sooner had she formed the thought, she sensed real danger.

"Follow me. Quickly!" Daze ran towards the flames in front of her.

"No!" Jax reached out and tried to stop her, but Daze was gone.

The others watched on in horror, gasping as the flames licked Daze's body all over. She roared with determination and passed right through them.

"Come through. It won't hurt you." To her companion's relief, Daze's voice came from the other side of the fire.

"After you." Nik gestured to her friend.

"No, no, I insist." Jax bowed graciously.

"Rock, paper, scissors?" Nik laughed.

"Just move!" Daze's voice was urgent, almost desperate.

They didn't question; they ran.

Dropping from the ceiling, small spikey balls fell all around them. They avoided some but two hit the fleeing warriors, piercing their skin. One stuck into Jax's shoulder, the spikes digging deep into her skin. Nik took one just above the knee as she surged forward to escape. They burst through the flames.

Daze already had her suit spread to form gloves to cover and protect her hands. She grabbed both the balls and ripped them from her friend's skin, and in a swooping motion, launched them back through the fire. Now Daze knew for sure that the spikes couldn't penetrate her suit. "Now go!"

They ran, tearing up the tunnel, knowing that any second, there would be an explosion. Daze let the others pass her then followed up behind them. The deafening boom echoed round the tunnel. The deadly spikes were sent hurtling, flung in all directions.

Daze tackled her friends to the ground and spread herself over them to protect them. The shockwave passed as the force licked her armour and the spikes deflected off.

"Okay, it's over now. Get off." Jax struggled underneath her.

Daze let them back up once the smoke cleared a little. They each had painful and bloody wounds where the spikes had dug deep into their flesh, made all the worse when they had been ripped out.

"This place is crazy!" Nik patted her body down to make sure she was still alive.

"If *you* think something's crazy, it's *really* crazy." Daze smiled. "But I have a feeling it's gonna get a lot crazier yet."

"Well, that's something for us all to look forward to."

The tunnels ran round forever, the dark always draining them, the tingle of threat ever lingering, the weight always heavily upon them. Before, these warriors had seen so much blood and despair, but this place felt like it could become their tomb. They stayed close to each other, each drawing comfort from the others, and without so much as their feet making a sound, they journeyed relentlessly onwards.

Isha's senses jangled with the now familiar sense of imminent danger, and if Isha sensed it, so did Daze. She warned her companions.

They slowed and prepared themselves for what could be anything. They searched the tunnel desperately with their eyes, but there was no sign of danger at all. With one more step, there was a crack, a spark, and a mighty fizz.

Daze was blown across the tunnel. She hit the wall and rolled down onto the floor. She lay there, unmoving and silent.

"Daze ... Daze?" Jax called out, but she was worried to move from the spot.

Daze didn't respond.

"We have to go get to her, Nik."

"But what happened to her?"

While Daze lay stricken with her arms outstretched, her light shone across the cave floor. Jax crouched low, and poking up from a crack in the rock, she could see a tiny tuft of what looked like fine hair. Then she spotted another one. The floor was littered with them.

"See them? That must be it. We can't touch them, and man, they're hard to see in here. What do you wanna do?" Jax asked.

A streak of light zipped past her head as Nik's whip went off. There was a huge spark and a crack. Her whip exploded onto one of the tufts, leaving it smoking.

A moment passed, then something came squirming up from the crack. It writhed and wriggled until it was completely exposed. It was a dark green and eyeless leech-like creature. The tuft of hair jutted up from its back, and slime glinted in the light as it oozed down its flanks. It was left pasted on the rocky floor. Frantically, it writhed in loops and figures of eight like an eel until, finally, it rolled over and died.

"Why is everything here so gross?" Nik did a gagging motion.

"Yep, don't need to be throwing up while I'm dying, thanks."

The two warriors glanced at each other, Jax drew her sidearm while Nik aimed her arm cannon, and they lit up every crack in the tunnel in seconds. Soon the disgusting creatures lay dead or dying, squirming helplessly in the tunnel, leaving their slimy carpet all over the rocks.

Nearly slipping over in the slime, they reached Daze. Crouching down next to her, they each laid a hand on her. Jax gently shook her, whispering her name.

Daze groaned and started to regain consciousness. Most beings would have been dead, but the symbiote made her even more resilient than she was before. Her heart was strong, and she fought back against the suffering.

"Are you okay?" Nik asked as she examined her for injuries.

She squinted with concussed confusion. "Huh?"

"Are you okay?"

"Yeah, yeah, I'm fine. Help me up."

They helped her back to her feet, but there she swayed, her knees threatening to buckle. She was dizzy, her vision blurred, and her head pounded. She leaned against the tunnel wall and took a few deep breaths.

"You're sure you're okay?"

"I'm good."

"You don't look so good."

"Thanks a bunch. That thing must have zapped me ugly." She laughed. "Nah, I'm okay. Don't worry. I just need a minute."

The others knew their friend well enough to know she would never admit it even if she wasn't okay. She could be half dead and she'd say she was fine, so there was little point pushing the subject.

"You take as long as you need. That was a close one. I thought you were a goner." Jax put her hand lovingly on her shoulder.

With that, Daze slumped down onto her backside with a sigh. "Okay, give me a few. I got a bit cooked then."

The warriors rested and ate what was almost the last of their food while they gathered their thoughts and their strength. The next part of their journey was bound to get tougher.

Smoke Screens

Daze couldn't afford to wait any longer. She got back to her feet. Her pain surrounded her, testing her heart and her determination. With every step, she suffered, but the symbiote, Isha, and Flick dragged her further than she could have ever gone without them. If it had been just Daze, she would have been killed. The symbiote gave her the strength to take the heavy blows she had. It fought back against her wounds, constantly repairing the damage.

Nik and Jax followed Daze's limping lead. Now the tunnels were sloping sharply downwards, all the time winding deeper and deeper into the mountain. The lingering silence was haunting, keeping them on edge, surrounding them in apprehension and uncertainty. It wore on their resolve, always probing at their spirit. At times, they may have silently teetered on the brink, but these warriors' spirits would never break. Together they were more formidable than they could ever be alone, and with the fearsome symbiote burning inside Daze's blood and Isha's senses that she could feel growing stronger all the time, they were almost unstoppable. This team, those without and those within, were an army on a desperate mission. Time was running out, but they could not rush. A lack of care or concentration would surely lead to their downfall, and without them, all would be lost.

They stepped carefully along, creeping through the tunnels, surrounded by now familiar darkness and silence. Daze caught movement in her flashlight by the ceiling. Something swooped quickly through her beam. With her lightning reactions, she followed it with her torch.

For a second it hung there, a ball-like creature with a long and whippy tail. A strange skirt from the underside of its body was waving and rippling like a flag in a gentle breeze, emanating mysterious electric blues and silvers.

It had huge shimmering eyes to penetrate the gloom. The creature's tale moved stiff and fast like a catapult with a noise that cracked from the tension. Three deadly spines left the end as fast as a bullet.

Daze pulled her blades in a flash and chopped down two of the spines with a clink. Jax kicked Nik out the way and dived full length to avoid the third. It stuck in the rocks behind them as Jax rolled and Nik crashed to the ground with a bump.

The creature swooped again. Daze launched her darts, penetrating it, deflating its balloon-like body and sending it floating gently down to the tunnel floor.

From above them, more of the creatures swooped through a gap in the ceiling. There were swarms of them. Daze set to work, and Jax and Nik were back on their feet in seconds with their weapons lighting up the tunnel. As long as the creatures didn't stop, it seemed they couldn't unleash their tails. The warriors expertly took them down, but still more kept pouring from above. Soon they were thick and circling around their heads.

Each creature started venting black smoke, thick like ink, from the skirt around their bodies. The warriors were choking and blinded.

Daze covered her mouth with her suit, but she couldn't see a thing. Then they heard the cracking noises one after the other as countless creatures released the spines from their tails. The warriors had no choice but to move. They rolled and zigzagged and did anything they could in the blindness to evade the deadly spines but to little avail.

Each of the warriors screamed out as the razor-sharp spines jagged into their flesh. They needed to worry about their wounds later; right now, they had to get away from those things before they were torn apart.

"Let's move. We can't stay here," Daze yelled. Through Isha, she could feel how many of the creatures there were, but Isha also had the ability to show her one other thing—the pathway out of there. "Grab hold of me."

Each of the warriors put a hand on her shoulder, and Daze led the way through the smoke, out the other side, and down into a smaller tunnel that was hidden in the wall. Each with numerous spines in their bodies and bloody wounds, they crammed inside. They scuttled through, ducking low as the creatures gave chase.

Through the darkness they went, spines hitting the rocks around them, rushing along. They couldn't keep running blindly as they were sure to run straight into another trap. They needed to make a stand.

They ran until the tunnel opened out and that was when they stopped. They turned and waited by the smaller part of the tunnel for the creatures to follow them through. As soon as the first one appeared, fury rained down upon it. The warriors whipped and sliced the creatures until a huge pile of them lay deflated, dead, or dying on the floor all around them.

The team stood panting, removing the painful spines from their skin, leaving their blood trickling down. While Daze's suit offered her some protection, the others did not have such a luxury. The holes were small, but they were deep.

"Can you help me, Nik?" Jax asked as she turned around. She had two embedded in her shoulder and one at the base of her neck.

"Woo, that was a close one." Nik plucked it out.

Jax sucked air through her teeth at the sharp pain. "This is starting to get really fun now." The sarcasm was clear in her voice as she stood feeling the back of her neck and watching the blood on her fingers. She opened up her first aid kit, and they helped each other treat their wounds.

"Well, we all have new scars and piercings now," Nik joked.

"You earn your scars," Jax replied.

"Shhh," Daze stopped her. She had a feeling of anticipation surging through her body. Isha sensed danger.

Without warning, the floor opened up below them and collapsed away. All three of the warriors fell, surrounded by boulders, down into the darkness below.

Shockwaves

"I'm trapped," Nik groaned as waves of pain shot up and down her arm.

The warriors lay on the ground amongst the boulders, winded and bruised. The fall had been a long one onto solid rock. Daze and Jax had no time to think about pain; their only thought was for Nik. They dragged their injured bodies from the ground, almost buckling as they did, and rushed to their friend's aid. The light from Daze's sleeves quickly found her, and the grimace on her face told a tale. Daze could see her arm trapped beneath a boulder.

"Just to warn you, when we move that rock, it may pinch a little bit," Daze half joked.

"Just do what you have to do."

As carefully as she could, Daze lifted the boulder off Nik's arm leaving her poor friend screaming out. Once she was free, it was clear her hand was badly broken. Her arm cannon strap became tighter and tighter on her quickly swelling arm. She reached up her good hand, and Daze pulled her to her feet.

"Ahh, how am I gonna juggle now?" Nik joked as Jax opened her first aid kit and wrapped her up in a bandage before giving her a pain killer.

"This'll help with the swelling and the pain, but basically, it's gonna hurt like hell. I'm sorry. Try and keep your hand pointed up, not down, if you can."

"Ah, a bit of pain never hurt anyone, and my whip hand's still good. And we all know that boulder could've landed on my head or my chest and then that'd be that. I was lucky."

They each took a moment to acknowledge their gratitude for their fortune.

Daze broke the silence. "Neither of you are allowed to die before me anyway because that's something I *never* want to see."

"But we need you, Daze, for direction, you see. We can't rock, paper, scissors every single major decision we have to make." They all laughed.

"Hey, that's a point." Nik looked at her hand. "That boulder took out my rock paper scissors hand, so you'd better stay around. I'm at a massive disadvantage now."

The tunnel exploded with laughter, and for just a split second, they forgot their woes and the mission that lay ahead. Unfortunately for the warriors, the mission was not about to forget them.

Aching, injured, exhausted, and with no end in sight, the three of them simply had to keep going. It seemed there were only two ways out of there—one, to complete the mission, and the other, death.

Daze went ahead and searched all around, knowing there was no way, especially with Nik's injury, that they could climb out. There was a tunnel high above them but far too high to reach. That left them with no choice; they simply had to find another way.

They searched every corner. The walls were green, slime covered, and dripping, but there seemed to be no way out.

Daze sighed with frustration and disappointment, loud enough for the others to hear. A hopeless feeling filled them all and silence fell amongst the group. They had come so far, just to fail here, like this. Not in a battle, but trapped and helpless. That was not the death of a warrior.

They stood in eerie contemplation. It was silent but for the occasional grunt of pain from Nik and the liquid dripping from the walls.

"Shh, listen. It's dripping through that crack." Daze shone her light from one end of it to the other. "There's a tunnel or opening below us. That's the way out."

"Daze, it's solid rock," Jax pointed out. "How are we going to break through that?"

Daze said nothing. She stared ahead, unmoving. The powerful symbiote burned fiercely inside her. Warmth built up and then flowed through her veins, filling her with energy. She closed her eyes and opened them again quickly.

She lunged over and grabbed a huge boulder while the others watched on in disbelief. There was no way she could lift a boulder that size. With a grunt, she lifted it clean off the ground and balanced it on her thighs. Her muscles rippled and strained as she hoisted it up to her chest, then with a final roar, above her head.

She braced the weight, crouched low, and then with a mighty spring, leapt into the air. She threw the boulder as hard as she could towards the floor from the very height of her jump. It exploded into the rocky floor, cracking it wide open. Daze vanished down through the rocks and into the cavern below.

The others ran to the edge, Jax's fizzing sword just about making out Daze's silhouette standing below. From the dark, there was the sound of a woosh followed by an almighty crack. Daze didn't move; she stood swaying.

"Daze, are you okay?" Nik called down to her. There was no answer.

Jax and Nik flicked a glance at each other, and without saying a word, they both jumped down into the hole.

Brown crab-like creatures clung to the walls all around them, each with a long tail finished with a ball at the end. No sooner had they landed than the tails flicked out in a flash. They moved, avoiding the blow, but the sound boomed through them, and just like Daze, they stood stunned and swaying. The shockwave through the air was like being hit in the head.

Daze snapped out of it first and went immediately on the offensive. The first handful of darts proved useless. They ricocheted harmlessly off the creatures' shells and rattled to the floor.

"Oh, I see. Time to get primal." She growled, swooped down, and picked up a rock as her weapon. Like a savage, she charged at the creatures. The clubbing tail flung towards her, and she dove to her right and rolled, avoiding the blow, but she didn't make it back to her feet. Again, she was stunned by the shockwave.

Nik awoke then, seconds later, Jax. As ineffective as Daze's darts may have been against the creatures, Jax's sword was quite another matter. The plasma fizzed and burned and slipped effortlessly through the hard shell as she expertly targeted the tails, rendering their weapons useless.

Nik's whip went off, blowing a hole right through the next creature, leaving it smoking but still clinging to the rock.

The creatures didn't move at all, apart from their tails. They gave themselves one chance to strike with their club, and a second to stun with the shockwave.

By now, Daze's blades were out, and the intelligent and battle-hardened warriors sliced off as many of the tails as they could. Occasionally one of them would be stunned, but always her comrades would come to her aid and protection.

All the while, as the battle raged, Nik was filled with pain. Each shockwave that flowed violently through the air jarred her bones, and it was only adrenalin and her sheer spirit getting her through. The painkillers worked to a degree, of course, but they were no miracle cure, and every movement was made through gritted teeth. At the moment she had broken her bones, she knew she was compromised and would have to work twice as hard for the others, but in turn, they would have to work twice as hard for her.

She felt like a burden now, but her friends certainly never felt that way. To them, a wounded Nik was worth a hundred healthy soldiers. They very much intended on walking out of there together, heads held high, ready to party like they never had before.

Soon the warriors had cleared the cavern of the creatures. They had overcome this enemy, just as they had overcome all before it. Grumbling, the warriors continued, now adding headaches to their ever-growing list of injuries. They struggled onwards, despite their pain, yet still with what felt like a million miles to go.

Patience

The Machine lay buried in the dark, the acid from the roots slowly melting its metal body. Had it been of flesh and blood, beneath the deadly tangle of plants would have long since become its resting place.

The foam oozed all over every inch of it, bubbling and fizzing on its metal armour. The plants were constantly moving, probing for a better grip on their victim like octopus tentacles.

"We're not strong enough to break them." Liam inside was impatient and frustrated.

"We do not need strength," The Fleck hissed back coldly, scolding him. *"We need patience. We have tried to break them. We cannot. Continuing to do so is futile."*

Angrily, Liam reacted. *"How can you be so calm?!"*

"Emotions are a waste of time and energy. We are in the situation we are in; emotions will not change that. The warrior that fights on anger is the warrior that loses. See inside yourself. Use your power not your emotions."

"I have no power. I'm a slave to this, aren't I?"

"You have much power, that is why you are the vessel. That is why The Fleck is within you. We will need all the power you have before this task is complete. Feel that power, not your emotions."

"You need my power? I know I'm not in control of this."

"Control matters not, the combined is what matters. The goal is what matters. Nothing else matters. You think like a human. You think about the me. How angry you are, how confused, how frustrated, but never about what really matters, never about why we are here. I knew that your humanity would be our undoing," it snarled with distain.

Liam boiled with rage and seethed to his very soul. He rumbled within his being, bristling to explode. Somehow, his logic won the battle, and he swallowed the fire into the pit of his stomach.

Slowly he calmed himself. He concentrated and let his consciousness drift out while, within, he felt the power surge.

Then there was nothing but Liam's thoughts, his darkness, and his silence. He would have given anything to hear his breath or his heartbeat in his chest, or the wind, but all around was nothing.

Time passed onwards and a cloud of depression closed around him. Hopelessness filled him. He questioned himself. He questioned his very humanity. He started questioning whether he was even alive or dead.

He wished he could close his eyes and find nothing, yet his eyes did not exist. He wished he could fall asleep and never again awaken. He didn't even know who he was any longer.

He missed Penny and his parents. He missed Earth. He even missed being an average student that most people ignored. Thankfully for him, the strength of the symbiote and The Fleck inside somehow kept him going.

He may have been a slave, but he dreamt that he was in another world and in another life where he could be himself again. The shy, half-crazy, awkward, semi-failure that was him, not some entity in the centre of a battle for existence. He could not fail—he sighed internally—he had to find a way. He simply had no choice; he had to see them again. He had to make this work, no matter how afraid and confused he was.

In its wisdom, The Fleck was right. Now was not the time for the "me;" it was time for those he loved. No matter how hopeless his situation seemed, he had to succeed.

Moments passed in silent darkness, and then as his hope was completely fading, with a bright flash and a fizz, the plants that entombed him split open. The Machine seized the moment it had been waiting for and burst out of the twisted nest of plants. In an instant, it was on its feet, at full height and surveying the scene.

Daze, Jax, and Nik stood before it, wide-eyed at its sheer size, slowly backing away. Both the Machine and Daze knew in an instant that standing before them was their one mortal enemy.

Pursuit

"Run, now!" Daze told the others, but she stood her ground, and as long as she did, Jax and Nik were going nowhere.

The Machine swooped out a huge metal arm without so much as a twitch of warning. The warriors scattered, diving ungracefully to avoid the crushing blow. Nik's screams of agony echoed out through the tunnels as the bones in her hand crunched. The tunnel rumbled when the Machine's blow smashed into the wall behind them. Chunks of rock crumbled to dust and dropped to the floor from the impact.

Daze jumped to her feet first and let fly her darts at the Machine's eyes. They bounced off harmlessly. Another strike was flung towards her, and she flipped her body over, leaping over the strike and landing expertly back on her feet. She ran, grabbed Nik's good arm, and pulled her up. Jax was already back on her feet, weapon ready.

Nik's whip lashed and cracked and sparked on the Machine's body. Jax jumped high and swift, bringing her blade swooping through the air and across the Machine's extended arm. The weapons slashed black gouges in its metal frame, but the damage was limited.

The Machine flung blow after blow with clubbing fists on extended arms so quickly that they arrived almost the instant they left.

The warriors moved expertly, ducking down, rotating their bodies, rolling on the ground. It took every ounce of skill they had to avoid the barrage of incoming blows.

The Machine rumbled forward, and Nik's arm cannon went off several times, lighting up its chest. She screamed as each blast jarred her injured bones.

Jax unloaded with her sidearm, hitting it in the head over and over. Daze released a palmful of micro-grenades by its feet. The warriors ran and rolled and were out the way of the blast before the explosion boomed out.

The Machine was knocked off its feet with the force, sending it crashing down onto the rocky ground. It leapt back up in an instant and stood menacing and bristling.

"This thing will rip us apart. We need to run!" Daze called out for a second time, but she no longer stood her ground. In that place, at that time, that machine would destroy them.

The warriors inside them twitched for the fight to the death, to fall in battle as is the warrior's way, but then and there, they knew their mission was far too important to fail. That was not the time to fight to the death. That was the time to ensure they survived. They had to find better weapons and some way of stopping the Machine before it stopped them.

They ran, skipping over the plants, cutting their way through them, avoiding the acid-like sap as they went. The roots twisted around anything that stood still for more than a second, so the warriors moved fast, away from the roots and through the tunnel. From behind, there was an electric-like buzz, and a violent wave of energy burst out of the Machine. The warriors scampered around the corner just in time to avoid it. Behind them, the Machine fell back into the plants that once again began to engulf it.

The warriors heard bangs and crashes coming from round the corner. That told them the Machine was engaged in battle with the plants. Such a fearsome and deadly opponent would not be distracted for long. They needed to get as much distance between it and them as they could.

The tangle of vines continued to swarm around the Machine. Its huge hands ripped them apart, fighting them from its legs and body. It snapped them, stopping them from completely swarming around it again. This was as close to angry as a machine could get, but this anger burned in the halithstord, and in Liam, and then through their host. Though it was something it could never understand, it burned with inner rage. For the first time ever, the metal warrior was desperate. It wanted nothing but blood.

It yearned to rip the warriors apart and wanted their very souls. It ripped wildly at the vines, spewing the white acidic froth everywhere. Never had this robot felt desire before. It had never known desperation, motivation, or a thirst for blood, all of which were now inside of it, fighting for their moment in the light.

Finally, its legs were free. It burst out of the jumble and immediately started to run. Each footstep thudded over the ground and rumbled the walls, echoing through the darkness of the tunnels. One-minded with perfect vision in the darkness, it set off after the warriors. The chase was on.

Alert, in an endless and exhausting state of readiness, the three warriors ran through the darkness. The pain from their wounds constantly begged them to stop. Their bodies were tired beyond measure, though these warriors would continue or die; they were the only options.

The weariness of the darkness and the anticipation was always around them. At any moment they could fall into another trap, they could be attacked, or worst of all, the Machine may catch up to them, and there was no doubt that it would, sooner or later.

Isha had felt the presence, just as she had with the Assassin before. She hadn't been able to know exactly where her enemy was, but immediately, she knew the Machine was there for the child. To stop Daze and her friends first was the only logical step for it.

They were now hunted. They had to find a way of stopping their foe, and all the while, the entire environment was fighting against them at every move.

The dark ahead grew thicker leaving the warriors with no choice but to slow. The mist once again lingered, and Daze's lights couldn't cut through it. Isha's senses tingled, and Daze put her hand out to signal the others to stop.

They stood unmoving for a second with their eyes alive, awaiting anything that could emerge from the dark. From above, a weight flopped down upon them. A cold, quivering mass swallowed them up, glooping down the cave walls and consuming them within.

In the blink of an eye, they were suspended and helpless. There they were, trapped in some gelatinous substance that rolled around them, squelching, sucking them back and forth inside it. They struggled, trying desperately to free themselves, but they were helpless.

The jelly-like substance hugged their bodies tight. No matter how much they squirmed, they couldn't move. The suction held them firm, and even worse, they couldn't breathe.

The goop sparkled like silver glitter, reflecting strange light that could have only possibly come from within it. It moved and breathed like it was alive. The sparkles fizzed all around them as the warriors fought to free themselves from the mass, growing ever more desperate to breathe.

The ground shook beneath the Machine's feet as it thundered through the darkness. The symbiote was burning deep within, pulling it along, leading it blindly.

It surged towards the warriors, dragging its damaged leg behind. The Machine's weakness in the tunnels, however, was its size. Many of the tunnels were tight for the warriors, and the Machine had no choice but to smash its way through the rock. Such was its power, it turned stone to rubble with its fists.

If the Machine couldn't follow the warriors, it would bring down the entire mountain around them. It would destroy everything in its path, fuelled by the symbiote, its thirst for blood, and the mission ahead. Willed along by Liam and The Fleck, nothing could stop it.

"We have to get free! She's running out of breath!" Isha panicked inside her host.

"Focus, Isha. Stay calm. Focus. We need to summon all the symbiote's strength. It is our only hope."

Isha turned her focus to the symbiote, poking it with her psychic stick, teasing it into action.

It brimmed with power, awake, alive, and angry. It would never quit on its host and fed Daze its power.

Isha filled the symbiote, in turn, with power, seemingly sucking energy from the cosmos around her and pouring it inside. Then, when the energy became too much to contain, a wave burst from within Daze, a blue wave, electric and bright. It surged through the jelly and out into the surrounding tunnels.

The creature around them squirmed, then bit by bit, released its grasp as the silver sparkles, once effervescent, became lifeless and faded. The creature was dead.

As soon as the jelly grasp loosened, Jax and Daze desperately sliced it open and slopped out of the creature, gasping. They rolled onto the hard cave floor, covered in slime. They panted, half-smiling, while relief filled their hearts and air filled their lungs.

They lay wet and cold with chests heaving in and out for a few seconds, then remembered their injuries. For a moment, each was glad of the pain because, if they were in pain, it meant that they were still alive.

The Wisp

Daze encouraged Nik and Jax to their feet and urged them on while all the time, behind them the Machine was making ground. They continued through the network of tunnels, still heading deeper.

The lights in Daze's sleeves were their only beacon in the cold darkness of that retched place. The inside of that mountain was a curse that tested every fibre of their being. The mountain itself wanted their souls, and they could feel it at every moment.

Isha could see an ominous shadow growing. She knew that something bad would happen soon. The feeling stayed heavy, now inside both Isha and Daze. Daze stopped and the others followed suit.

The feeling inside Isha grew and evolved and the shadow appeared again, looming and menacing. This time, the shadow was not only in her vision, but physically, in the silent darkness, where the three warriors stood.

The shadowy haze, deep black yet with a tinge of purple, silently snaked around the warriors' legs. It made no noise, it had no smell, it had no warmth or coldness, and in the dark, it could hardly be seen. The warriors didn't even know it was there. The shadow was nothing but a wisp.

It crept slowly, rolling and tumbling up their bodies and around their heads as they breathed it deeply in. Soon they felt an unnatural calmness. Their fears and anxieties lifted away, and slowly, they slipped into blackness.

Strange patterns swirled inside Daze's mind's eye. Thoughts crept in, unhelpful thoughts, adding always to the confusion. Was she a soul or a dream or a spirit? This warrior feared nothing it seemed, but she feared this. She felt as though she was drowning, but like someone drowning who didn't know what water was. Like one who had no idea how it would feel, or how it would react as they hit it with no concept of stopping themselves from sinking into the deep.

She was sinking, yet floating, drowning silently, yet without limbs to fight against the forces. She drifted through the moments, at first afraid and fraught of what she did not understand, void of a point of reference, with no means of escape. She was no longer of body, silently wondering if she was dead.

The fear that had wrapped her melted away, and she started to accept her fate. If she was dead, if she was to die, the mission had failed, but she was free of her burden. A warrior without body has no power. She couldn't make the darkness around her cower or run in fear, nor could she hurt it.

She was little more than a helpless baby, yet a motherless baby, unprotected, floating in nothingness, lost.

There in the haunted dark, forms appeared to Daze which became faces. They were faces etched with harrowing tales of pain and misery. These were not strangers, although of many she did not know the name. They were the lost souls of the beings she had laid waste to over the years. That most often she'd killed for money, stealing them from life with her fury and her deadly wrath.

She was forced to watch on, unable to close her eyes or turn away from them. She longed to see her friends beside her, but this was a comfort she did not have. In that place, all she saw were the lost souls, and for a second, she felt the pain she inflicted and fear she instilled.

These were emotions lost on her, locked behind her internal walls of iron, her own secret box of trauma that she didn't even tell herself about. The images and emotions of every life that had been taken by her hand revealed themselves. Those were torturous moments that lingered an age with hundreds of souls flashing before her, each with their moment to shine.

She wished she could scream out or that the tears would flow, but she was trapped in nothingness. All Daze knew at that moment was pain.

"Where am I, Flick?... Flick?"

"Do not fear, Isha. I am here."

"I've lost Daze. I can't feel her anymore. I don't think we're still connected."

"We are still connected. The Wisp has stolen her and the others. She floats in what, to her, seems nothing."

"Is she trapped? Will she die?"

"Trapped? Yes, for now. Die? Not like this. Not here."

"What is the Wisp?"

"A higher being and a gateway, all in one. It can smother you or carry you. It can poison you or give life. It can take you to places."

"But I can't feel her anymore."

"Search, Isha. She is still there, just lost in darkness."

Isha was too afraid to search. Thoughts kept running through her, not structured and clear, but fraught and frantic. Her thoughts were of the child, and how her host was lost with no time to lose. Worst of all, she couldn't feel Daze. She searched desperately in nothing, but it only felt like she was drifting further away, like they were ripped apart by the tide.

Her mission was in peril, hanging over her like a dark cloud. She panicked. The weight poured down upon her, but like Daze, she felt nothing at all. She was suspended in nothing, wrapped in her own fear, but unlike Daze, Isha was not alone.

"Calm yourself. This is no time to panic or fall into fear or despair. You see, we are where we are. How we got here and why we got here are questions that no longer matter. What does matter is where we're going and what we must do when we arrive."

Isha didn't respond. She imagined she was in her body, in the comfort of her own skin, forgetting for a moment where she was. Images like a never-ending slide show zoomed relentlessly through her.

"I need to find Daze. Save the child. Complete the Mission. Stop the Machine!"

Entities Reconnected

The Machine rushed through the narrow tunnels, at times smashing through solid rock with its fists. Soon enough it came to the same place the warriors had been an hour before, and just as the warriors had, it stopped dead. This wasn't a decision it had made. There was no reasoning; it was a feeling.

Slowly the Wisp crept up its huge metal legs, growing all the time. It snaked around it, twisting the contours of its hard shell, and eventually wrapped itself around its head. With that, even with the Machine's amazing vision, everything went dark. The Wisp wrapped tighter and tighter around its massive form. Darkness normally didn't affect the Machine's vision at all—it could see in all spectrums of light—but the Wisp wrapped it like a cloak.

The Machine ran the situation through its computerised mind, trying to decide the best course of action. Since this situation was unprecedented, it was not one for which the metallic warrior had an immediate answer. With a mangle of computerised confusion, the Machine did the only thing it knew it safely could—it stood completely still.

Around and around the Wisp went, growing ever thicker, surrounding the Machine's body, getting tighter all the time. The robotic being was frozen, but a voice came from somewhere within it.

"Run!"

The Machine surged forward and burst from the mist, leaving it swirling and lingering. The Wisp reached out again, but it stormed out of the blindness, and once again it could see.

With Flick's quiet coaching, Isha was finally calmer.

"Forget where you are and what's around you. Just focus on the path back to Daze. The Wisp confuses, that's what it does. Be silent, thoughtless."

Isha drifted through the nothing, gently searching, not with her eyes or mind but with her soul, following a path of energy. The energy was within her, and now not a moment went by she couldn't feel it. It was her guide, and eventually, she knew she had found the place that she belonged. Her host that she both loved and hated, that she both feared and admired, was there. Silently, effortlessly, like nothing existed at all, she slipped back inside the warrior's being.

At once her energy bound with Daze's, and the symbiote warmed to her, almost wagging its tail like a dog whose master had returned. Once again, Isha felt powerful. Once again, she felt brave, and she knew herself, the symbiote, Daze, and Flick were connected.

Daze shook her head, and for the first time in what seemed forever, light streamed into her eyes. This was bright artificial light. She had no idea where she was. It was only a split second between emerging from her dream to knowing that she had to move.

She leapt backwards as the electric explosion flashed angry white, rippling through the air. She hit the ground and rolled. Her suit took the edge off the blast, surely saving her life as it had countless times before.

"Daze." Her ears were ringing. The voice wasn't clear, like someone was speaking under water. The ringing quietened, and the voice became clearer. "Daze!"

A hand reached down and pulled her to her feet. She staggered, but Jax pulled her along. In seconds, so many things had rattled her senses that when she finally realised her friend had her, suddenly, despite the pain she was in and the confusion that surrounded her, she felt relief. That was something real.

They ran and jumped in the crater that the explosion had created, joining Nik in there. They wedged themselves tight, lying flat, ducking down inside the hole. In this huge white room, this was the only cover. Plasma fire started to rain down on them from gangways above.

"Oh, man, we are so screwed!" Nik said almost light-heartedly.

The explosions rang out, sparks flew, and they felt the heat close to them. They ducked as low as they could, covering their heads with hardly even room to breathe.

"Daze!" Jax had to yell to be heard above the explosions. "Now would be a really good time to do that explodey head thingy again."

"I'll think of something. Give me a sec."

"Isha, she needs you. Now is your time," Flick said with the matter-of-fact calmness that always soothed her. She seemed to guide her without words, preventing her from panicking or getting flummoxed, calming the fear and confusion. As long as Flick was there, she was never alone.

Isha focused. She had no idea what she needed to do, but she drifted away to find out. She completely ignored the explosions and battle raging around her; that was Daze's job. Hers was to find a way out.

Flick only ever seemed concerned about Daze, but Isha was taken with her friends, and she wanted to make sure they all got out of there in one piece. This gave her even more motivation. They hadn't let her down, so she wasn't about to let them down.

On the outside, Daze was staring into nothing, unblinking, almost miles away from the fury that raged all around her. She forgot the sounds of explosions and sparks, she forgot her pain, she forgot her body entirely, then warmth swelled within and filled her. The symbiote inside her was brimming, and darkness started to rise from Daze's fingers like smoke, slowly at first, then pouring out, expanding all the time. It had no taste, no smell, and made no sound. It slowly filled the room while fire still poured from above.

Slowly, it smothered the beings that were on the gangways, and the weapon fire stopped. The soldiers had vanished where they stood. Finally, the warriors could safely come out from their hiding place.

"Well, that was completely awesome!" Jax laughed.

"Where'd they go?" Nik asked.

Daze shrugged. "Who cares? Let's go."

"Where did they go, Flick? Did I kill them?"

"No, they are not dead. You sucked the energy out of the Wisp we were in. You created a Wisp of your own, but this Wisp was born. It is its own living, breathing thing, with will of its own. You have not decided their fate, but you have managed to buy us some time. It feels as though our goal is close."

Ruthless

A clank echoed out and the huge metal door warped. The Machine tore into the locked entrance over and over, thrashing hard against it. There were countless enemies, weapons trained, ready for when the door finally gave way. They twitched to unleash the savage volley and take down whatever emerged from the wreckage, but the Machine didn't care. All it cared for was the completion of its deadly mission knowing the target of its mighty wrath was on the other side of that door.

Eventually, the sound of metal twisting and then breaking was loud, and the door gave in. Awaiting guards that stood shivering, fingers nervously twitching on triggers, watched on.

The Machine held the door in its grasp and surged forward. Not a second passed before the room was lit up with plasma fire and explosions, blackening the Machine's door shield. It flung the door forward with all its might, smashing into the guards that stood in the way, crushing their frail skeletons under the weight. Most were dead, some were injured and wailing in agony.

The Machine swooped to the side, diving and rolling over, constantly grazed by the plasma, and clanked behind a stairway that led to a gangway above. The metal warrior stayed on its knees for a moment, calm, as all hell broke loose around it. The sparks fell like rain from the unrelenting plasma fire. The Machine was far from the shiny metal being that it had been. Now its exoskeleton showed the scars of the battle.

It rose back to its feet and moved quickly, heading for the bottom step. The plasma fire grazed it constantly, but its shell was thick enough to protect it from all but direct hits. Those would damage it. With so many guards, there was no way it could avoid all the weapons.

The Machine ran up the metal stairway and to the gangway above, flinging out its enormous fists on extended arms as it did.

The nearest guards were flung from the gangway. The ones that survived the bone-crunching impact would not survive the fall.

Quickly and expertly, the killing machine swooped down, grabbing a fallen plasma rifle in each hand in one flowing movement. The fury was mighty as it unleashed a deadly barrage against the rest of the guards on the gangway. Some tried to fight and returned fire, others ran, but neither option did them any good. This cold warrior just as readily took down the ones fleeing as the ones fighting. Soon the gangway was clear but for one guard.

The Machine fired its weapon. The guard fired back, and then was hit and sent hurtling off the gangway. The guard's shot zipped, flashing through the air, hitting the Machine in the head. It left a smoking hole by its eye, but that couldn't stop it.

The guards below fired upwards, rocking the metal floor beneath the Machine's feet. It rained plasma back down upon them with unrelenting fury. With the advantage of a near perfect aim and the high ground now firmly the Machine's, it indiscriminately ripped through the guards. Some held their ground and died where they stood, others ran for the door in a bid to save themselves.

The Machine didn't care; it was unremorseful and ruthless. It happily shot them in the back running, if that was indeed how they desired to die, like cowards fleeing the battle. It would leave no one alive.

The room below was black with explosions and small fires burning on dead bodies. The smell of charred flesh wafted upon the smoke that lingered. Apart from the occasional scream of pain, silence fell.

Little did the screamers know that all they had succeeded in doing was telling the Machine where they were. It wouldn't let them live, not on this day.

Inside the symbiote, Liam reeled in horror. The killing was so unnecessary. Why couldn't the Machine let the ones that ran away live? His humanity screamed, but something inside him, somewhere dark and twisted, liked that power. The symbiote around him burned hot with an insatiable blood lust.

Liam was losing his sanity. Half of him was drenched in terror and guilt as if the murders had been by his own hands, the other half brimmed in tandem with the symbiote, excited for the next battle, yearning for more blood.

Maybe it was The Fleck that had control of him and forced him to do unspeakable things against his will, but as more time passed, it seemed The Fleck's, the symbiote's, the Machine's, and Liam's will were all entwined as one. He didn't even know who he was anymore.

He hated himself for enjoying the power, but power can corrupt even the strongest individuals, including Liam. He was strong—how else could he have got through all that he had without completely snapping? —but he wasn't even close to strong *enough*.

He'd been pushed to the very brink. He had taken as much as any young man could ever endure, and still the goal was the only thing that was clear. The mission was all that mattered, and if he focused upon that, maybe somehow, he would get through this.

The Guardians

It was as though the warriors floated on the wind. Nothing seemed real, and moments passed in an instant. Miles they'd walked, turning the endless tunnels inside the mountain, but they felt like they had not travelled at all, almost like they'd floated through a dream.

Something was dragging them on now. Their own thoughts and feelings didn't matter. They were pulled along by a higher purpose, by a task with so much more meaning than their own lives.

It seemed for those hours, their bodies didn't exist, like the pain and fatigue melted away, and they floated onwards. Even though they trembled under the mighty physical burden, somehow they were unfeeling, like their own weight meant nothing, like they drifted.

They were hungry and unrested, weary and weakened, and all the while, they could tell that things would get harder yet. The promise of more punishment and pain stalked them like a shadow, awaiting its moment to strike. It wished them on, towards doom, towards misery, towards a future that at that moment was in the balance.

They had no idea how long they'd marched; all they could know was the goal grew ever closer. Daze and Flick could both feel it, but most of all, Isha felt it. Her consciousness tingled with anticipation, knowing soon enough, their destiny and the destiny of all things beyond would be met. Each knew they couldn't let that pressure break them, the pressure of countless souls out there across the galaxy, unknowingly and silently calling out.

The lack of resistance they had recently met was welcome after battling almost every moment since they arrived, but it also left them uneasy. Things felt strange, like a buzz of energy surrounded them.

Moments passed, then hours, always with the energy in the environment building until they felt it inside their bodies. They could tell their time of reckoning was nearly upon them. Their silence spoke the loudest. The jokes and banter had subsided. Whether they were saving their energy for the coming battle or they simply had nothing to say could not be clear. Each of them was focused and waiting, ready for anything. This place was one they'd never known, and the events that had unfolded were unpredictable to say the least, and that made them nervous.

Time slipped away in a haze, and the electric buzz that filled the air was thick around them and within them, growing heavier all the time. Inside Daze, Isha felt uneasy. She sensed that a great power was in the air, and from wherever this great power came, they were getting closer to it every moment. The threat ran through Isha and, in turn, through Daze, and though outwardly she would never show any sign of fear, inside she was apprehensive.

Slowly the buzz in the atmosphere became a crackle, and images flowed into the warriors' minds. Not full images, like they couldn't quite stay. It was as if they were stuck between frames, a fuzz of static, they'd flicker and then fade out again, followed closely by the next. Their vision was blurry, like they were trying to focus on two worlds at once, a world in front of their eyes and one inside. Confusion filled them followed by fear. They didn't like this at all.

At any other time or in any other situation, they would turn back, but there and then, they had no choice. They had to keep going. The thought always lingered that they were up against powers they didn't understand, yet they had to battle it, and more importantly still, they had to win.

Staggering on, half blind, half going crazy, the images began to linger for longer. There was no way to block them out. If visions are inside the mind, there's little point shutting the eyes. They stayed close to each other just to feel the presence of their friends.

They went through rooms that were lit up, brilliant white, but to them, it was like they walked through smoke. Nothing was ever clear, neither the forms in their eyes nor the ones in their minds. It was like their consciousness was the white noise between stations on the radio dial, or the world around them was badly drawn, nothing in proportion or focus.

The images came again, but this time stayed. The warriors were blind to the outer world. They stopped.

"Move!" Daze crouched down as within her Isha sensed danger.

The others moved a split second later, but it was a split second too late. Something struck them, burning yet solid like steel, sending them sprawling to the ground. Daze heard the breath being knocked out of their lungs and heard them hit the floor, but she couldn't see them.

Inside, Isha fought with everything she had.

"*Stay calm. It's telepathic energy. You can fight back. Use your own powers,*" Flick gently coached her.

Panicking would cause the strength of Isha's power to waver, and she could little afford that. She needed to regain control for Daze. She needed her cloudy mind back now or it would be too late. This was immense power they faced, and one they did not understand, and to defeat one's enemy, one must understand them.

Instead of fighting against the force inside Daze's mind, Isha tapped into it. She followed it with her psychic energy, from Daze's mind and then off on nine pathways that led to their powerful enemies.

Isha understood. She absorbed their energy, reading their thoughts and their intent.

The nine Guardians were mighty and hidden behind their telepathic cloak, sneakily attacking the minds of the warriors, changing their perception, changing who they were. These guards were small yet fearsome, using their two-pronged attack of both body and mind in the name of that which they protected.

Isha could feel a familiar presence, one that excited her to the core. It was the child, and they were nearby.

For now, she had to fight hard to protect Daze from the psychic attacks. She needed to even up the odds.

She pushed back against the Guardians. They fought her, but she raged with everything she had, blocking the confusing visions so they could no longer reach Daze's mind.

The instant Daze's psychic blindness lifted, she moved, ready and bristling for battle. The symbiote inside her once again yearned for the fight.

She glanced over her shoulder to see her friends struggling back to their feet, and in her heart, she felt relief. At that moment, they could look after each other. She had a job to do. If any of them would make it out of there, it was up to her to stop the Guardians that stood like predators in wait.

She ran, drawing blades, and roared her fearsome war cry. The nine Guardians stepped towards her. They were short forms with spindly legs and arms that glowed. It appeared they were not quite solid as they sparked in random patterns. Wiry, glowing hair hung in strands, ever morphing, unsolid. Two huge green eyes burned brightly in the middle of their heads. She couldn't tell if they were living or mechanical, but to Daze, that didn't matter. She simply had to defeat them.

Before she even reached them, in flashes and pops, their savage weaponry was on full display. The hair flicked out, extending far from the head and hurtling through the air towards her. She moved without thought and desperately avoided the exploding hair tips. The blasts spread far beyond their limits and sparks dropped, fading, to the ground.

She rolled and flung her darts from each sleeve, arms outstretched. Her enemies moved like nothing this brave warrior had ever seen. They morphed and skewed their form, and gaps opened up right through their bodies, leaving the darts passing harmlessly through.

The Guardians ran in all directions, surrounding the warrior. Her huge eyes flicked left and right, trying to take in every movement. For a calm second, Daze and the Guardians awaited the inevitable clash.

They attempted their mind attack again. Isha duly blocked them, protecting her host. Daze didn't know that Isha was inside, stopping the attacks, and the Guardians couldn't know either, which gave her an advantage.

Isha launched an attack of her own, sending clouded visions like smoke that swirled inside the Guardians' minds.

While her nine foes were dazed and confused, Daze flung her darts from her sleeves once more. This time they left jagged holes through their bodies, but they passed right through the semi-solid glowing limbs and hair.

The Guardians were stunned for a second. They didn't know how their attack had failed or their defences had dropped.

Jax and Nik now joined the battle, standing by their friend's side with their weapons ready.

The Guardians summersaulted and darted from place to place so quickly they were almost impossible to hit. Even when they were dead on target, they could open gaps in their bodies and weapons would pass through harmlessly.

The Guardian's hair and limbs came all at once, everywhere. Although Isha could stop the attacks in Daze's mind, she could not offer the same protection to the others. Quickly Jax and Nik were overcome and out of the battle.

Daze protected her stricken friends, flinging darts and flashing her blades, but she was soon entangled with strands of hair holding tight round her arms and legs. The Guardians started to drag her closer. Their eyes burned like fire.

She struggled and fought back ferociously. The strands that held her were hot, and the more she struggled against them, the more her skin burned beneath her suit, leaving her screaming out in pain. She fought with everything she had, but still, she was dragged towards them. Her frantic eyes watched on while her body fought a seemingly losing battle.

The Guardians' eyes flamed as they dragged her closer and closer, so close she could feel the heat coming off them.

At that moment, her heart sank. She knew she couldn't break the bonds that held her, and she was being dragged helplessly to a fiery death. In her heart, Daze knew then that she had failed.

Isha searched desperately and, somehow within the jumble of entities, found a connection that she recognised. It was the connection to the child. The child, far more psychic than Isha, knew who she was in an instant. She may be inside a different body, but her spirit and presence the child knew well.

Daze was pulled closer, and the Guardians fizzed, awaiting eagerly to finish her.

Jax and Nik had regained their feet and were pulling back on Daze, trying to stop her momentum to no avail. They tried to cut the strands that held her, but all their attempts failed. She had stared death in the face so many times and evaded it, but this time, it seemed her death was certain.

She was mere inches away from the glowing fire when, just like that, the Guardians stopped pulling and released her from the painful bonds. The three friends hugged each other in relief.

The child stepped forward as the Guardians separated to let them through. There they stood, radiating power, an almost kingly magnificence, but in the body of a youngster.

Daze looked upon them, filled with awe, such a frail looking being, but one that was so strong. They exuded energy, and slowly they spoke, though not in words but in mind.

"*I know you.*"

"No, you don't know me," Daze responded with her voice.

Jax and Nik looked at each other and shrugged. It was just Daze talking to nothing—what else was new?

The child boomed, *"Not you! I was speaking to the other one."*

"Huh?"

"Yes, I'm here," Isha responded from within the warrior.

For the first, time Daze heard her words. She swirled as confusion reigned, and her mind flashed uselessly from place to place to try and make sense of the senseless.

She was confused, but in another way, it made sense. She had known someone was there with her. She'd felt the presence and called upon her power many times. She could have easily felt invaded, but what she felt was kinship and gratitude. Now it made sense that Isha, all this time, had fought with her, not by her side but from within.

"You have come to set me free? You have come to get me away from Dark Space?" the child asked.

"Yes, now we must leave. There's something else here to kill you. It's coming!"

"The Guardians shall protect me, just as they did from you." The child swept their arm as if to show them who she meant.

"We were not finished yet." She was angered at the suggestion. *"And your Guardian's strongest weapon is telepathy. This thing is a machine. It will tear them apart. Then it's one step away from you. We have to get you to safety and just hope the Guardians can stop it. It'll follow you to the ends of the universe."*

"Okay," the child agreed. *"I trust you."*

"We need a way out. Where can we go?"

"There's a transport, over there." The child pointed to a door in the wall.

"Right, let's move," Isha said. Daze echoed Isha's thoughts with her words to her companions.

The Guardians waited for a moment then swarmed, forming a barrier in the path. Daze took the child by the hand and rushed towards the door.

Only minutes had passed before the Machine burst into the room. Unhindered by the Guardian's telepathy, it stood face to face with them. The rifles still in its hands were rapidly firing plasma explosions all around. The Guardian's quickly moving and morphing bodies avoided most of the damage even though the metal warrior was deadly accurate.

They flicked out their hair and limbs in a blur. The tips of the hair exploded on the Machine's body, blackening the metal. It dropped one of the plasma rifles and extended an arm with an enormous clenched metal fist, striking one of its assailants and knocking it flying through the air.

The Guardian crashed into a wall then hit the floor. It tried to regain its feet, but sparks spat from its metal interior. Finally, it fell twitching, and then lay lifeless.

The other eight Guardians flew wild at their enemy, jumping towards it. The Machine swatted one away, and it hit the ground hard while the other seven attached themselves to its body, winding their strange limbs around it, setting to work gnawing through the protective shell. It bucked and thrashed, but the Guardians were stuck fast and started to cause damage.

As they dug into its hard metal shell, the Machine was left with no choice but to pluck them off. It reached down and grabbed the Guardian that was on its chest with its free arm, simultaneously crushing it and ripping it from its body. Shards of metal came off its exoskeleton along with the guardian. The mechanical assassin squeezed hard until there was a crunch and then threw it down with disgust. Its foe lay lifeless on the ground.

Soon the mighty robot pulled another two off, damaging itself and killing its enemies in its crushing grasp. The five that remained hanging let go and zipped out of the Machine's reach.

The hair flew out, fast and deadly, aiming for the holes in the Machine's armour. It blocked many with its solid forearms; some made it through and sent waves of power running through the Machine's circuits, stopping it for a split second in its tracks. Another volley was unleashed from the weapon that remained in its hand and extended its other arm, making a grab for one of the Guardians.

Though it moved like lightning, with the distraction of avoiding the plasma fire, the Machine caught hold of it. It flicked out its hair and legs and fought furiously. With one hand, the Machine lifted it off the ground. With the other, it blew its head apart with the plasma weapon. It released the headless body, glowing eyes now dull, and turned its fire upon the remaining Guardians.

The Guardians would never surrender. They would fight until they could fight no more, but with their telepathic attacks rendered useless, this machine with the symbiote on board was too powerful, even for them. The Machine was fast and devasting, taking out their brethren like they were mere insects, as though they were little more than an annoyance. The Guardians would still fight with fury, until the very last one of them was lifeless.

The flurry of hair and limbs wrapped around the Machine's legs and arms in an effort to restrain it, but with robotic power, it was far too strong. They were left being swung around the room like balls on the end of strings, smashing into one another.

The Machine flung them at the walls then swung its arms up and sharply down. The two Guardians in its grasp flew up, then crunched into the floor, leaving them smouldering and twitching with sparks coming out of their metal innards.

The other Guardians released the Machine again. Now only three of them remained. Two jumped, spinning in the air like tornados, flicking out their weapons at the Machine's head. It grabbed their hair in each of its hands as they sparked on its face. It opened its arms wide and then closed them quickly, bringing the Guardians crashing violently together before flinging them lifelessly onto the ground.

Only the last Guardian remained.

It flew at the Machine, jumping, spinning over and over as it did. The Machine swooped an arm towards it, but the arm narrowly missed its flying assailant. The Guardian jumped again, latched itself onto the Machine's face, and jabbed its hair-like weapons into the hole near its eye.

The Machine's whole body tingled and jolted. It reached up a trembling arm and grabbed the Guardian from its face. With the sound of ripping metal, the Machine pulled it off along with some of its own armour. The Guardian was crushed right there in its hand.

Smoke came from the Machine's head, and its armour was ripped. The Guardians had at least, in part, done their job and left their mark on the Machine, creating vulnerabilities for the first time.

"Where's a transport?" Daze ushered the child to show them the way.

"This way." The child spoke verbally for the first time and pointed the direction.

The child ran freely, but unfortunately the warriors did not. Each of them carried many injuries. They were struggling and tired beyond measure. Each would have given anything to stop, to lay down, or to give up, but their hearts drove them on.

They ran for what seemed forever through white rooms until finally, up ahead, there was what appeared to be a transport hanger.

Behind them, the Machine dragged its compromised body, but pain and fatigue were no barrier for it. It didn't need heart or determination; it was just relentless in the purest form. It cared not for the mission or the fate of others. It just did what it had to do, what it needed to do—kill the child.

"It's coming!" Isha silently told her host.

Daze warned the others. They sped up to a full sprint. Well, at least the fullest sprint they could manage while limping. When they finally reached the hanger, they each felt a slightly misplaced sense of relief.

The child rushed over and pushed a button on the wall and a light scanned their face. With a hiss, the huge hangar door started to retract. They didn't wait for it to fully open before they ran inside. There was a transport ready and waiting for them on a platform.

They headed up the ramp, and Jax threw herself into the cockpit. She fired up the engines, and slowly the craft started to lift.

An explosion rang out. The craft rumbled.

"Go, Jax. Go!"

She tried to speed up, but there was no thrust. They were levitating there like sitting ducks. The bursts of plasma fire kept coming and hitting the ship.

"Abandon ship!" Jax yelled. "Jump out now. Go. Go!"

The ramp was half open, and Daze jumped first, then the child, whom she caught in her arms. Nik followed closely with a roar as the bones in her hand crunched again, and Jax went last. Just as her feet left the ramp, the transport tilted to its side and dropped down, crunching into the hangar floor.

"Run now. It's gonna blow!" Jax screamed out again.

They ran as fast as they could. The flash and the heat rushed past them as they ducked down low for protection behind the platform.

"What now?" Nik whispered.

"Now, we fight!" Daze growled.

All or Nothing

The warriors stepped out from their cover and were joyous when they saw there was another transport at the other end of the hangar. It was right there, their escape, but there was never any chance of them getting out unless the Machine was no more. They needed a plan above and beyond a suicide mission.

"Jax, take the kid to the transport, and get ready to start it. Nik, you and me will have to try and stop this thing."

"I want to fight, not run," Jax snarled.

"But the child, the child must be safe."

"Do you think that thing will just let us fly out of here? Been there, tried that." She pointed towards the still burning wreckage around the hangar.

"Okay, but, kid," Daze crouched and looked into the child's eyes, "you better find somewhere to hide, okay?"

The child nodded and quickly scuttled away.

There was a thud and a screech of metal. The warriors came out into the open and only then could they see the full image of the raging inferno the transport had become. It was a wall of fire spread right across the hangar. The metal within moved, and a looming blackened silhouette emerged from the flames, tall and menacing. The Machine smoked as it stood towering over the wide-eyed warriors.

"Erm, yeah, this looks fun. I nominate Jax to go first." Nik let out a little titter.

"Rock, paper, scissors?" Jax quipped back.

The Machine clanked closer.

"Its armour is damaged, so aim for the weak spots. We can do this," Daze said through gritted teeth with a voice of determination.

"Okay, got it. Last one to kill the big scary robot has to buy the drinks," Jax offered with a giggle.

The Machine was now close. It stopped. It stared. The warriors stared back. Just for a lingering moment, each entity took in the enormity of what would be at least somebody's last battle. The only question that remained was… whose?

The Machine raised its plasma rifle and tried to fire, but the heat from the transport explosion had damaged it, and the weapon exploded in its hand. It left jagged, glowing metal strands hanging on the bottom of its arm.

"Man, I hate it when that happens," Nik joked.

The others laughed, but the Machine didn't seem to see the funny side of it, and it was nowhere near done yet.

The warriors split to create a triangle around the Machine. Their metallic foe flung its remaining fist on its extended arm towards Nik, who jumped out the way, flinging out her whip as she did. The whip cracked and fizzed and contacted the inside of the shell on the Machine's chest where its armour had been damaged by the Guardians.

The Machine staggered for a second, just long enough for Jax to lunge in with her sword and sever the dangling strands of its useless arm. Then in a swooping motion, she leapt up from the ground, stabbed her plasma sword deep into the Machine at stomach height, and withdrew it as she landed expertly on her feet.

The Machine flung out a leg. Jax avoided it, but it caught her and sent her sprawling towards the flaming debris. She lay still for a second.

The Machine turned to face her and ran, jumping high over the stricken warrior. The shadow of its mountainous frame loomed as the Machine flew down towards her. She closed her eyes.

There was a flash of light so bright that Jax could see it through her closed eyelids. The sound of metal hitting the ground was welcome in her ears. She opened her eyes. The Machine was down on its back surrounded by a green glow that froze it in place. She was up and ready in an instant.

The Machine emerged from its frozen state and expertly flipped itself back to its feet. It flung its fist again, this time at Daze. She backflipped away from the crushing blow.

Jax and Nik took that moment to attack. Again, the whip tore through the holes in its armour, leaving glowing metal smouldering within. Again, Jax's sword ripped a gaping hole inside the Machine.

Daze leapt, blades out, higher than she ever had before, driven on by the symbiote. It seemed the more injured and tired she was, the stronger the halithstord became.

She placed a foot on the top of the Machine's outstretched arm and pushed off it. She went higher as the Machine tried to swat her away like a fly. She reached head height and, with a scream, sank her blades deep into the hole in the Machine's face. Electricity sparked and buzzed and, there was Daze, stuck, convulsing, with her blades jammed deep inside her foe's head. The sound crackled fiercely, and black smoke started to pour out from both the Machine and Daze.

There was a huge popping explosion. The Machine stood rocking with only half its head remaining, and Daze was flung across the hanger in the blast. The Machine stood for a moment longer and then fell, tree-like and stiff, crashing to the ground. The force sent debris scattering everywhere.

Jax and Nik wasted no time making sure the Machine was finished. The warriors jumped upon it and set to work making sure it would never move again. They leapt down from their smouldering and broken foe and ran to Daze.

Her friends found her in moments, but immediately their hearts sank. She was laying unmoving on the hangar floor. They slowed and knelt beside their comrade.

"Oh, no! Is she breathing? Hang on, Daze." Nik's voice was filled with desperation.

"Only barely," Jax said with her head on Daze's chest. She took her by the hand. It was blistered and blackened, but Daze gripped back at her friend's touch like the pain had melted away. Tears welled in both of their eyes. They could only fear the worst.

"Hang on, Daze. We'll get you out of here." Jax reassured her. "Find something to carry her on." She looked at Nik, whose eyes were already darting round the room looking for ideas. She released her hand and started to stand.

"No, no, please, stay with me," Daze croaked, and her voice trembled.

Nik knelt back down beside her and took her other hand in hers. Daze gripped back at her. She held her two friends' hands so tight, and through the touch, the warmth of love poured into their hearts. They each prepared in her own way for the feeling they knew all too well—the feeling of loss. Daze's eyes couldn't focus any longer; her wounds were choking the life from her.

"We did it, didn't we?" she whispered.

"We did it, my friend. You did it." Jax squeezed her hand a little tighter.

She managed a weak smile, just from the corners of her mouth. "Thank you for being there for me and with me, to the very end, my sisters. I think I'm going on a journey soon, one that you two cannot come on with me."

"I wish we could," Jax sobbed.

"We would in a heartbeat," Nik assured her while her heart broke, and the tears flowed from her eyes.

Daze needed no assurance; this she already knew in her heart, like it was engrained within her. "I... I... I," her voice trembled. "Just wanna say..."

Her voice was cut off by a gurgling noise, and blood bubbled from her mouth and nose. Her head fell back, limp, and the child's hand emerged from her body with the squirming symbiote clenched in their fist. The child screamed in agony as the writhing halithstord entered its body, crunching within their head until it finally popped.

"At last, we are one. My destiny is here!" the child roared.

Isha awoke, silent and shivering, the realisation of what had happened dawning with her. Her heart was lost and aching from betrayal, from failure. Immediately, tears fell from her eyes.

"Flick, no! You tricked me. How could you? How could you?!"

"Silence, human! We used you to do what needed to be done. Now you have to go somewhere."

"I don't..."

She was cut off, like her inner voice had been gagged. She wanted to scream, she wanted to yell, she raged on the inside, but she was being supressed from within. Her body moved against her will, forcing her helplessly on a journey.

The journey came and went in what seemed a flash. She had no memory of it at all, but Isha stood on the clifftop. She looked over the edge. The sheer faces fell vertically down onto the rocks and the raging grey ocean. The wind howled wildly and ripped at her hair. She gasped as the tears fell. She knew with all that she had done, her time was at an end.

For just a moment, her will was her own again.

"Flick, you knew along, didn't you?"

"I knew. I know there is no choice."

"But I thought you cared about me. I thought you loved me."

"The Fleck is not capable of love, Isha. This is a concept for which The Fleck cares not. Our goal is far greater than the one. You humans are always obsessed with the one. You were a tool. We needed you, and now your use has run out."

"But you told me I was special."

"You are special, that's how we have achieved what we have achieved. You have done what no other could, but you are still an insignificant human. You are expendable. Your usefulness is no more."

"Why must I die? You said you didn't control me, and yet, you put me here."

"You must die so The Fleck can leave your being. Enough! Now is the time."

"But..."

She held her breath as she involuntarily went forward, dangling her toes over the edge. Her heart raced and fear filled her body. She stared down at her fate, towards her mortality, her end. She fought it with all her might, with everything she had, pushing back against Flick, but this was a battle Isha lost. She took a step forward into silence.

To Be Continued...

Stars light the cosmos so if you enjoyed this book, you can show it some love by leaving a rating or review on Amazon or Goodreads today!

Up Next: The adventure continues in Entities Part II: Entities Divided. Step into an intergalactic war, skip to Earth's past, and hold onto hope for the future. The battle is coming, and the galaxy will never be the same.

The Reptilian's planet has long since been destroyed, and they mean to take a new one, Earth. Now, a diverse alien coalition and a fearsome army of clones are edging closer to a violent conflict.

With humanity on the brink, Penny is thrust into the midst of a fight that shouldn't be hers. She must team up with a new friend, an alien alliance, and a group of warrior mercenaries to defeat the coming storm. Everyone is relying upon them, but can they succeed against seemingly insurmountable odds?

Subscribe to Barry's newsletter for monthly updates, crazy polls, poetry, jokes, laughs and general shenanigans. That's Just the way I like it! - **http://eepurl.com/gkYk5P**

Check out Barry's blog The Diary of a Wizard: It's weird wacky wondrous wizardry weekly (almost) from the Enchanted Woods! Adventures and laughs abound and, all for FREE! - https://imaginationgeneration.fun/category/blog/diary-of-a-wizard

Other Works by Barry

Novels

The Entities Series

Entities Part I: Entities Connected
Entities Part II: Entities Divided

The Dreamland Trilogy

Part I: The Fabric of Dreams
Part II: The Masters of Light
Part III: The Veil of Shadow

The War of the Turnips

Short Reads

Home
Flesh and Blood
Savage Wild

Contact

Website
https://imaginationgeneration.fun

Twitter
https://twitter.com/BarrySBrunswick

Facebook
https://www.facebook.com/Barry.S.Brunswick

Goodreads
https://www.goodreads.com/author/show/16765230.Barry_S_Bru
nswick

Amazon
https://www.amazon.com/Barry-S-Brunswick/e/
B07PLBMLVL

Email
barry@imaginationgeneration.fun

Subscribe to Newsletter
http://eepurl.com/gkYk5P

About the Author

'Once upon a time, there was a wizard and that wizard had a dream. His dream was to spark kid's imagination through the telling of amazing tales. So, with his pointy hat on his head and his long and slender fingers, he picked up a pen and began to write. The candle flickered as the pages turned one after the other, night after night.

He journeyed long and journeyed far. He went all the way to the mountains, through the forests and valleys. He travelled through the mists of time and through the wonders of space. He met dragons and ghosts and a myriad of magic creatures along the way. And, he did it all without ever leaving his chair.

As the images ran wild through his mind, his pen scratched away on the paper. Then one day, after many years and much toil, he had done it. He had created wondrous books to ignite kid's imagination and to help them to think and grow and dream.

And just in case you wondered, the wizard still journeys through story world and scribbles by candlelight to this day.'

Barry S. Brunswick

www.ingramcontent.com/pod-product-compliance
Lightning Source LLC
Chambersburg PA
CBHW071233250626
47163CB00001B/162